ROGUE

SAILOR

HEATHER HANSEN

I0667040

Book Design By Zoe Mellors.

ISBN: 978-1-7355637-3-2

THE ROGUE WAVE SERIES: BOOK 3

ROGUE SAILOR

HEATHER HANSEN

1

Benjamin caught the look in Catherine's eyes as he felt the shot hit just above his chest. The shock and fear matched his own. His back hit hard against the railing, losing his balance he felt himself falling from the ship. The pain in his shoulder choked his words as he tried to call out. The sea rushed over his head. He did not have a chance to take in a breath before the water flooded around him. Fighting against the pain, he pulled himself to the surface, fallen men and debris from the ships flowed on the waves making it hard for him to make his way to the edge of the ship. The water around him turning dark with the blood from his wound. Benjamin reached for the hull of the ship, feeling the lines from a fallen mast tangle about him. With the sway of the ships there was nothing he could do, they pulled him under once more, dragging him along with the current. He grabbed for the surface but could not reach it, his vision blurred and the waters around him went black.

He could feel the sway of the water below him, the cold and wet wood he lay upon keeping him afloat. Some of the debris from the battle still floated around him, the canvas sail draped across his body, protecting it from the hot sun. He raised his head as best he could, faintly hearing the voices of men. Trying to turn in the direction the noise was coming from. The thoughts of the battle came flooding back to him. He knew Alaric likely thought him among the dead. Benjamin craned his neck more, he needed to draw the attention of the ship. He needed to return to the West Indies, and he had to get word to *The Trinity*.

The voices from the sailors on board the ship filtered down towards him. He heard one man call out that he was alive. Relief flooded through Benjamin, if the ship had not slowed and spotted him, he may not have made it until the next ship passed. A rope was thrown down, landing on the wood he lay upon, pulling the loop around his body, he did what he could to grip it firmly, grateful they had thought to tie the end, so he did not have to rely much on his strength to hold on. He knew he would not have been able to do so.

Benjamin fell onto the deck of the ship. Men gathered around looking him over with curiosity. "What ship did you fall from, boy?" A man said, his voice course.

Benjamin opened his mouth to speak but no sound came out. Clearing his throat, he tried again, "*The Trinity*, sir." The words were raspy and now that he was out of the cold waters, he could feel every scrape and cut that lay upon his body. His head throbbed and the pain in his shoulder felt near to exploding. Blinking, he tried to clear his mind. He needed to get his bearings and be alert. He did not know these men or what kind of ship he had found himself on.

"A privateer ship, is it not?" The captain asked, waving a younger lad over, "Fetch some broth and grog for our new friend, then let Mister Brumage know he has a patient with shot in his shoulder." The sailor nodded, rushing off to do as he had been ordered.

"Aye, tis that, Captain…" Benjamin let the words fall short, waiting to hear the name of the man he now found himself under the command of.

"Forgive me, I am Captain Stoll, Mister Brumage is our surgeon, he will see to your wounds once you have finished your meal." The captain ushered, nodding to Benjamin, before turning, his hands neatly folded behind his back. He leaned over to a larger man who had stood at the back of the crowd of sailors that had gathered around them. "When Brumage has finished with him, send him to my cabin."

An uneasy filling set in the pit of Benjamin's stomach, causing the grog and broth to threaten to come up. He scrunched his nose against the sour smell of the broth, finishing the contents of the wooden bowl. He knew he needed it but reckoned he would regret swallowing the fair. Perhaps he had been spoiled by Cook's meals on *The Trinity*, he thought, spitting on the planks in an attempt to rid his mouth of the fowl taste. Benjamin looked about the deck, it was not as big as *The Trinity*, but it was not as small as many of the merchant vessels he had seen and was more equipped than most.

Benjamin handed the bowl and cup over to the young sailor as another led him to the surgery, or if you could even call it that. A tattered curtain hung in a doorway, leading into a small cabin, hardly more than a few feet wide. Herbs and ointments lined a shelf, tools that sat in a tangled mess in a crate, lay in the other corner.

"Please, have a seat," Mister Brumage said, pointing to the small wooden table. "Did your ship see battle then?" He asked, gesturing at the wound.

"Aye," he mumbled through gritted teeth. The surgeon, unceremoniously scrubbed at the wound, pouring an ample amount of salt onto it. He let it sit for a moment as he gathered the tools he needed. The retractor had clearly seen better days. The salt was rinsed from the wound with a splash of sea water.

"Steady yourself, lad, this won't feel too pleasant." Brumage's face contoured in concentration as he fished around for the ball. Benjamin felt himself grow pale. His body swayed against the pain. A small clink brought him back just as blackness had begun to close in. Looking down, the wound flushed with fresh blood, the small ball now lay in a tin dish. "You done well, lad, most of 'em find themselves on the ground before I be done getting' the ball from the wound." He chuckled, "Now's the easy part, I'll sew you closed, and you can see what the captain wants to do with you."

Benjamin grimaced once more, Brumage had not been wrong, though. The stitching hurt far less than retracting the ball had. "My thanks," Benjamin said, examining the stitching. It was roughly done, enough to ensure the wound was closed but no more. He would be lucky if the wound did not fester.

"Right then, you best git yourself on deck and see what

needs to be done." Mister Brumage replied, his voice tight, as if he had noticed Benjamin scrutinizing the job he had done.

Benjamin did not hesitate, though he had little strength and knew he would not be much help to the rest of the crew. Despite of that, he rather be on deck where he could get a clearer idea of their location and be away from the surgeon who was making him feel increasingly uneasy.

"Here, you can do some of the scrubbin'," a sailor, a few years older than himself handed Benjamin a bucket with a rough brush inside it. The contents sloshing about. Benjamin looked from the sailor to the rest of the crew, several of them glancing at him in curiosity. "Don't get caught standin' 'bout. Capt'n won't tolerate no slackin'."

Benjamin nodded in response. It was reasonable for any captain to be firm on his crew. No one sailor would be allowed to sit back and watch while the rest worked, no matter what ship they were on. He set the bucket down, crouching beside it, all the while watching the crew. Most of them were a bit more unkempt than the crew of *The Trinity* and seemed almost weary.

"You're wanted in the captain's cabin." A gruff man approached Benjamin, his hand on his blade. He looked Benjamin over, a smirk appearing upon his face. "You ain't much, are ye?"

Benjamin stood up, stepping closer to the man, his eyes hard. He walked past him towards the cabin, ignoring the goading. For the most part, the crew seemed alright enough, aside from the man he had just spoken with and the surgeon, if he could even be called such.

Benjamin knocked, awaiting the captain's response. The hoarse voice sounded, bidding him entrance. "Come in and have a seat. I imagine you are quite exhausted from your ordeal." He said, gesturing to a chair that sat opposite his desk.

"Aye," Benjamin replied, his expression guarded. He knew that Lucas and Alaric had done no wrong and therefore had nothing to hide. He even knew little of the letter the Governor had given Lucas to deliver so if this man had any connections with him, he would not be able to answer any questions the captain had regarding it. "May I ask where exactly this vessel is bound?"

"Aye, of course. You are aboard *The Arbiter* and we are bound for Georgetown in the Carolinas." The captain said simply, waving a hand in the air as if to dismiss any further questions Benjamin may have.

"I see." He hesitated, "You seem to have heard of *The Trinity*, but I don't recall ever hearing about your ship. Is this a merchant vessel?"

"You do ask many questions." His face hard. "As I am the one that rescued you, I rather thought I'd be doing the asking." He replied, sitting back in his chair, gazing across the table at Benjamin.

"I apologize, I am only trying to get a better judge of where we are and just who my captain is now." Benjamin glanced about the cabin. It was smaller than the one on *The*

Trinity. A hammock swung steadily in the corner, a chest sitting near it. A simple wash basin rested on the opposite wall.

Captain Stoll let out a laugh, "I suppose that's fair. You ought to know a little of your captain, though, I believe a captain should know even more about the crew he commands. Those who will be faithful to their captain and do his bidding," he paused briefly, "And those that may be less careful and perhaps too reckless." He stood, turning to gaze out the window behind the chair he had been sitting in. "See, reckless behavior, particularly in those men that are younger, can be dangerous. They can create a stirring in the crew that can develop into troubles that benefit neither the captain nor the crew." Turning his attention back to Benjamin, resting his hands on the back of the chair. "I suspect you will no be one of those lads though. You seem able bodied and have your wits about you. I dare say you will make a fine asset to my crew, so long as you head my warning, and don't ask questions." He finished pointedly.

"Of course, Captain Stoll." He nodded, not taking his eyes from the captain. He had not intended to challenge the man but found he could not help himself. "We can't be too far from the colonies, from there, I'm sure I can find a ship to take me on to the West Indies."

"I dare say it will all work out for the best." He nodded in agreement. "Go see to your duties." He said, dismissing Benjamin without another glance.

2

"Sailor," a voice sounded behind Benjamin. "Head to the galley, you're to take the grog and bread below." The man stood level with him, but several years older. His face cracked and worn from the years at sea.

"Aye," Benjamin acknowledged, letting the stone fall back into the bucket. He had learned quickly that it was no merchant vessel he now sailed on. After having spoken with Captain Stoll, he had returned to the deck to continue with his tasks. That night he had been informed he would need to find a spot on the planks to lay until the bells rang out to change shifts again. He had inquired about hammocks below, only for the sailor to laugh at him. Shaking his head, he informed Benjamin that below decks was for the slaves and there was no room for even one more soul below. Benjamin had been shocked. He had never set foot on deck of a slave ship, and it had not occurred to him that *The Arbiter* was such a vessel.

A couple of years before, *The Trinity* had been a few weeks from port when the mournful sounds came floating on the winds. It had sent an eerie chill down Benjamin's spine. Alaric had explained it was a slave ship headed for the West Indies. The words they had heard being sung were not sung by the crew of the ship, but from those that had been taken from their lands. He of course had seen the ships in the docks often enough but had paid little mind to them as the islands had always held rich entertainment, distracting him from the sorrow.

Benjamin made his way below, the hot and stagnant air hitting him before he could make out the shapes of the men and women below. Covering his face briefly, trying to gain his composure, he let his eyes adjust to the darkness. The bucket full of grog sloshed in his hand, the other holding a bucket filled with dried bread. Setting them down in front of a woman, her hair whiter than the sands on the beaches. He edged the buckets closer, allowing her to take the scoop from the grog. Taking a long, slow drink, she passed it to the girl next to her before grabbing a piece of the stale bread.

Benjamin watched the girl, she had to be about his age, her eyes not lifting to look at him. Gingerly, she lifted her hand from her arm, taking the scoop from the elderly woman. Blood was dried and crusted to her arm, the skin beneath looking swollen and discolored. Benjamin made a move to take a closer look. He did not know nearly as much as Miss Catherine or Doc, but he had learned enough from them to know she needed the wound to be cleansed and taken care of.

"May I take a look?" He asked, he voice echoing through the large cabin. He flinched, not wanting the captain or crew to hear him. He knew little of the goings ons of slave ships but knew enough to know his efforts to help those in need would not be welcomed by the captain or possibly even the rest of the crew.

The girl shrunk back, looking up at him. Her eyes filled with fear, pain and anger. He nodded, "I'm Benjamin. I have many injuries as well," he said, showing her, the wound on his shoulder. "I know you must be in pain." He moved slightly closer. "I may be able to help if you allow me." He whispered, gesturing towards her arm. In truth, he did not know how he could help her. Even if he managed to get in the surgery unnoticed, he doubted the herbs and tools in there would be very useful.

The elderly woman next to her spoke to her, her voice too low for Benjamin to make the words out. The girl looked Benjamin over, a guarded look in her eyes. "Are you a part of the crew? I have not seen your face before."

Benjamin shook his head, "No, the crew pulled me from the sea. The ship I was on was attacked. That is how I got this." He explained, gently tapping his shoulder. "The ship I belong to is *The Trinity*. My captain is a fair and decent man, not like the men aboard this ship. I am a privateer, we are different." Benjamin was not sure how much to say or if she understood what he was trying to tell her. Glancing at her arm again, he asked, "Can I take a look?"

The girl paused, looked to the woman next to her who smiled and nodded, gesturing for her to do as he asked. Lifting her head, a bit higher, she removed her other hand from the injury once more, allowing for him to see. Gingerly touching the torn and bruised flesh, he felt around, trying desperately not to cause her any more pain but knowing it was not possible.

"Can you move your arm?" He asked, already knowing the answer but wanting her to confirm it.

She shook her head, placing her hand protectively over the arm once more. Her clothes were ripped and stained. The dress fell limply to one side, exposing a shoulder.

"I am sure you already know, but your arm is likely broken. I may not be able to do much for it, but I can try and clean the cut and perhaps even sew it up." He had assisted Miss Catherine and Doc set many broken bones but he himself had never actually done it and he feared he may cause more harm, particularly if the bone had already begun to heal. He had a strong feeling that the pain, bruising and swelling was not just caused by the broken bone but that the cut had begun to fester. He looked her over, her skin was very warm to the touch and sweat beaded from her forehead as if her body was answering his questions for him before they could be asked.

"One of the sailors that came down, he held a stick. He was in a fierce mood and tried taking Imani," she explained, looking over at the elderly woman. "He was angry that the crew's rations had been cut once more and blamed us. Saying we were eating too much and drinking all the grog. He planned to throw Imani overboard to lessen the mouths." She stopped, her eyes were a bright gold, filled with anger and pain. "I couldn't let him take her. He beat me with the stick. I fell, my arm hit something sharp." She finished, her gaze shifting from her injured arm to Benjamin.

Benjamin's jaw tightened. Anger filled him with every

word she spoke of the story. He wished desperately that Doc or Miss Catherine was there to tend to the girl's wounds. He knew the surgeon aboard *The Arbiter* was not gentle and would likely not help, even if he could. "If I'm able to gather the supplies, will you allow me to clean and mend your arm?" He felt terrible, knowing there was nothing he could do for pain but if he could clean her wound, then maybe he could save her arm and even her life. If the arm got much worse, she may not even make it to the colonies.

The girl stared back at him, her eyes softening a bit, the fear still lingering. "Yes," she finally said.

Benjamin smiled weakly, hoping he was doing the right thing and would not be causing her pain for nothing. He stood up, gathering the buckets that now sat at the other end of the enormous hold. It reeked of a combination of smells he did not wish to think too long on. Carefully stepping around the bodies, he made his way slowly through the hold and towards the stairs where the surgery sat at the top of, just before the main deck. He would have to wait until the surgeon was not in his cabin and Benjamin did not know the crew well enough to know who, if anyone he could trust or ask for help. He would need to be vigilant and move quickly when the time came.

3

Benjamin adjusted his body against the planks, trying to find a position his could fall asleep in. His shoulder throbbed and ached. During the day he could push himself to ignore the pain while keeping his mind on working. At night though, the pain seemed to consume his entire arm. The snores from the crew around him did not bother him much, he was used to such sounds. It almost helped to sooth his worries. He knew Alaric was most likely punishing himself, thinking Benjamin dead. He had heard Miss Catherine's cries as he fell over and no doubt, she told Alaric and Lucas he had been shot by Banning. He hoped that once they reached the colonies, he could find a naval officer willing to help get word to the West Indies so that once *The Trinity* arrived, they would know Benjamin lived. He would then seek passage, either on a naval ship, if they would have him, or some other vessel taking on a crew.

The waves steadily lapped against the hull, the dark waters below meeting the night sky. Save for the sliver of moon that remained high and the stars that lit the way, the world around the ship seem like nothing more than a black cave that stretched on for miles. Leaning his head back, he allowed his eyes to close, letting the feel of the ship relax his body into sleep.

"Git up," a low voice sounded in his ear. "Capt'ns comin' on deck. You best git up and look more awake. I reckon someone's times come." A sailor, a few years older than Benjamin and about his same height stood next to him. His hair was tied back as best he could get it and had a long scar running down the side of his face.

"What do you mean by that?" Benjamin asked, a sickening feeling sitting in his chest.

"You'll see," he replied, his eyes locked on the captain, who was steadily assessing the crew. A moment before, he had been speaking closely with a burly man that went by the name Skraag. Benjamin did not know much about the man, only that he had been sailing with the captain for a few years and that they had met during one of Captain Stoll's ventures to Africa. "Names Archer by the way. I saw 'em pull you from the waters. You looked near to death. How's the shoulder?" He asked, tipping his head towards Benjamin.

"Better, I suppose." He knew his wound needed cleaning but there was not much he could do about that. "At least the shot is no longer in it." He glanced at Archer for a moment before switching his gaze back to the captain. Skraag had come back on deck from going below, his grip tight around a man's arm. "I'm Benjamin." Archer nodded in response, his face growing tight.

Benjamin watched as Skraag moved forward, shoving the

18

stumbling man towards the edge of the ship. The man was pale, his eyes half closed. He swayed slightly, giving away his weakening state. "They aren't…" His words fell limply from his mouth.

"Aye, he's sickly and they don't want him spreadin' whatever he's got to the rest of the slaves. They are supposed to be in prime condition when we reach the colonies. 'Tis not right, but there you have it." Archer shook his head, a look of disapproval and disgust upon his face.

"And no one will do anything to stop this? He could be healed. He's not sick, merely starving." Benjamin looked about the deck, the surgeon leaned comfortably against the railing, patiently waiting for the man to be thrown overboard. "This is ridiculous, he has to be stopped." Not waiting for Archer to reply, he pushed his way to the front. "You can't just throw a man over like this. There is nothing wrong with him." Benjamin protested, his anger rising with every breath. "If I could be allowed to give them another ration of grog and something more than just stale bread, they would live longer."

The captain's face was hard. He stepped down from his spot near the helm. "Do you hear that man? This boy wants to take away from your rations and feed them to those below. What do you say to that?" The tension on the deck grew. Benjamin could feel the angry looks driving into his back from his shipmates.

"If I could tend to them, surely you wouldn't lose as many. Wouldn't that be better for you? You would make more of a profit at the colonies." Benjamin tried reasoning with Captain Stoll, though he knew by the look on his face, it would not make a difference, no matter what he said.

The captain laughed, "A few thrown overboard during a voyage is to be expected and accounted for. It will be you losing more than you bargained for if you keep this up." Captain Stoll stepped closer to Benjamin. "Clap him in irons. If he has such sympathies for them, he can join them below." He said, his eyes not leaving Benjamin's.

Skraag stepped forward, readying to take him below. "Wait," the captain said, holding up a hand. "First, we need to set an example, make sure no one else is willing to step out of line. Bring up the whip." He said, watching the rest of the crew in case any of them showed their sympathies. His gaze shifting back to Benjamin, "I warned you, boy."

Benjamin clenched his jaw, his hands balled up into fists so tight he could feel his nails biting into his palms. The whip came down again, he had not kept track of how many lashes he had received. His head fell limply against the grate that had been lifted up. If it had not been for his wrists being tied, he would have fallen over long ago. He felt the vessel pitch, though he was not sure it was the waves causing the motion or the pain. His stomach turned and his eyes rolled back. The world around him darkened, the sounds faded, all he could hear was the crack of the whip before his mind went blank.

"Benjamin, here, drink this." Archer helped Benjamin sit up. "You've been out some time, mate."

"Aye," Benjamin winced as he sat up. Looking around, he saw he was in the hold with the others. "I thought I was to be clapped in irons as well."

"Captain Stoll thought the whippin' was enough for now. You passed out and they drug you down here. I was told to fetch you when you awoke and bring you above. I reckon the captain has something in mind, worse than being clapped in irons for the rest of the voyage." Archer placed the scoop back in the bucket and allowed it to be passed around. "The captain doesn't show any sympathy for his crew. He can always recruit more and sees no sense in keeping them alive, if he has enough men to make it back to the colonies. The more men that die along the voyage, the less men he must pay once they reach port."

Benjamin scoffed, "I suppose we best get on deck and see what more punishments the bastard has in store." He shook his head, biting back the searing pain that lit into his body as he stood. He could not think of what more the captain would do to him, and dreaded finding out, but he rather get it over with then wait down below imaging what more could be done. He stood a moment, bracing himself against the wall. He glanced around the room, he spotted the girl with the injured arm, her eyes held concern. Shifting his gaze back to Archer he nodded, "Let's get this over with." He said between gritted teeth.

He squinted, letting his eyes adjust to the bright sun outside. Despite the clear skies, the air held a chill to it, the breeze was cool and stung the broken skin on his back. Archer handed him the shirt Benjamin had been wearing before the whipping. It had sat, disregarded on the planks near the spot they had tied him up. He nodded his thanks and gingerly pulled the garment over his head, letting the lose material slide over his wounds. He hissed out a breath as the fabric met with the wounds.

21

Captain Stoll's voice echoed over the deck. He had waited until he had spotted Benjamin to begin his speech. "As most of you know, I do not hold with disobedience or insolence. If you dare to cross me, you will be dealt with in the strictest of ways, as you witnessed earlier today. I am the captain of this ship, and my commands will be seen to, and my warnings will be headed. Yesterday, you saw a sailor, a lad, a mere boy," he spit the words out, "Dare to try and argue with me. He was whipped and thrown below, for what? For trying to save an already dying slave. To try and take your rations from you and give them to those below." A roar of anger and shouts erupted from the crew, several of them shooting Benjamin, dark looks. "I dealt with his disobedience justly and my orders that I had originally spoke will be done." He turned, gesturing for Skraag to step forward.

Benjamin's stomach dropped, the sickly man he had tried and failed to save earlier, stood against the railing. Skraag's grip hard against his arm. Captain Stoll locked eyes with Benjamin. He brought his hand down, signaling for Skraag to do his bidding. Benjamin made no move, he held his body steady, not wanting to give the captain the satisfaction of seeing him sway. Skraag let go of the man's arm, without hesitation he shoved the man overboard. The splash sounded, causing Benjamin's stomach to flip. He still made no move, his expression blank. He would not let Captain Stoll see how it angered him, it was what the captain wanted. He wanted Benjamin to react again, wanted an excuse to rid his ship of him.

"Back to work!" Captain Stoll commanded, not looking back as he made his way to his cabin.

"I suggest you keep your head down and your mouth shut if you hope to make it to the colonies alive, mate." Archer said, going back to his duties, his face grim.

The light from the sun was fading on the horizon. Benjamin lifted his head, his body was stiff, his back felt dry and crusted with blood. Cool evening air bit deeply into his torn flesh. His thin shirt giving him little protection against the wind that swirled fiercely across the deck. He let out a sigh, he had not had a chance to get the girl the supplies to clean her wound and he knew she could not wait much longer. Now, he had to worry about his own wounds festering. It had been bad enough with the shot in his shoulder. The pain from that still had not subsided, now he felt as if he could barely move, let alone sneak around the ship, hoping to go unnoticed as he cleaned the girl's arm. He also knew the captain and Skraag would be keeping a closer eye on him.

He let out a long breath, waiting for sleep to come once again. He stared at the stars, trying to get his bearings. He remembered Alaric spending hours teaching him about the stars and how to find his way on the ocean, where there are no landmarks, no way of knowing where on the endless seas he could be. He had an idea at least. He knew that it could only have been a day or so after the battle when *The Arbiter* had picked him up. Since that day he had been aboard Captain Stoll's ship for only a matter of days.

Benjamin heard the bell ring out. Wiping the sleep from his eyes he groaned, if possible, his back felt worse than it had the day before. Benjamin heard the bell ring out. Wiping the sleep from his eyes he groaned, if possible, his back felt worse than it had the day before.

"Git scrubbin' lad. The capt'n won't like it if you are found lying about. He hasn't taken a shine you."

Benjamin let out a rough laugh, "The feelings mutual."

The sailor scoffed, "I imagine so," he replied, seeming to soften a bit. He reminded Benjamin of Ol' Shorty, though this man was not as wide around the middle and appeared to have seen far better days. "Don't worry, the capt'n doesn't usually emerge til midday. He and the doc spend all morning drinking all the rum and whiskey they want and gambling in his cabin."

Benjamin's head snapped up at the mention of the Doc. "You mean to say the Doc is not in the surgery?"

The old sailor laughed, "He ain't much of a doc. He keeps the men alive when it suits the capt'n." The sailor shook his head in disgust.

"Aye, I can testify to that." He replied, rubbing a hand over his shoulder. Benjamin waited until the older sailor had walked off to busy himself with the lines, before moving away from his post and towards the surgery. He only had one chance at it. He glanced in the tiny cabin, looking around, he quickly found herbs and salves hidden safely away in the cabinet. The tools he needed to mend the girl's wound were in the chest on the wobbly table. Benjamin scrunched his face.

The table, even the implements were crusted with old blood. Finding a needle that looked to be unused or at least cleaner than the rest, he made his way below decks. The smell from below fogging his senses, causing him to cough.

"Miss," Benjamin whispered gently touching the girl's shoulder, the urgency clear in his voice. "Please, we don't have much time. I need to clean the cut on you arm." He said, showing her the ointments and needle.

The girl nodded silently, stickering her chin up and preparing herself for the pain to come. Benjamin swallowed hard. He knew that if he were caught the girl would suffer too. He set to work, cleaning away the dried bits of blood and dirt that had filled the cut. Benjamin bent lower, trying his best to see in the darkened hull. As he cleaned, fresh blood slowly began to seep from the cut. He tried desperately to remember everything Doc and Miss Catherine had taught him.

"What's that?" She asked, nodding to the oil he was gently applying.

"Oil of juniper, it should help, though I'm afraid there is nothing for pain, but as it heals, that will lessen." He readied the needle, glancing at the young woman's face. Her eyes the color of dark, golden sand. The determination in them nearly overpowering the fear. He steadily pulled the needle through, hearing no more than a slow and shaky intake of breath from the girl. The woman that sat next to her, held tightly to her hand, giving her what strength she could. "What's your name?"

The young woman looked up at him, gathering her

thoughts through the pain in her arm. "Amara," she whispered. "My name is Amara."

"I like that," Benjamin replied, smiling. He was finishing up the stitching and pleased with how it went. He hoped that the little he had done for her would be enough. Looking down at her arm, she returned his smile before showing the older woman next to her. She patted her hand, assuring her she was alright.

Benjamin made his way back to the surgery, quickly replacing the items. Exiting the small cabin, he took a few steps up the companionway, nearly bumping into the doctor. "What you doin' down here?" He asked, pointing a narrow finger into Benjamin's chest.

"I thought to look for you, to see if you had something for my back," he paused looking the doc over, "But I rather take my chances with a fever than let you touch me again." He pushed passed the doctor without another word, returning to his spot on deck. The coarse brush and stone sat in the bucket of salt water, awaiting his arrival. Clenching his jaw against the pain that shot through him at bending his back, stretching the already raw flesh, he began scrubbing, doing as Archer had suggested and keeping his head lowered to the deck, the rest of the day.

4

"It can't be," Alaric whispered, stepping forward, ignoring the fray that continued around him. He could not be seeing straight. Benjamin stood before him, sword and flintlock in hand. He blinked, shaking his head, wondering if at any moment he'd wake on one of Doc's tables and realize it was all just one of his dreams.

"Aye, it's good to see you too." Benjamin grinned, quickly glancing around at the men that continued to fight.

"I don't understand, how is it possible? Catherine, she saw…" His words faded as a sailor approached him. Shifting his gaze to the man, Alaric blocked the blow, holding his stance firm. A shot fired, smoke streaming from Benjamin's flintlock as the man before them dropped to the deck, his head making a cracking sound as it hit the planks.

"Perhaps the questions can wait, mate." Benjamin suggested, laughing at Alaric's still stunned expression.

Alaric nodded, trying to regain his composure. Looking back at *The Trinity* he saw a couple men being carried below but thankfully the battle had not spilled over to his ship. Molly remained below with Doc and a few of his younger crew members. Glancing about the deck, he tried spotting Banning but the battle was too thick. He waved Benjamin forward. Pushing through the men, making his way towards the hatch that led below.

Ethan came bursting through the open hatch, just in that moment. He held Thomas firmly by his arm. Blood streamed from Banning's mouth and nose, and Ethan's shirt was coated in red. Whether the blood was his or not, Alaric could not tell.

"Not another step," a man growled, his flintlock raised at Ethan.

Benjamin lunged forward, knocking the man's wrist up with his sword, causing the pistol to fire into the air. Benjamin pulled his sword back, only to draw the blade into the sailor's chest.

"Anyone else wish to challenge us?" Alaric bellowed. The fighting had stilled. Bodies lay lifeless about the deck, the rest of the three crews watched on. Alaric caught movement out of the corner of his eye. He recognized the sailor. He was the same man that had once been aboard *The Trinity*. "You there," his voice gravelly "I remember you," his anger rising. "Take him below, along with Banning and anyone else you see fit. The rest of *The Amity*'s crew can be locked in their brig. We will take it back to the colonies where the remainder of the crew will be tried and hanged for piracy." Alaric said, watching the rest of the men for any signs of raising up arms against them once more.

Ethan moved quickly, followed closely by Ol' Shorty and Joseph. Red and Jim held fast to Jonathan, not giving him a chance to fight against them. Men moved about, taking the remainder of Banning's crew below and locking them in their own brig. The rest of the sailors checked the deck for injured men, taking them to Doc as they were found and separating the crews' dead. Alaric looked around, Thomas did not have a large crew and many of them had died during the battle. He dreaded to know how many men he had lost and how bad the injuries were.

Turning towards Benjamin, Alaric swallowed hard. He still could not believe what he saw before him. The scraggly haired boy he had saved those years ago, once again stood before him. His hair was longer now, tied back, much like Alaric's was. There was something different about the boy though that he could not explain. He had changed, his eyes not as carefree and he now held himself with more confidence. Alaric stepped towards him, hesitating only a moment before drawing the lad into an embrace.

They stood together a moment, watching the crews do what was needed. The silence between them growing stronger with every breath. Suddenly, Benjamin turned, his face hard, "Why let him live?" He asked.

"We need him, to prove our innocence and clear our names. We will be taking him back to the West Indies with us." Alaric explained, looking the young man over. *How could little over a year change him so much?*

Benjamin's brow furrowed, "I see." He replied, "You said the rest of the crew would be taken back to the colonies? I cannot return there, not for some time at least."

"We will talk it over, first, let us see to our crews." He reassured him. He had many questions for the lad and would get to the bottom of all of them in time. Looking about the deck though, he saw that the young man had more pressing matters to attend to. While Alaric's crew cleared the deck and saw to their duties that they knew well. There were several other men that Alaric did not know, that stood on the deck of the other ship, watching their young captain and awaiting further orders. "Do you have a proper surgeon aboard?"

"I'm afraid not." Benjamin admitted, shuffling his feet and glancing over at his ship.

"Bring any of your wounded to Doc, he can see to both crews." He offered, watching the young man head over to his vessel and giving a burly man orders.

"How on earth do you suppose he made it that day? And still more impressive, be here the very day we are with his very own ship and crew?" Ethan asked, coming up to stand beside him.

"I haven't the slightest idea. I'm not even sure this is even real." He murmured, his eyes still watching the young man he had believed to be dead. "Thomas secured?"

"Aye, along with Jonathan. I had wanted to take Grady with us as well, but he died in the battle." Ethan replied, "With your permission, I'll question him once we are underway."

"Aye, of course. I'll come with you, just let me know when you go below. I need to check on Molly and the crew and it will be a bit before we can leave. The crew will need to fix up *The Amity* enough to get it to the colonies." Tearing his eyes from the other ship, he headed below.

Alaric prepared his senses for the smells and sights he was sure to see in the hull. No matter how many years he had been privateering, seeing his friends and crew in pain or dead did not get any easier. Approaching Molly who stood at the first table, drawing a damp cloth against one of the younger sailor's foreheads, he spoke quietly, not wanting to wake the men that were resting. "How are you fairing, lass?"

Her eyes went wide at seeing him. He knew he must look dreadful. His clothes were stained with blood from the battle. "Tis not mine, lass." He assured her as if reading her thoughts.

She nodded, looking away quickly and turning back to the sailor that lay upon the table. Clearing her throat, she found her voice, "He was brought down not long after the battle began. They said he was knocked down. A man had hit him on the head with the end of a flintlock." She whispered, gesturing to a large lump that had formed and split open on the side of the sailor's head. "He still has not awoken and Doc is concerned he may not." She whispered, her eyes shifting to Alaric's.

"I'm sorry, lass. You should not have to carry that burden. You have done what you can, time will tell, and Doc will see what more he can do once he's seen to the rest of the crew."

31

Alaric said, his voice low and filled with concern. "I should speak with Doc and see how everyone is fairing." He looked her over. She looked exhausted and worried. Leaning down, he placed a kiss on her forehead, hoping to wash away the sadness in her eyes. "Why don't you go see if Cook needs any help." He said, wanting to spare her from seeing anymore of the injured men.

"Aye, I will be back down shortly to bring in some broth for them." She replied.

"I take it, that is not your blood, as you do not appear injured." Doc said, looking up briefly. His eyes rising above his spectacles for a moment, before returning to Gordy's still form. His skin was pale, and his eyes were shut tight against the pain. Doc gently twisted the tool in his hand, drawing the small ball from the sailor's side. Fresh blood streamed from the wound. Gordy let out the breath he had been holding. Doc examined the ball, peeling the bit of fabric from the ball and matching it to the hole in the shirt. "Clean," he said, smiling down at Gordy. "I'll stitch you up and you can rest."

Alaric squeezed Gordy's shoulder, "Well done, mate." Glancing about the room before resting his eyes on Doc once more. "How are the others?"

Doc shrugged, "We've seen worse, though many of these injuries you see before you will take some time to mend. We will be short crew members for a couple weeks at least. It would have been far worse if we had not had the mysterious alley aiding us today." Doc said, finishing the stitching. Looking up at Alaric, he placed a hand on his back, twisting in a way to loosen the tight muscles. "Who did our friends turn out to be?" He asked, confused at the very pleased looked upon Alaric's face.

"That's just it, you will never believe…" His words were cut short.

"It was me," Benjamin's voice travelled through the cabin. "And I'm afraid I've got a few more for you, Doc." He gestured to the men behind him, some of whom held each other up. "There are several more aboard my ship, I knew you would not have room to treat them all in here."

"I don't believe my eyes." Doc adjusted his spectacles, "How is it possible, lad?" Walking up to Benjamin, he placed a hand on either shoulder, appraising the young man. Shaking his head in shock, he looked back at Alaric, "I just don't believe it." He laughed, clapping Benjamin on the shoulder. "Well, I suppose you best get your men in here, find a spot to place them and I'll look them over and see what we can do. Once all are settled in here, you can take me aboard your ship so I can have a look at the others." Immediately getting to work on the first man, his leg badly cut.

5

Alaric watched as hammocks were sewn up around the still bodies. He had Red fetch canvas and hammocks from *The Amity* to stitch up the men from all three ships. Looking across the decks, he saw Benjamin speaking to a young woman, her hair tied back in patterned cloth.

Stepping across the plank that joined *The Amity* to Benjamin's vessel. He wanted to see how he was getting on with repairs and if there was anything else he or his crew needed. Cook had made another pot of broth to take over to the other vessel, Benjamin had mentioned they were not as well prepared as they should have been but that he would explain why at a later time.

"What is it you are having them do there?" Alaric asked, pointing to a couple of men that hung from the bowsprit.

"The figurehead was badly mangled. They are removing the rest of it as well as the name. The more unrecognizable the vessel, the better." Benjamin answered, watching Alaric's reaction.

He leaned over the rail, watching the men scrape the splintered wood away from the ship. "What will you name her?"

"*The Croga*," Benjamin replied, pride deep in his voice.

Alaric grinned, his own pride rising within him. Placing a hand on his shoulder, "Tis a good name, lad." He looked about the ship, the crew focused on the tasks in front of them. He had a fairly good idea of what had transpired, of how Benjamin had become captain of the ship, but he wanted to hear it from him. He needed to know the details of his story if he had any chance of helping him and keeping him out of further misfortune. Taking a ship by way of mutiny was never a simple situation and depending on who the previous captain was, there was sure to be more trouble and clearly Benjamin expected there to be. "Come have your meal with us when you are ready. I am eager to hear your story."

Benjamin turned, "Aye, I'll be over in a bit, I want to be below when Doc comes aboard."

"Very well," Alaric said, returning to his own vessel. The look upon Benjamin's face had been grim. Clearly there was more weighing on the lad's mind then he was letting on. Running a hand through his hair, he headed towards Ethan.

"We best go down and see what we can learn." Alaric suggested, knowing that Ethan was anxious to begin questioning Banning.

"Ah, I have been waiting for you to grace us with your presence." Thomas said, his voice dry. "Seeing as how you did not kill me when you could, I suspect you need something from me." He drawled on, "So, what is it I can do for you?" He asked, leaning against the back wall, glancing between the two captains that stood before him.

"How is it you came to be in possession of the ruby bracelet?" Ethan asked, stepping closer to the bars, his expression hard.

"That's right, I remember you had a particular fascination with it the last time we spoke, though, situations were reversed." He replied, unamused. "Tell me, did it belong to a lover? She must have been quite something for you to go to all this trouble to find and capture me, just to ask about a piece of jewelry, no matter how fine it tis." Thomas had stepped forward, away from the back wall. The bracelet swinging from his fingertips.

Alaric caught movement out of the corner of his eye. Glancing at Jonathan, he watched him a moment. He had also stepped closer, his eyes fixed on the ruby bracelet before shifting his gaze to Alaric and leaning himself against the bars once more.

"It belonged to my sister. She was attacked one night in

Barbados when I was away at sea. It was said a pirate that matches your description was the culprit, but that cannot be you as you were off the coast of Africa at the time. So, tell me, how is it you came to be in possession of that very bracelet?"

Banning laughed, "As much as I wish it had been me that had gotten to know your dear sister, I confess, I had nothing to do with that night. I came to be in possession of this lovely bit of jewelry during a fine night of gambling and drink. That bastard cheated me at dice and so I killed the fool, taking his loot and being on my way. I did this, the very night before I set out to find you and your brother." Banning explained, pointing a finger at Alaric. Raising his hands in mock defeat, "The rest my friends, you know." Returning to his place against the wall, he added, "And before you ask, no, the man I killed did not resemble me at all," he shrugged, "He was much uglier."

Ethan turned to Alaric. His jaw tight. He raised a brow, tipping his head towards the hatch. Alaric followed him out, not bothering to look back at the prisoners. They both knew Banning was telling the truth and knew no more. At this point, it appeared Ethan would not find the answers he sought.

"After all this. All this chasing him down, risking our lives and that of your crews'. Risking being branded pirates ourselves. For what? For it to all come to an abrupt ending?" He slammed a fist against the railing.

"It was not all for nothing, mate. We did what we sought out to do and now we have him and can clear our names, even if he does not have the answers you need, this trip was not for nothing, and we could never have known what he knew of the bracelet." Alaric knew his words meant little and he could not blame Ethan for being angry. He would never have forgiven himself if they had not captured Banning. Even now, knowing Benjamin was alive and well, he still wanted no more than to bring Thomas in and see him hung for the crimes he had committed over the years.

Leaving Ethan alone in his thoughts, he headed for the galley. He wanted to be sure Cook had all the help he needed since he was now providing broth for both their crew and that of *The Croga's*. Benjamin had said they had what provisions they needed but no more than that. He had sent over two women and a young boy to help distribute the food amongst the crews. Alaric also wanted to be sure the cabin would be set up to host more than just he and Molly.

"Molly," he said, entering the small galley. The smells of steaming broth, biscuits, savory pies and softly cooked vegetables filled his senses. "We will be having a few others dine with us tonight, I hope you do not mind. I would like to introduce you to Benjamin, he will be amongst those joining us tonight." He informed her, watching her pour a pot of thick gravy into a separate bowl that would be set on their table. The rest of the gravy being left for the crew. "You two have really outdone yourselves." He said, dipping a finger into the warm sauce.

"Oui, but of course we have. We have much to celebrate this night. Our young Ben has returned to us, and we have captured the notorious pirate, Captain Thomas Banning." Cook said with a wave of his hand, splattering a bit of potatoes on the opposite wall.

"Aye, we sure do. If you need more assistance, just let some of the younger sailors know." He said, watching Molly mix more biscuit dough, before leaving to see to his cabin.

As his guests sat down around the table, he could not help but wish Lucas where there to share this moment with him. Molly sat between him and Doc, much more comfortable now than she had been a couple of months ago when the officers from the Royal Navy had sat about his table. The food was brought in, filling the cabin with warmth. Wine and whiskey were brought around the table, filling the glasses. Alaric could hardly take his eyes from Benjamin, still not believing the sight before him.

"I do not think I can wait much longer. How is it you survived? How is it you became the captain of that vessel out there and came upon Banning at the same time as us?" Alaric asked, leaning forward eager to hear the response.

"Tis a long story." He began, raising his brows, his eyes fixated on his plate, aimlessly moving the food about with his fork. "I was shot, just above the chest. I was fortunate." He began, showing them the scarred flesh. "I got pulled down by debris from the battle. A bit of canvas covered me and the bit of planking that I clung to." He shook his head, looking up at Alaric. "You couldn't have known." He said, his voice barely audible. Understanding in his eyes, knowing Alaric hated himself for not checking the debris in the water for his body. Alaric remained silent, his voice refusing to work. He felt his jaw tighten, his throat moving but no sound came out. He shook his head, taking a long drink. "A ship came by, perhaps a day or two after the battle, I cannot be sure how long it had been. The ship was *The Arbiter*." His voice now hard. He pushed the plate from him, clearly having no appetite as he relived the events that followed. "The captain was a man named Stoll. He was as vile as Banning, perhaps even more so. I did not realize it at first, but quickly found out that the ship I was aboard was a slave ship." He shook his head, swallowing hard. "I tried to save them then, but I couldn't." His voice was tight. "Captain Stoll had promised he would deposit me at the colonies," Benjamin let out a laugh that sounded more like a rough choking sound. "He kept his promise, I suppose." Running a hand over his face, he continued. "He sold us to a plantation owner. He was not a pleasant man either, but it was not he we had trouble with. It was his man, the foreman and Captain Stoll's best sailor. He wanted to ensure that we obeyed the foreman and gave no reason for the plantation owner to regret his purchase."

"Christ, lad." Alaric whispered. The table was silent, all that could be heard were sounds outside as the waves lapped steadily against the hull of the ship and Aoife scratching about the chairs, searching for scrabs that dropped.

"I found my opportunity, Alaric. I took it. I got as many of them out as I could. We had a plan. We headed for the shipyard. I had heard that Captain Stoll was back to retrieve his man and venture out again to Africa. I wanted revenge for what he had done and not just to me. We escaped the planta-tion, some of the slaves choosing to remain in the colonies, headed into the woods to hide, hoping to make it to other parts of the colonies. The rest joined me." Benjamin finished.

"Bravely done, lad. Bravely done." Doc said, taking a sip from his own cup.

"Aye, he's right." Ethan began, glancing from Benjamin to Alaric. "However, a mutiny is not a crime easily forgotten and you say this Captain Stoll was a vicious man. I very much doubt he will allow you to get very far if he can help it. That's also not to mention, you are an escaped slave and helped many others escape as well. It is an offense worthy of a hanging." Ethan explained solemnly.

"I know," Benjamin replied, raising his head a bit higher. "I do not regret my actions or take them back though. I did what I could and what I needed to do." His voice raising with every word. "I could not stay there any longer and I could not allow them too either." Clearing his throat, he continued. "That is why it is so risky for me to return to the colonies and why I am having the name and figurehead changed. With that, I had not intended to go after Banning so suddenly, especially with so many women and children aboard, but I heard at the docks of a man, matching your description," he pointed at Alaric, "Looking for a ship called *The Amity*. I decided right then to go after him. I took the chance, and lucky for us, you showed up when you did, as I had hoped you would." Benjamin confessed. "It was Banning's fault, all that happened to me after that night. I couldn't just let him get away, not when I found out he was so near."

"I'm glad we showed up when we did, then, and I'll say, you were doing a mighty fine job before we arrived." Pride filling his face. "Ethan's right though, and somehow, we will find a way to keep you and your crew out of harm's way and changing those pieces of your ship is a good start. One thing you have on your side is us and the fact that neither the plantation owner nor your previous captain will expect you to return to the colonies so soon. They will expect you to be on your way to the West Indies, not you heading north, only to return to the place you ran from."

"Aye, it's a good point you make." Ethan agreed, "Perhaps that alone will be enough to hide you."

Alaric sat back in his seat, taking the information he had just heard in. Much of the story is what he had feared it would be, only hearing it spoken and seeing the emotion on Benjamin's face had been far harder to watch than he had imagined. Catching Molly's eye, he winked, reassuring her. He knew he must look troubled, despite trying to hide it.

"How about a game?" Ethan suggested, bringing out his chess board and laying it on the table. Alaric grinned, happy for the distraction.

"Aye, it's about time the lad learned the game." He replied, gesturing to Benjamin and pouring each of them another cup of whiskey.

"If you don't mind, I'll see to the animals." Molly whispered, shyly, leaning in closely towards Alaric.

"Of course, no, I do not mind." He assured, his gaze resting on her lips that were a deeper shade of red from the wine. Clearing his throat when he noticed her cheeks flushed, he turned his attention back to the men around the table. Benjamin's attention on the board in front of him, curious about the game and just as glad as Alaric had been for the distraction.

6

Molly choked out a breath. The smell in the hold was terrible, despite the fact that the women that had remained below were doing their level best to clean the area and void it of the smell. As Doc and Molly entered, the hold had grown quiet, several children hiding behind their mothers or older siblings. Molly did her best to smile, unsure of how else to respond to so many curious and frightened faces.

"It's alright," Benjamin spoke up, "This is Doc, he is a very old friend and is here to help." He explained, looking about the room, his eyes resting on a young woman who stood near the front of the group, a bundle in an old quilt lay in her arms. "And this is Miss Maclean. If you should need anything, I've been assured that they will help in any way they can." A high-pitched cry sounded from the quilt, drawing their attention to it. Benjamin beckoned the girl forward. "May I present Amara," he smiled reassuringly at the young woman. "This babe's mother unfortunately did not make it. She was unwell when we left, and the babe needs to be fed. We've given her what milk we have but it's not much and there are no other nursing mothers with us." Benjamin explained, a look of sadness and guilt upon his face. Looking at Doc, he let his shoulders fall. "We had been desperate to leave and had no time to prepare." He admitted.

"You did well and showed great bravery, I'm sure. Not to mention, probably saved more lives than were lost," Doc comforted. "Now, let us take a look at this wee babe." He said, slowly approaching Amara and pulling the quilt back, revealing a baby no older than a month or two. She squirmed in the blanket, letting out another cry.

"I will fetch some milk from the goats," Molly announced. "And if you have a cabin where a goat can be kept, we can lend you one of ours so you can feed the babe as needed and not have to wait for us to bring you more." She suggested. "How will you give the baby the milk?" Molly asked, curiously.

A woman next to Amara held up a think leather bag. A small hole had been poked into a corner of it. "We have this." The woman responded.

Molly and Doc exchanged a glance. It would not take long for the leather pouch to grow filthy. They would need a much better way of getting the milk into the babe.

"It is a wonderful idea, but I can see from here it will need to be thoroughly cleansed, and soon, or else you risk making the babe sick. We will find a better way once we reach the colonies. Perhaps a tin bottle can be found. Until then, please, use a spoon to ladle the milk in her mouth or attach her directly to the utter of the goat." Doc advised.

Benjamin nodded his thanks, moving through the group, explaining to Doc what ailed them or showing the injuries that had been made during the battle.

Doc opened his bag that he had brought over. The scent of herbs, ointments and vinegar wafted in the air. "Ben, hold this firmly to his leg as soon as I remove the cloth he has on the cut. Once I remove the cloth, the blood will likely begin to flow again." He explained, handing Benjamin a wad of clean bandages. Doc poured a generous amount of the vinegar water on the cloth that remained on the cut. Slowly loosening it and pulling in gently from the wound. Benjamin did as he had been told, seeing the fresh blood immediately come to the surface of the cut. Doc worked quickly, sewing up the wound. "It will be sometime before he can use this leg again. The blade that caught him cut deep into the muscle. He will likely have a limp."

Molly moved about the hold, greeting each person she came to, desperately trying to bring a smile to the children's faces. One little girl in particular caught her attention. There was something in her eyes. Something that reminded Molly of herself when she was wee. She could not tell if it was the desperation, the hope, or the determination that struck her so or perhaps it was all of it. "Would you like to come with me to fetch the goat for the babe?" Molly offered, holding out her hand and looking up at the older girl next to her, guessing by the resemblance that she must have been an older sister. The girl nodded eagerly, peeking around Molly, and awaiting Benjamin's assurance. She slipped her small and delicate hand in Molly's, eager to leave the hold and see the animals.

"Have you seen many chickens, goats or cows?" She

asked the child as she led her across the plank that led to *The Trinity*. The girl simply shook her head in reply. Her eyes were wide as she looked about the ship, watching the sailors go about their duties. Her eyes growing wider still when they entered the cabin holding the animals. A smile slowly and tentatively spreading across the young girl's face. She looked to be younger than Mackay, possibly by a few years. Her tiny hand fitting perfectly in the palm of Molly's. Opening the gate, she led the girl into the cages, motioning for her to go ahead and see the goats, the kids bounding around excited for the new and extra attention. The girl let out a squeal of delight when one of the kids came up to her, affectionately pressing its nose against her cheek.

"Here, let's tie this around her and we can bring her to the other ship." Molly instructed, showing her how to tie the lead around the goat's neck. "You hold tight to this now and be sure to not let it go." Molly handed her the rough, fibrous rope. "I'll be right beside you." Together, they made their way back to the other ship. Molly would bring over the straw later, once they got the goat settled in a cabin and tended the rest of the crew. She would also need to aid Cook, with so many mouths to feed, he would need the assistance, even with all the extra food he had prepared ahead of time, it still would not be enough.

Returning to *The Trinity*, Molly stood at the rail, breathing in a deep breath of the sweet, salty air. The chilly breeze blowing steadily across the deck. She wrapped her coat tighter about her. Hearing Alaric's voice, she turned, watching him stride across the deck, speaking to his men, seeing to it all was in order. She had never met a man that showed such confidence and kindness, nor had she ever met a man that demanded such respect and loyalty from those that found themselves in his company. Her mind went to the kiss he had given her just before the battle had begun. Her lips tingling at the memory. Footsteps drew near, drawing her attention back to the present. Her face flushing at his approach, surely, he had caught her watching him.

"How are the repairs coming?" She asked, her voice shaky.

Grinning, he replied, "Fine, but rather than speak of repairs, I rather know what you were thinking a moment ago."

7

Alaric glanced up at the hatch. Molly had still not returned from checking on the animals. He had not thought much of it at first, knowing she easily lost herself in their company and easily lost track of time. He ran a hand over his face, something about it this time did not sit well with him though.

"She sure does get caught up with the beasts. She enjoys their company as much as they enjoy hers." Doc said, a knowing look on his face. "I'm sure she will return to your side soon." He teased.

Alaric ignored the snickers that traveled around the table. "That's just it, something isn't right." Standing, he strapped his sword and flintlock to his waist, the others quickly following suit. "Benjamin, you're with me. Ethan, Doc, you check the prisoners." He ordered, his jaw tightened, flinging the hatch open, he bounded down towards the large cabin that held the animals, Benjamin close behind him.

Slowing as he neared the cabin, he drew his flintlock,

raising it as he entered. His heart stopped. Molly squirmed, a hand covering her mouth and a small blade pressed dangerously against her side. "Not this time, Captain." Jonathan grinned, "It appears the tables have turned once again." A shot rang out from above, followed by shouts. "We may be outnumbered but I believe we have a bit of a leverage this time." He pulled Molly closer to his body moving his hand that held the blade, travel the length of her body. "I must say, Captain Stein, you and your brother do have a lovely taste in women."

Alaric met Molly's eyes, her body stilled, trust and calm filling her gaze. Throwing her head back, it clipped Jonathan's chin, causing him to flinch and draw in a hissing breath. Alaric moved forward without another thought. Shoving Molly aside and onto the soft straw, he brought his full wait upon Jonathan, bringing him quickly to the ground. His fist hitting its mark against the side of the sailor's face. A loud crack echoed through the cabin as Alaric brought the butt of his flintlock against Jonathan's head. The man's body went limp. "He won't stay like that for long. Benjamin, tie him up with this." He said, throwing a lead at the young man. "Are you alright?" He whispered, placing a hand on either side of Molly's face.

She nodded, "Aye, but you are not." A look of fear and worry filling her eyes.

Alaric looked down, placing a hand against his side, trying to halt the flow of blood that came from a deep cut. "Tis nothing, simply got a bit too close to his blade." He assured her. Urgently, he gestured for her and Benjamin to follow him. Judging by the sounds above, they were not in the clear just yet. "Stay close," he whispered. "Benjamin, follow behind, if you will." He commanded, moving forward steadily, through the companionway. His mind whirled, trying to figure out how the men had escaped and wondering how he would keep Molly safe in the fray. He had sent Doc with Ethan to check on the prisoners, that meant both men were likely caught up in the battle, leaving Alaric little choice but to brave the fight with Molly close in tow. He would need to get her to his cabin but doubted by the sounds on deck that he would be able to.

Turning, he handed Molly his flintlock, "Remember, don't hesitate." He said, his voice rough. His gaze shifted to Benjamin who stood with his sword drawn, ready to protect his crew and that of *The Trinity's*. Throwing the hatch open, they entered the fray. He needed to find Thomas before he found a way of escape. He knew the slithery bastard would find a way if he got the chance. Keeping one hand on Molly, the other gripping his sword, he looked about the deck. Spinning around, he stopped, a splash sounded. Racing to the railing, he glanced at Molly then Benjamin.

"Ben!" He yelled. The lad had leapt over the edge, landing in the skiff, knocking Thomas over the edge of the small boat and into the waters below. A shot sounded next to him, whipping around to face Molly, he saw the smoke streaming from the tip of the barrel, her eyes wide. A sailor, his sword raised above his head ready to strike Key, suddenly dropped to the planks, a pool of blood growing quickly under his fallen form. Key quickly scrambled to his feet, his face pale with shock.

Alaric let out a shaky breath, relief, and pride evident on

his face. "Very well done, lass." He pulled her closer to himself and grabbing hold of the rope that still remained attached to the skiff below. How Benjamin had managed it, he could not say. The young man hulled Banning's unconscious form onto the skiff, he himself falling into it as he pulled himself up. The battle around them had slowed. Ethan was next to him now, pulling the skiff back up.

"Shorty!" Alaric bellowed, "You and another man take Banning below and lock him back up. This time, tie his wrists and check him for anything he could use to pick the lock." His anger and fear rising at the thought of nearly losing Molly and Thomas so close to escaping.

"Ethan, come with me." He breathed out. He needed to check on Jonathan. He had a feeling it had been he and not Banning that had led the escape.

"I should have killed you when I had the chance." Ethan growled, approaching Jonathan who had awoke from the blow to his head. Benjamin had tied him securely to one of the posts, not allowing him another chance at escape. Placing the tip of his blade against Jonathan's cheek, he stepped closer. "I saw you, saw your reaction to the bracelet Thomas wears. You know it. Where have you seen it before?" Ethan asked, his voice steady and hard.

Alaric looked Jonathan over, stunned at Ethan's observation. He too had noticed Jonathan's actions when Thomas had held the bracelet up, but he had not thought too much on it. Looking at the man now though, he realized just how much Jonathan resembled Banning. Their hair, dress, mannerisms were all very similar, Jonathan even had several large tattoos that Alaric had never paid close attention to until that moment.

Jonathan laughed, "Aye, I know it." He smirked, "I lost it later that night in a dice game to the very man Banning said he later shot." He looked briefly down at his feet, his gaze returning to Ethan. "She was more beautiful and softer than I had imagined. Pity she only had a small purse and that bracelet on her. I had rather hoped to come upon a heavier bit of treasure in that carriage that night. In the end though, I admit, I was quite pleased." His eyes were dark, nearly unreadable. He leaned his head back against the post, as if relaxing. He smirked, "I was within your grasp once before, many months ago and your friend and his brother simply sent me from their ship." He laughed, drawing his shoulders up and letting them fall once more. "Now you have me within your grasp again and now you know the truth." His voice challenging.

Ethan swung his blade, splitting the ropes, allowing them to fall from the man's body. Jonathan stood, watching Ethan, his eyes void of all emotion. "Alaric, your sword, please." He requested.

Alaric stepped closer handing Ethan his blade, their gazes locked. Alaric nodded his understanding, stepping back to give the two men space. Ethan tossed the sword to Jonathan without uttering a word, his stance and gaze being challenge enough. The sounds of the swords meeting each other caused the chickens to scatter. Jonathan pushed Ethan back, closer to the other side of the cabin, not relenting. Alaric kept his body still, not wanting to distract either man. He knew Ethan. Knew his ability with the sword and had little doubt Ethan would succeed, but he had also seen Jonathan fight, and knew he was just as skilled.

Ethan brought his sword up, blocking another forceful blow. Jonathan reached out with his fist, knocking Ethan's head back against the wall he had become pinned against. Alaric took a tentative step towards them, his jaw tight. Ethan shoved forward suddenly, causing Jonathan to momentarily lose his footing and stumble back. It was Ethan's turn, his face strikingly calm. He moved Jonathan back with each swing of his blade. Jonathan's body met the fencing, just as Ethan drove his blade through his middle. The moment seemed to last an eternity. Alaric took another step nearer, bringing Ethan back to the present. Pulling his sword from the man's body, he let the sailor fall to the straw filled planks.

Alaric retrieved his sword from Jonathan's limp fingers. "Well done mate. You had me worried for a moment there." He admitted, shaking his head. Giving Ethan's shoulder a brief pat. He left him to be alone in his thoughts. After all the questioning and chasing for the last couple of years, he finally had his answers, finally gained the vengeance he sought. Whether it would ease the pain and guilt Ethan had felt, Alaric did not know.

How are you fairing, lass?" Alaric asked, a grin beginning to show upon his lips. "You really are quite something." He laughed, "You saved young Key tonight. You acted brave-ly." His voice husky, he leaned in, wanting no more than to draw her to him, hesitating only a moment before allowing his lips to meet hers. He did not want to think of how close he had come to losing her that night, he only wanted to act on the very moment they were in.

"Let's see how Benjamin is getting on and I need to check on Doc. He isn't usually in the thick of the battles." Alaric explained, praying both of them had made it through unscathed. He led her from the deck and down to the surgery.

Benjamin sat on the edge of a table. His shirt spread out next to him to dry. He looked up as Alaric approached, sitting up a bit straighter and clearing his throat. Alaric felt his mouth go dry. Upon the lad's shoulder was the scar from the shot he had received from Banning, just above his pant line, on his left hip was the scar from a cut he had received during his first battle. Alaric stepped closer, unable to speak. There were several new marks that Alaric had never seen before. Three thick, dark marks ran a couple inches along his ribs, as if someone had taken a hot poker to his side and a large, pink, fresh scar spanned the length of his chest. Walking around the table, Alaric drew in a breath. Benjamin's back was all but covered in what were once open wounds from lashes that he had received.

"My God, lad. What did they do to you?" He whispered, his voice catching. He looked over at Doc who gave him a sympathetic look.

"Thankfully for him and surprisingly so, all his wounds, even his most recent," he said, gesturing to the pink mark that ran along his chest, "Have all healed remarkably well. "Whomever stitched him up from that one did a mighty fine job." Doc spoke, not pausing in his work. He set a cloth down that he had used to wipe his hands clear of the vinegar water he had rinsed them in. "Right then," he announced, "I believe that will be all of the new injuries seen to. How about a quick drink before turning in?" He offered, smiling kindly at Molly who had been watching Alaric's reaction to the lad's scars with great concern.

Alaric agreed numbly, leading the way back to his cabin, still unable to get over the shock of seeing Benjamin's scarred body. Running a hand over his face, he poured them each a cup of rum.

8

Benjamin walked about the deck, the hammocks with the still bodies in them lined the planks. The fallen sailors from all three ships were ready to be sent to the depths. Catching movement out of the corner of his eye, he turned, seeing Amara slowly approaching. Her eyes shown in the morning light, making them even more striking than they typically were. "How are they fairing below? Any improvement?"

"Yes, much better. You were right about your friend and Miss Maclean. They are very kind." She confessed, uncertainty returning to her face.

He turned further, stepping closer to her, "What is it?"

"It's just," she paused, "What happens next?" She asked, glancing over at the canvases and hammocks.

"There will be a small ceremony. The bodies will be buried in the waters below." Seeing the confusion upon her face, he explained. "It's not like on the ship over to the colonies. This is a proper burial, one fit for a proper sailor." He assured her. He watched her a moment, hoping his decision to bring as many with him as possible, was a good one. "There is nothing more that can be done." She nodded in understanding. "Would you like to join me on *The Trinity* for the ceremony or would you prefer to remain here?"

"I'd like to be with you," she replied, a small, unsure smile appearing.

Benjamin returned the smile, his gaze going back to his ship. He was pleased with the repairs. A few splintered fragments lay scattered about the deck, but the ship appeared none the worse, much to his relief. There was still work to be done but it would not be long now.

"Benjamin," Alaric yelled from his ship, waving him over.

"Aye?" He asked, stepping down onto the planks of *The Trinity*, holding out a hand to help Amara down.

"I think you should perform the ceremony." He stated, his gaze shifting between Benjamin and Amara, a look of curiosity on his face.

"Me? But why?" He asked, taken aback. He of course had seen Alaric and Lucas perform the ceremony many times but never thought he would have to. Even when he took the ship, he had not once thought of having to be the one to send his crew to the depths. To watch the faces of his men and know that he had not been able to save them all. It had been different before, different standing beside his captains knowing Lucas and Alaric would do all they could to ensure the safety of their crew and him. Now, he was standing there beside Alaric once again, but not just as one of the sailors aboard their ship but as a captain as well. A man of equal duty. Looking over at Amara, she smiled up at him, urging him to accept the duty for the sake of the crew they had lost.

"I believe you are more than ready to, and it is one of the most important and hardest tasks you will be forced to perform as captain." Alaric acknowledged, looking again between Benjamin and Amara before handing Benjamin an old a worn Bible. Benjamin swallowed, holding the book tightly in his grasp. It was the same one he had seen Lucas and Alaric use since he was young.

Clearing his throat, Benjamin faced his crew and that of *The Trinity's*. His hands shook. When he had decided to go after Banning's ship, he had asked his crew if they stood with him. If they would be willing to fight alongside him in an attempt to gain revenge and rid the waters of a vile man. They had agreed to stand with him, even seemed eager to assist him. At the time, he had felt great pride, in some ways, he still did, but looking at the hammocks that lined the deck, he could not help but feel the guilt. Looking down at the book in his hands, he began. The words echoing solemnly across the deck. Aside from the occasional cough, shuffle of feet or a squawk from a seabird, the ships remained silent. The sound of the hammocks sliding across the boards, under the flag and dropping into the water below made his chest tighten with each one.

As the ceremony came to an end, the crews went back to their ndividual tasks. Benjamin gently closed the Bible in his hands, handing it carefully back to Alaric.

"No, it's yours now." Alaric said, holding a hand up. "You spoke well," Alaric whispered, as the crews continued to disperse.

"Thank you, it certainly brings things into a different light when standing in this spot." He admitted. "Alaric, I'd like you to meet Amara." He gestured to the young woman standing next to him. Having noticed the glances he sent between the two of them.

"It's a pleasure to meet you," he replied, his curiosity peaking once more. "I take it you two met on the plantation?" He asked.

"No, we actually met on the ship," Benjamin jutted his thumb at *The Croga*. "Amara, and many of the folks aboard the ship now were on there when I was pulled from the sea."

"He saved my life on more than one occasion, on that voyage and several more times while on the plantation." Amara voiced. Her tone full of admiration. "Please, do not think badly of him for taking the ship or helping us all to escape." She pleaded.

"I don't, in fact. I think he did the right and noble thing, and I couldn't be prouder." He confessed, reaching out to give Benjamin's shoulder a squeeze. "How is it you all ended up at the same plantation?" He asked, shifting his stance, relaxing a bit in the cool breeze.

"That was down to Captain Stoll. It was fortunate for us he made it happen, though his thought was that we would suffer most under his buyer's foreman and that was what he wanted, particularly for me. In the end though, it allowed me to help them escape." Ben explained.

"And you saved many of the slaves from suffering terrible injuries." Amara said, "You protected us as best you could. If you had not been sent with us, none of us would have made it."

Benjamin smiled weakly at the young woman, his guilt rising once more. He did not feel like he deserved such praise, particularly from Amara. As often as he had tried to help her, he had also failed to be there for her, and he would never forgive himself for it.

The hatch to Captain Stoll's cabin flung open. Stumbling out, a bottle of rum still in his hand. Staggering onto the deck, he squinted up at the bright sun. Though there were no clouds, the breeze that blew across the ship was cold, biting through Benjamin's thin shirt. Captain Stoll bumped into one of the sailors, angerly blaming the man for being in his way. Swinging a fist at the sailor, he missed his mark, nearly losing his balance. A stream of a vile words slurred from his lips. Regaining his footing, he looked around, spotting Benjamin.

Keeping the thick needle in his hand, he tried to focus his attention back on the canvas he was mending, hoping to avoid yet another unpleasant confrontation with the man. He felt a bump on his back, glancing over his shoulder, up at

Archer, who nodded in the direction of the captain. Hesitantly, he returned his gaze to Stoll who was heading through the hatch, going below. Benjamin clenched his fist. Shaking his head, he stood up. Cautiously he and Archer followed the captain below. They watched from the companionway, Stoll stood over the slaves, shouting words that came out more like unintelligible noises rather than actual sentences. Stoll kicked at one of the slaves, once again nearly losing his balance. The man remained still, simply watching the captain, unphased by the outburst.

Captain Stoll continued to walk amongst the crowded room, catching sight of the young woman that stood against the wall. Staring straight ahead, she refused to move or appear frightened. Benjamin took a step closer, unsure of what he should do next. Captain Stoll reached for the girl's arm, pulling it away from the other one. The stitches Benjamin had placed a few days before, staring back at the captain.

"What's this?" He demanded, his face inches from hers. Her eyes unwavering, she refused to speak. Captain Stoll looked around the room, gauging the reactions of the others. All of them remaining silent and unmoving as if they had been frozen. "Very well." He said, grabbing her under the arm and pulling her to him. You can come with me until you are ready to talk.

Benjamin stepped closer, now blocking the companionway. "It was me." He shrugged. "I know a thing or two about healing and if I hadn't mended her arm, she would not have made it the rest of the voyage and you would be out a valuable bit of cargo." He reasoned. "We both know she'll fetch a good price." Benjamin caught the slight movement the girl made at his words. He knew it hurt her to hear him say it, but he hoped his words would keep the captain from harming her.

The hold grew achingly quiet, before the captain let out a roar of laughter. "You're a clever lad." He mused, letting go of the girl and stepping up to Benjamin. His breath wreaking of drink. He patted Benjamin's face, "Cross me again though and you'll not make it to the colonies yourself." He threatened, looking back at the woman. Captain Stoll pushed past Benjamin, knocking him hard into the entryway. Benjamin watched the woman for a moment, before turning and walking back on deck.

Benjamin settled himself down, a plate with a dried biscuit and a bit of hard meat in one hand, a cup of grog in the other. Laying his head back against the planks, just below the railing, he let out a long and slow breath. Dipping the biscuit in the grog in an attempt to soften it, he looked over and at Archer who had come to sit next to him.

"You'll likely starve before we reach the colonies with as little as that to eat and drink, that is, if the captain don't kill you first." Archer commented, slipping Benjamin an extra bit of meat from his own plate that had several more pieces of food on it than Benjamin's had. He scoffed, laughing weakly in agreement.

He watched the men settle in for the night with their own rations of food and grog. The ship was much bigger and more equipped than most slave ships. From what he could tell, the captain was not unlike Banning. He did what he pleased and cared little for his crew. Probably taking out whatever other ships he came across, no matter the cost and only for his own, selfish gain.

9

Benjamin awoke to the sounds of humming, sitting up straighter, he looked about the deck. Many of the men were also just waking, some seeing to the last of their duties before resting and letting the next shift take over. The deck had grown quiet, the humming continuing, growing louder. The words in the song were inaudible, but the message coming across clearly. The solemn and lonely voices drifting up from below decks.

The hatch flew open, Captain Stoll bursting out from inside his cabin. "Will someone stop that infernal noise, at once!" He bellowed, his voice carrying over the silent deck. Sailors exchanged glances, unnerved and unsure of how to proceed. No one moved. Captain Stoll moved forward, catching sight of Benjamin and shooting him an accusatory glare. The captain lunged down the stairs, yelling for them to cease. Stepping up to one of the men, he raised his hand, bringing it down upon him. The singing only continued. Pushing through the crowded hull, he grabbed hold of the older woman that had held onto the girl while Benjamin had stitched and cleaned her wound. Yanking the older woman forward, "I demand silence aboard my ship. There will be no uprising, no mutiny this day." The slaves lowered their voices, but several continued. "Very well, an example shall be made." Hauling the older woman up the companionway, he shoved passed Benjamin and the on looking sailors.

"String her up!" He demanded, picking a long roped up and tossing it at a couple of sailors that stood nearest him.

Benjamin walked toward him through the crowded deck. "Is no one going to stop this?" Benjamin asked, his words hard and demanding. He looked at a man next to him, who quickly looked away.

The sailors did as they were bid, tying the rope around the woman's ankles. Benjamin could see the one sailor's hands shaking as he did so. The woman remaining motionless, her eyes void of emotion. She looked straight ahead, out at the dark waters that stretched on for miles.

Benjamin moved past the men, knocking them to the ground. "None of you agree with this!" He yelled. "You are all standing here like cowards, about to allow an innocent woman to be flung overboard. Only the worst of sea crimes are worthy of the punishment she is about to endure. Will none of you stand forward?" He questioned, challenging each of his shipmates. His voice cracked, never had he seen such treatment or fear. Shaking his head, he untied the rope from the woman's leg. Still the crew made no move.

Benjamin felt the cold metal of a pistol being brought to his head. Slowly standing, he faced the captain. "Killing me will not make an example and harming those people will only cause further troubles for you." He seethed. Wishing now more than ever he could feel the strength he so often saw in Alaric and Lucas, to have his words and courage spread through this crew like even the smallest look from either of those men could with the crew of *The Trinity*.

"Doesn't look like anyone is coming to your aid, boy. I guess the crew still prefer a real captain over a whimpering child." He looked at the other sailors that Benjamin had pushed down. "He can take her place, string him up instead." Shoving the old woman towards the companionway. "Return to the others before I change my mind." He spat out. Giving a quick, sorrowful glance at Benjamin, she rushed below.

Skraag stood next to him, holding a fistful of Benjamin's shirt in his hand, ready to push him over the railing at the captain's orders. "Should learn to keep your mouth shut, kid." His thick accent making it difficult to understand. "I'll try and make it quick," he laughed.

Benjamin swallowed, contempt, hatred and fear filling his numb body. He could not think of a way to get himself out of this. The knots around his ankles were skillfully tied, not allowing him to wriggle from their tightening grasp. His hands were bound as well, his arms falling limply in front of him. Looking out at the sea, he vowed to himself that if he lived, he would find a way to seek revenge on Captain Stoll. Not just for himself, but for the rest of the crew and those chained belowdecks.

He heard the command given by the captain, his body feeling light, before smacking hard into the rushing waters.

He tried curling his body in on itself, trying desperately to minimize the damage that was sure to be done by the rough barnacles that clung to the bottom of the ship. Feeling the side of his body connect with the hull, he did his best to not let the breath leave his body, thankful it had not been his already injured back or his head that hit the bottom of the ship.

He felt himself being lifted from the raging sea. The cold air hitting his face. He sucked in a deep breath, preparing to be dropped once again. This time, his feet hitting the hull. The rope slacked, flowing in front of him. Grabbing hold of it, he pulled up on it. Allowing himself to pull his body up to the point he remained just under the waves but above the level of the majority of barnacles that would tear away at his body if he hit them again. The rope bit mercilessly into his hands, the waves pulling hard against his body.

As he was pulled from the water again, he released the rope so they would not see that he had not been fully submerged the entire time. The wind stung every inch of his body, causing him to shiver violently. The cold making his chest feel tight and nearly impossible to take a deep breath. Clamping his teeth together, he felt himself drop into the waves, his head hitting hard against the hull, just above the water line. He wrestled with the rope, knowing it was the only chance he had at preventing his body from being totally mangled. The blow to his head making him to swallow a mouthful of the salty water. Angling his body as best he could against the strong pull of the rushing water, he managed to pull himself up enough to draw in a quick breath. He felt sick, not sure whether it was from the icy waters, the hit to the head or the large quantity of sea water he had just inhaled. He tried desperately to focus on nothing more than the rope he clung to, knowing if he let go, his flesh would be roughly torn by the crustaceans and if he allowed his body to give in to the growing feeling in his stomach, he would surely drown. As he was pulled up, he saw blood dripping into the water below. He closed his eyes against the pain and exhaustion. Twice more, he was dropped back under the moving ship. The final time, his hands slipping from the rope. Unable to hold himself up any longer, just as the rope tightened, pulling him back aboard the ship.

His clothes were torn, a few cuts lined the side his body from the first hit. The blood from the injury on his head streamed down the side of his face and onto his soaked shirt, mixing with the salty sea water, making his injuries appear far worse. He laid his head against the planks of the ship. He willed himself not to spill the contents of his stomach. He did not wish to give Captain Stoll or Skraag the satisfaction.

"Leave him," Stoll shouted to a sailor that tried to help him sit up. "Leave him there. If he dies, so be it. Any man that tries to help him will suffer the same fate."

Benjamin heard the captain's footsteps fade as he entered his cabin. Relief flooded his body. His eyes falling closed, despite the nausea, the pain that radiated in his skull and the chill his body endured. He drifted off, his mind taking him to an island. The sands were warm. The smell of pigs and iguanas roasting and the sweet, smooth taste of the fresh milk from the coconut filling his senses.

10

"Once we arrive in the colonies again, what will happen?" Molly asked. She sat upon the bed, the night shift, falling delicately about her shoulders. Her hands ruffling the blankets, playfully teasing Aoife, who mercilessly attacked each foe with great vigor.

"Ethan will alert the Royal Navy, letting them know what has transpired with Banning and Jonathan. From there, they will send a message to his Admiral." He replied, stretching in the hammock. There was a loud snap, followed by Alaric's body thudding to the ground. Molly looked over at him in shock and disbelief. His hammock lay on the planks in a mangled heap, one corner still strung up to the planks on the wall. Alaric stood up muttering curses under his breath. Molly bit back a smile. He gazed over at her, knowing she had witnessed what had just happened. The look of embarrassment and annoyance on his face, making it impossible for her to contain herself any longer. Sputtering out a laugh, she quickly looked away, avoiding his good-humored glare. Flinging back the covers on the bed, she gestured to the spot next to her, offering it up to him.

Leaning over the water basin. He looked her over, a sober look in his eyes, returning his attention to the basin. "Have you given much thought to whether or not you would like to stay in the colonies or remain on the ship a while longer?"

Molly swallowed hard, her chest tightening, all the humor from a moment ago, dissipating. They had not discussed what she had preferred to do since he first asked her, and she had no idea how he felt on the topic. At times, she believed, hoped, that he wanted her to stay, but she also knew that he had his doubts and did not wish to put her in danger, that the colonies may be a safer choice. In truth, she did not even know how he felt about her. She had grown to love the ship, the crew, and animals aboard it and could not imagine leaving it, leaving him. For the first time in her life, she felt happy, felt safe. "I want to stay here. On this ship, with the rest of the crew, with the animals," she paused, looking up at him now. "With you." She whispered.

Alaric stared at her a moment, letting out a soft laugh, he walked over to her, brushing her hair over her shoulder. "Christ lass, you had me worried there for a moment." Pulling her to him, he met her lips with his.

Molly awoke the next morning to Aoife mewing at the edge of the bed, begging for her morning feeding. "Aye, wee beast, I'll fetch you some scraps." She laughed, going to the chest that sat at the end of the bed. She pulled one of the dresses Alaric had purchased her, from it.

The hatch opened behind her, allowing Alaric to enter,

a large tray in his hands. "Oh, I was just about to fetch our meal." She acknowledged, nodding towards the food. "You should have let me see to that." She quickly took the tray from him, setting it on the desk where they typically took their meals.

"Nonsense, you needed your rest, and I was in the galley, seeing how Cook was getting on." He sat down, beckoning for her to join him. "Cook has hardly slept at all. At the rate he is going, we will run through all our stores before making it back to the colonies." He laughed, "I expect he's making it up to Benjamin. He has always been a scrawny lad, but seeing him now, he is all bone and not much else." He voiced, shaking his head at the thought.

"Are we returning to the same town we just came from?" She questioned, feeling sorry for Mrs. Banning. Judging from their brief meeting before, the poor woman did not know any truths about her husband's exploits.

"No, Banning has too high of connections there for us to risk bringing him there. No, we will head south and return to the Carolinas. There, Ethan will alert the Royal Navy, but we will not hand Banning over. However, we will hand his crew and ship over." He answered, taking a bite of eggs.

"I see," she nodded in understanding. "His crew, they will be tried and hanged, no?" She could not help feeling pity for them, though they are the ones that chose their fate.

"Aye, so they will be. Don't you fret over it none. They knew the risks and joined his crew anyway." He reasoned, dropping a few bits of sliced meat down for Aoife.

"And what of Benjamin and his crew. It will be dangerous taking them there." Her mind going to the little girl.

"It will be, but it would be more dangerous having them sail to the West Indies without our accompanying them. With both our ships sailing together, they will be less of a target and will not draw the eye of those searching for them as it will not be suspected that they are with another vessel." He explained "We, and they, also need to resupply before heading towards the islands. It's a long voyage and this battle took it out of us, and they had little to begin with anyway."

"How will it work? At the docks, when they ask to register the ships. Surely Benjamin's age and the ship's crew will raise questions, will it not?"

Alaric laughed, "You've thought of it all, lass." He sat back in his chair, "I will have one of the older mates pretend to be captain of his vessel for the time being, that way if a description is going around, they will not suspect it to be that ship. I will also split the crews before we dock, making it less conspicuous. They will list the ship as *The Croga*, just as Benjamin named it but it should put off any turned heads."

"Tis a sound plan." She replied, feeling a bit better, knowing what was instore. She marveled at how Alaric always seemed to have an answer and solution for nearly every problem they faced. "I'll take our tray up. Leave those there," she pointed to the pile of clothes that he had worn the last few days. They lay upon the floor, possibly unable to be salvaged. The extent of damage they had sustained, she was not sure she would be able to clean or mend them. She planned to gather the clothes from the rest of the crew. She knew what it

71

was like to wear worn and damaged clothes, the same ones for weeks, even months at a time. She felt sorry the crew had to do the same, especially since their captain had spent so much, making sure she would be warm enough and have every bit of clothing she could possibly want or need. It was also the least she could do for them, to thank them for coming to her rescue when Lord Willington had taken her. "I'll bring them on deck and gather what other clothes need to be washed and mended." She informed him, heading for the hatch, tray in hand, clothes tucked under her arm.

Her hands dipped into the salty, soapy bucket, scrubbing the remaining sweat out of a well-worn shirt. Several others lay out, drying in the breeze that swept across the deck. She was growing accustomed to the cooler weather and finding she even enjoyed it. Tucking a stray bit of hair behind her ear, she wrung the shirt out, laying it next to the others. Reaching up, she adjusted the cloth she had used to tie her hair back. Taking a breath in. The air felt different, not as heavy as it did, nearer the islands and it smelled sweeter, remanence of the lands that sat just a day's journey from them. In truth, she was rather looking forward to visiting the colonies again. The lands their vibrated with excitement and adventure, mingling with a sobering reality of hardships that kept the men, women and children immersed in their new daily lives. She admired them for their hard work and skills they had learned, to make their lives and their family's lives as rich and fulfilling as they could.

She settled herself on a crate, picking a shirt up from the pile, in order to stitch up the sleeve. Charlie had caught it on a sliver of wood that had been sticking out. Lucky for him, it at only caught his sleeve and not torn into him as well.

Molly carefully stuck the needle and thread through the fabric, steadily patching up the gaping tear in the garment.

11

"We will be swapping a few of our crew, including some of the women, with *The Trinity*. It will make it less conspicuous once we arrive at the docks. I advise that you keep your head down, you may be recognized if they are searching for us. Amos, one of the mates from *The Trinity* will be acting captain as well. Unfortunately for him, he does not look a thing like me," Benjamin grinned, causing Ajani to cough out a laugh. "He will not be questioned or draw any attention, unlike you or I would if we signed our names in the books." Benjamin explained, informing his friend of what was to come. Archer and some of the other men that remained with us will stay below, hidden from sight, along with the rest of the crew and the women and children."

"It will be risky, going back, but we stand by your side no matter what is to come." Ajani replied, placing a hand on Benjamin's shoulder in way of showing his gratitude and loyalty. "It is good to be on the waters, to be a free man." He closed his eyes, feeling the breezes blow over his form.

74

"I'm glad to hear it," his grin returning. Walking off, he went to find Amara. He felt more comfortable having her aboard *The Trinity* while they were at the docks. He knew that Ol' Shorty, and the others that would remain behind would look after her and that no one would go looking about their ship, where it was still in question that suspicions would be raised with *The Croga* in the docks.

"Amara," he spoke up, quickly grabbing the bucket of water from her that sloshed in her hands. "Allow me," he said, gesturing for her to lead the way along the companionway. The contents of the bucket were to be used below to continue the ongoing cleaning. He felt, though the smell had improved, the ship would not be rid of it unless the very planks were stripped. "You and a few of the others are to head over to *The Trinity*. You will be safe aboard it while at the docks and no one will dare to board it without permission of the crew that is to remain on the ship. You can trust them. You will be safe and hidden away. You will not have to worry." He wanted to take the fear away, wanted her to know he would never allow her to be taken back to any plantation. "You have my word. I will not let any harm come to you again and you will never go back to that place." He assured, stepping closer to her. "They won't be looking for us in the towns anyway, they would not think we would stick around. They'll believe us long gone."

"I believe you and I trust you," she admitted. "It's just that, I wish we were long gone already. I want to put the colonies behind us. To start a new life, a free life." She paused, "With you."

Benjamin brushed a finger softly against her cheek, "Aye, me too. It won't be long now." Someone cleared their throat, half coughing, alerting the two of his company. They stood in the middle of the companionway still. Looking over his shoulder, Benjamin felt his face redden. Amara refused to meet Alaric's eyes. She took the bucket back from Benjamin and rushed past.

Benjamin faced Alaric, who now stood, leaning against the wall, pretending to examine his fingers. "Have any more to tell, about your time away?" He mused, a teasing smile on his face.

"I could ask the same of you?" He retorted, biting back his own smile.

"Aye, so you could." Laughing, he beckoned Benjamin to continue up the companionway. "Best start sending some of your crew over. I do not wish to be anchored here long." They had been sailing towards the coast, now within a few hours journey of the Carolinas and had stopped to transfer some belongings, provisions, and crewmembers.

As they neared the docks, the sea birds became more plentiful. Sounds of the ships and crews busy loading and unloading the vessels, being carried on the winds. Benjamin stood, looking at the nearing town. He could feel his hands growing slippery as they gripped the wooden railing of *The Croga*. Alaric had suggested he switch over to *The Trinity* and stay below, hidden away with Amara and the others, but he had not agreed. He wanted to go ashore, to face the fears and images that invaded his thoughts. He felt it would be the only way. He also needed to see for himself if anyone was looking for him and the others like he suspected they were.

Keeping his head down, he grabbed hold of a large crate like other crew members did, placing them in a pile on the dock. Amos had registered the ship and came quickly back to the vessel, ordering what supplies were needed and going over the books. Benjamin continuing with the crates, making it appear he was just another sailor. In a way, it helped him to relax, it reminded him of the days when he helped to restock *The Trinity*. He would always be buzzing with excitement, eager to be on the waters again, and keen to see what adventures their next voyage would bring them.

"Careful with that crate," Molly yelled out sternly to a sailor that was bringing crates and boxes of chickens and other livestock out for them to load onto their ship. Benjamin quickly turned, going towards the man and taking the crate from him, placing it gently on the dock.

Molly strode over, looking over each chicken that lay in the crates, picking out the ones she wanted. The chickens that had been aboard *The Trinity* had been put into their own boxes to be traded for new ones, a few Cook had claimed.

"Why trade out the chickens now?" Benjamin asked Molly curiously. From what he had heard, Molly really enjoyed the feathery animals.

"They are no longer laying the way they should. They likely have gotten too old. Alaric says they have been aboard *The Trinity* for a couple of years and had been adults when originally purchased. It is time for fresh layers." Molly explained setting the ones she wanted aside, for the men to bring up to the ship. "Soon, we will need to sell the wee goats as well," Molly said mournfully. "There will be more though,

Doc is to find a fine buck while we are here. The one that had been on board before, no longer performs the way he should."

"I see," Benjamin had never paid too much attention to the animals before but was beginning to understand there was more to them then he had always thought. Lifting a crate and balancing another on top, he made his way up the plank and onto *The Trinity*. Molly continued to look about the animals on the dock, separating a couple more for Benjamin to put aboard *The Croga*.

Benjamin stalled his footing as he came back down the plank, catching the eye of Ethan who was quickly approaching. He sent a letter, alerting a man he knew in the Royal Navy to the capture of Thomas's ship. "What is it?" He cocked his head, unsure he truly wanted to hear what he had to say, by the look upon Ethan's face.

"This," he replied, his voice strained. He handed Benjamin a paper, turning it over, Benjamin felt the blood drain from him. He swallowed hard, glancing up to Ethan, only to stare down once more at the paper in his hand. A sketch of his likeness upon it as well as his name and a large sum of money to be given to anyone that turned him in. "Mate, you should go back on deck and wait for Alaric. Take the parchment to his cabin. I will see what I can do." Ethan ordered, turning his back to Benjamin and striding off, disappearing into the crowds moving about the docks.

Benjamin paced in the cabin, pausing briefly to look out the window, all that could be seen were other ships, mostly merchant and passenger vessels. Many of which were coming in from the West Indies or England. Benjamin grabbed for the rum that lay in one of the drawers of desk. Pulling it out, he took a long, slow drink. He felt terrible for bringing this trouble down on Alaric, Ethan and the crew. If they were caught being associated and even more so, helping him and the rest of the escaped slaves, it would brand them criminals as well, and that was not what Benjamin had wanted or had planned. He also feared what would happen if they were caught. He would never allow Amara or the others to be taken back but he had not thought as to how he would keep them safe or from being found out.

The hatch opened and Alaric strode in, his face grim. Ethan followed close behind. Benjamin slid the parchment across the desk for Alaric to see. "I am sorry. Sorry for the trouble this is causing you. I had never meant for it to fall onto you. I will do whatever it takes to make sure they," his voice a tight whisper as he pointed towards *The Croga*, "Make it safely to the islands and are free. If it means me handing myself in, then so be it." He stared hard at Alaric not knowing what else to say or do. He would never let any harm come to Alaric and the others and did not want the blame falling on them. "I knew they would be looking for me but did not know they would plaster wanted posted all about the towns."

"It will not come to that, and I will see that it doesn't. Ethan was able to take a few more of the posters down and we have sent some of the men out to see what more they can do and find out. With luck, we will be meeting with General Cunningham in a day or two and can hear what he has to say about all of it. He may know of a way we can get you pardoned. Some way Ethan and I do not know of." He reasoned, pouring them each a cup of rum.

"Aye, alright," He replied, his mouth dry, despite the drink.

The next couple of days went by quickly, Benjamin stayed on *The Croga* making much needed repairs, making the ship his own and more unrecognizable by the minute. He anxiously awaited the meeting that was to come. He had figured he would have had to stay aboard the ship, but Ethan insisted he come with them to meet his friend and tell him the whole story, so nothing was left out.

They sat around a table at McCady's Tavern, awaiting the arrival of General Cunningham. He had sent a note requesting they meet him there. The door swung open, and Ethan stood, looking pointedly at Benjamin, signaling for him to do the same. A man approached them, dawning a Royal Navy uniform. Benjamin shuffled his feet, looking over at Alaric who smiled encouragingly.

"It's good to see you again," Ethan greeted, gesturing for his friend to have a seat. "You have met Captain Stein," he waved a hand at Alaric, allowing the two men to say their welcomes before pointing to Benjamin, his voice lowering. "And this young man is the very same lad we believed dead, by the hands of Thomas Banning. He is the reason Captain Stein went in search of Banning and without this lad's skills and bravery we may not have been able to capture Thomas."

"Well then, it is a great pleasure to make your acquaintance, lad." He acknowledged. "How is it you lived and came to be in their company once more?" He leaned in, curious to hear the story.

"Uh, I was swept under the ship and covered by a sail."

He began, taking a deep breath. "Sometime later a ship came upon me. They pulled me from the water. I, for a short time became a member of the crew while we made our way to Georgetown. The captain was a cruel man and slave trader, among other things."

"I see, sounds as if you did not get on well with this man. What is his name and the name of his ship?" General Cunningham cocked his head, looking over at Ethan who raised a brow, indicating he should continue to listen carefully to the story.

"His name is Captain Stoll, the ship was *The Arbiter*."

"Was?" A questioning look on his face. The tone of his voice giving away that he suspected what the answer would be before Benjamin clarified it.

"Aye, myself and a few others, some that had been part of his crew before and some that had not been, took it. It is now under the name, *The Croga*." He raised his chin, holding his breath and waiting for the general's reprimanding.

"Ah, a mutiny. I am sure since you have spent many years already under the tutelage of Captain Stein, here, that I do not have to explain the seriousness of such a crime." He gazed at Benjamin, his head tilted in an almost sympathetic way.

"No, I am aware." He replied, glancing at Ethan who gestured for him to continue with his story. "We did not mutiny at sea, in fact it was at the docks in Georgetown where it occurred, but that was several months after I was sold into slavery by Captain Stoll himself." He watched the general's expression. Shock taking over the man's features. "The slaves that were aboard his ship and I were sold to a plantation owner in Georgetown. From there we lived, if you can even call it living. It was more like surviving, for several months. I escaped, taking as many of them as I could."

Realization dawning on the general's face, "You are not possibly saying you are the very same lad I have been hearing about?" His voice stern, disbelief evident.

"Aye, I am," Benjamin pulled the folded-up parchment from his pocket and placed it on the table for General Cunningham to view.

Carefully unfolding the paper, he kept his eyes on Benjamin, flicking them quickly to Ethan who only confirmed the details. He looked from the likeness to Benjamin and back again. "I do not have to tell you that I should hand you over this minute. You and the rest. The crimes you have committed these last few weeks are punishable by death and that is only if the plantation owner and foreman do not wish to claim you and have you punished by their own hands first."

"Aye, again, I am well aware of the circumstances and appreciate you hearing my story. We did not have too many dealings with the owner himself, it was mostly the foreman and his wife. They sought to punish us when not one person had done wrong. I could not stay there any longer, nor could the others. I apologize from the wrong I have done, but if you had witnessed the wrong that had been done to us, General, I believe you would understand my motives."

"I do not have to witness what you went through to understand. I have seen more than you know, over the years, both on land and sea, lad." He looked directly at Alaric, "Unfortunately, there is very little that can be done to pardon you and many a man will be on the hunt for you to claim the generous reward your hide will bring." He sighed, "I will see what I can do to help but to be quite honest, even trying to clear your names," he said, pointing a finger at Ethan than Alaric, "Has proven difficult, and you didn't even commit any crimes." He shook his head and snorted, "You three certainly know how to draw unwanted attention to yourselves."

Alaric laughed, "We do have experience with that, aye. Now, about Banning's crew, they are already in custody here and we are awaiting word from the governor on what he chooses to do with the ship. It will not be long before his wife finds out his ship was taken, and the crew tried. I do not wish anyone to come after us in an attempt to free the man. We ask that it remain in confidence that we are taking him back to the Admiral. Let it be believed that he died in the battle."

General Cunningham agreed, "That would be for the best. You may run into more trouble than you bargained for, with this lot with you, anyway." He wagged a finger disapprovingly at Benjamin. "I have to say though, I am quite curious, how did you escape, and with so many women and children in tow. Not many manage an escape, let alone from that particular plantation or of that magnitude."

12

"Amara," Benjamin gently shook her arm as he crouched beside her. "You must wake up. Quickly and quietly gather the others. It is time, we can't hesitate." He whispered, his voice catching. He did not want her to know how unsure he was. He knew this was their only chance, knew it had to be now but could not help but think of what would happen if they were caught.

Benjamin stood outside the small shack, keeping a watch while the others were roused from their sleep. They had spoken since arriving at the plantation of how they might escape, of when and who would choose to go with them. Too many feared the repercussions and asked to remain out of the talk of it. Others though, mostly the ones that had been aboard *The Arbiter* with him did choose to go with him. There had been a large dinner party at the big house, many of the guests were deep into their drink and Benjamin would wager, so was Mister Luggnar, the plantation owner. With luck, the distraction of the party would give them the chance they needed to escape. He had not seen the foreman or Skraag all evening and guessed they were either in attendance as well or had gone into one of the taverns for the night. He guessed it was more likely the ladder, as the foreman's wife remained at their house at the edge of the plantation.

Amara and the others began to slowly emerge from the shacks, the smaller children were strapped to their mothers with strips of fabric so they could be carried and not have to worry about growing tired. One of the women, Amara had grown close to had only recently given birth. She had wrapped the small babe up tightly and kept her latched to her chest so she would not cry out and alert anyone that may hear.

Benjamin caught sight of Ajani, signaling for him to take up the rear of their group to ensure no one got lost or fell behind. The sounds of the night made it eerie. An owl could be heard in a nearby tree. Benjamin had found that he rather enjoyed their calls but in that moment, it sent a chill down his spine. They kept their footsteps quiet, there were other men that watched over the slaves and the plantation during all hours. Benjamin had kept an eye on them that night though. They were taking advantage of their foreman's absence and were drinking and gambling in their own huts.

They slowly made their way through the buildings at the back of the plantation property. The wall was built up too high to hope to escape that way, they would need to get to the front gate. They kept low, crouching in the shadows along the edge. The very crops they were made to grow and harvest, protecting them momentarily from sight. Soon though, the crop line would end and there would not be as much cover.

Benjamin stopped, listening. At the edge, nearer the big

house there was movement. In the darkness it was difficult to see who it was. He held up a hand, gesturing for the others to stay behind, nodding for one of the men to follow him. They crept behind a large rose brush, the thorns poking out dangerously close to Benjamin's face. Peering through the bush, he watched the man for a brief moment, being sure it was one of the men charged with guarding the estate and not a guest that had found himself lost out in the gardens. The man turned and he saw the whip strapped to his hip, answering his question. Benjamin did not hesitate, moving forward and out of the cover of the bush, he came up behind the man, covering a hand over his mouth so he could not alert the others. He grabbed for the club that rested in the man's belt. Bringing it down with force against the man's head, he felt him grow limp in his grasp. Slowly lowering him to the ground so as not to make any noise, he inched forward, waving for the others to follow.

There was a large, open area at the front of the estate where carriages could roll in. The heavily laid gravel making it hard to keep their steps silent. Very little shrubbery lined the wall. Trees spread out, making a canopy like effect down the path that they were headed towards. The gate sat up ahead. With no place to hide behind, they had to make the last bit fast, in case a watchman appeared, or a servant or guest happened to peer out the window and spot them. Looking over his shoulder, he made sure everyone remained with him. Taking a breath in of the cool night air, he quickened his pace. The sounds of their feet on the tiny pebbles, breaking the almost peace of the night. Save for the croak of a frog or the chirp of the crickets, the night had grown silent, even the owl seemed to have settled.

Making their way up to the gate, Benjamin peered around it. Not seeing anyone, the path remaining bare. The shadows from the tree branches above them casting their arms out across the path as if they were reaching out, ready to grab anything that got within their reach.

Stopping, Benjamin felt his heart begin to pound harder, the thundering in his ears nearly drowning out any other sounds. Skraag stood in the middle of the path, his hand gripping his sword. He had stepped out from behind one of the trees, a smirk upon his face.

"I thought I heard sounds of escape," he laughed, the noise as rough as the gravel beneath their feet. "You will pay dearly for this, boy." Waving his sword in the air, he continued, "And so will your friends." Lunging forward he swung at him, missing. A snarl escaped his lips. Benjamin was leaner, quicker on his feet and had more experience in battle than the other man had anticipated, giving Benjamin the edge.

He waited for Skraag to come at him again. Stepping to the side, Benjamin swung the club he still held in his hand, smacking him hard in the shoulder and causing him to stumble. Skraag scrambled to find his footing again. Drawing his flintlock, he pointed it directly at Amara who stood with the others in the middle of the path. Ajani and the other men trying to keep the women and children hidden behind them. Benjamin sprang forward, he caught the smile on Skraag's lips and realized his mistake too late. Benjamin felt the blade slice deep across his chest. A blazing pain radiated across his middle. He blinked, a scream that was quickly silenced, sounded behind him. He felt his feet go out beneath him, causing him to fall to his knees onto the gravel.

Skraag stepped around him, flintlock and sword still in hand. Benjamin closed his eyes against the pain. He could not let them be caught. Could not allow them to be taken back. He had seen the look in Skraag's eyes too many times when he gazed upon Amara. He could not let him near her, not again. Benjamin opened his eyes, something glinted on the ground in front of him. The light from the moon, catching the small blade just right. It had fallen from Skraag's person when Benjamin had hit him. Reaching for it, he wrapped his fingers around the hilt. Placing a hand hard against his middle, trying in vain to stop the flow of blood. He raised himself to his feet. Turning, he called out. "I haven't finished with you." He stepped closer, hiding the blade against his body.

Skraag faced him, bellowing out a laugh. "Is that so?"

"Aye," drawing his hand up, he plunged the small blade deep into Skraag's middle. Surprise registered on his face as he fell to the ground, his flintlock discharging at the sudden impact, his finger squeezing hard against the trigger.

Benjamin swayed, he felt himself falling but never reaching the ground below his feet.

13

His head felt heavy, like the cannon balls aboard a ship. His chest was tight, as if something clutched it firmly, not releasing its grasp around his middle. His eyes fluttered open, everything around him blurred. He vaguely heard a soft voice calling out to him. Gentle fingers brushed against his cheek.

"Amara," he whispered, "Did she make it? Tell me she is alright." His throat was dry and the words barely audible.

"I'm here," she replied, pressing a cup to his lips. "I'm alright, but you need to drink this." Lifting his head, a little with her hand, she tilted the cup, allowing the warm liquid to pour slowly into his mouth.

He coughed, desperately trying to swallow more of the broth. He could feel the warmth from it travel the length of his body, slowly bringing life back into it. "The others? Where any captured?"

"No, we all made it safely away, thanks to you. Ajani and

another carried you. It took time, but we are in a cave, safe. For now, at least." She explained, allowing him another drink of broth.

"We cannot stay long. We are too close. They will find us." Benjamin tried to sit up, a searing pain shooting through his torso. Looking down, he saw his chest and stomach had been wrapped. "Who did this?" He asked, knowing that none of them carried bandages with them, nor did they know how to dress a wound so efficiently.

"I did that." A deep voice rumbled through the cave. A man came over, dressed in animal hides. "Names Leon Cutter, son. You were badly injured and near to your grave when I came across you and your companions." He knelt beside Benjamin. "You are safe here for now. I have hidden the entrance well." He assured, pointing to the far end of the cave. "There aren't many who know about this place, and you are lucky I killed the bear last winter when it awoke early and came after me." He said, lifting a necklace from his chest to show a row of large bear claws that hung from it.

"How long have we been here?" Benjamin asked, forcing himself to sit up, doing his best to ignore the pain.

"A few days, but don't think you'll be leaving yet. Your wound still needs time, or you'll risk reinjuring yourself and then you won't be any good for anyone." Leon advised. "I'm fine with you lot staying here for as long as you need and you mustn't worry 'bout them coming to look for you none, not this way anyway."

Benjamin accepted the bowl of broth that Amara handed

him, helping him to sit with his back against the wall of the cave. He realized for the first time that he lay upon furs. "I have no way of repaying you for your generosity." Benjamin said, feeling a bit uneasy about the situation. "Why risk your life for us?" He asked, watching the man. He seemed genuine and he had not given them any reason to doubt his motives, but he could not risk Amara and the others being taken back to the plantation and after being thrown into one bad situation after another since he was pulled from the ocean, he could not help but be cautious.

"Tis a tough country, son, and I believe in helping honest folk that are in need of it. And them plantation owners and their foremen are not among the honest." He replied, "You have nothing to fear from me. You and your friends are safe here for as long as you need," he said, standing. "Now, I must check on my snares and I'll be back to bring more provisions after dark."

Benjamin looked about the cave, it was larger than he would have imagined, the mouth of it making it appear quite a bit smaller. A couple of the children had found some small rocks to roll around. They had drawn a circle in the dirt and were seeing who could get the rocks to land in it. Benjamin could not help but smile. He remembered playing a similar game with the other children he lived with while Alaric was away. If no rocks could be found, they would then toss sea-shells or kick around coconuts instead. Despite being trapped in the cave, everyone seemed relaxed for the first time. They had rested, been well fed and had the hope of freedom within their grasp. He let his head fall back against the cool, stone wall of the cave as he watched Amara scoop up a bit of broth for Makena. Benjamin felt sorry for the woman. He had wished for Miss Catherine and Doc when the woman's time had come. Amara and a couple of the other women on the plantation had been with her. She refused to say who the father was, though Benjamin had his suspicions. He had been relieved when he heard the babe's cries that night, but his thoughts had turned to the story he had heard tell of Miss Catherine's mother. She had taken ill with fever and her body had never recovered from the birth. Makena now had a fever of her own and he did not know what could be done for her.

"How's she fairing? And the babe?" He whispered when Amara returned to his side.

"Not well, I'm afraid. Mr. Cutter brought us willow bark for tea and other herbs, but they have not done much. He says there are tribes nearby that he is friendly with. They provided the medicines and furs," she busied herself with the infant she held, her eyes hidden from his view.

He did not miss the trembling of her shoulders or how she now avoided his gaze. "Amara," his voice soft. "What is it?" He asked, only loud enough for her to hear. Pushing himself up more, he tried to move closer to her. Drawing in a breath at the pain.

"We almost lost you again." She shook her head, wiping the tears fiercely from her cheeks. "You've risked yourself too often for us."

Benjamin smiled, "Aye, tis the way I was raised. The man that brought me up and his brother would do anything for those they care about." He paused, awaiting her response. "Besides, I lived, again." He choked back a laugh at the indignant look she shot him.

The days passed soundlessly. Benjamin was grateful for the chance to regain his strength and he was pleased the others, had time to rest. He needed to get word to Alaric and Lucas and had asked Leon to send a letter to the islands, explaining what had happened but he was not sure when or if they would ever receive it.

They had planned to leave the cave within a day or two. Leon had given them a pack with dried meats and had told them he would guide them towards a path that was rarely used any longer, leading them further north and away from the plantations that dotted the lands to the south. That night, Leon had come to the cave, telling Benjamin that Captain Stoll was in port and would be for a few days. Together, they planned what could be done. It was their chance at escape and his chance at revenge on the man.

The light from the sun, peaked over the far mountain, illuminating the path in front of them. The golden glow shining like a beacon of hope. Not everyone had come with them, a few had chosen to remain behind, wanting to try and start a new life for themselves. Benjamin did not blame them, their plan to take the ship and sail to the islands was near to mad. If their plan worked though, they would be far from the men seeking them and the memories that plagued their thoughts.

Even in the early morning hours, the docks were busy with sailors, though most rested on their vessels or in the inns and taverns that were scattered along the edge of the port. Benjamin led the group, *The Arbiter* sitting tantalizingly close. There was no telling who or how many sailors remained onboard or if Captain Stoll was in his cabin.

Leaving the women and children behind several large crates, barrels and stacked canvases, Benjamin gestured for the men with him to follow. Quickly making their way up the plank, Benjamin and Ajani heading to the cabin, the others going below.

Reaching for the hatch, he cautiously opened it. He carried a large knife, resembling the dirks Lucas and Alaric owned. Leon had given it to him before wishing them luck and saying he would keep an ear out; in case any trouble came their way.

The hatch opened easy enough, but there was no sign of its captain. Muffled shouts could be heard below. "Let us help the others. With luck, he will return soon." Benjamin said, leaving the cabin. His steps froze. Standing just outside the cabin was Captain Stoll.

"Well, well. I had heard you and your friends had escaped, but I did not think to find you back aboard my vessel." Pulling the sword from his belt, he cautiously approached Benjamin. His eyes near as black as the night had been. The anger on his face was evident as the sounds below drew nearer. It would not be long before the battle below spilled over onto the deck. "I see your…time away did little in teaching you your place." He spat out.

A man stumbled onto the deck, several others following closely behind. Not one of them making a move when they saw Benjamin and Captain Stoll, their blades locked together. Stoll pushed forward, not allowing Benjamin a moment to do anything other than block each blow. "I'm impressed," Benjamin breathed out, "You are lasting longer than your man did." Stoll faltered momentarily, giving Benjamin the chance, he needed. His middle burned deep, the wound was healed, but only just. All the moving and twisting had the newly formed skin stretching, pulling against the tender muscle below. He caught the captain's blade with his, sliding it in a way that caused the other man to stumble. Catching on the crates, Stoll fell to the planks. Benjamin placed the tip of his sword carefully against the captain's chest. "Doesn't look like anyone is coming to your aid, captain." He mocked, remembering the very words Stoll had said to him. "I guess the crew still prefer a real captain over a whimpering child." He paused, letting his words sink in. "I'll be taking your ship now." He raised his blade, stepping back. He wanted to show Stoll what mercy was, wanted him to live, knowing Benjamin had bested him in front of his own men.

Benjamin turned, to see the crew, one by one smiling and saluting him. "Bout time you did that. Sure, had us waiting long enough." Archer grinned.

He watched Stoll and a couple of his more loyal men rush off the ship, no doubt to tell authorities. Benjamin, nodded to Ajani to fetch the others who remained hidden on the docks. They would not have time to gather more supplies, they must leave as soon as everyone was on board. Even if Stoll did not alert authorities, no doubt the many sailors that had watched from the docks, would be eager to claim any reward they could from the plantation, for spotting the escaped slaves.

"You allow him to get away?" Ajani asked, confusion and frustration upon his face.

"Aye, he'll be sitting, licking his wounds for some time to come. And that will cause him more pain and embarrassment than us killing him would." Benjamin stated, helping the women onto the deck from the plank.

14

Alaric stood amongst the crowd, Ethan and Benjamin on either side of them. The crew from Banning's ship had their trial, proclaiming them guilty of being the pirates they were. Each man stood, shackled, and awaiting their turn on the stand. The ropes tied in a way that would allow for a quick and sudden death, though, he wagered that thought did little to settle the nerves of the men in line. He did not enjoy this part of privateering but given the crew that had been captured and the fact that he himself and Ethan's reputations were in question, they needed to make a clear show of where their allegiances lie. General Cunningham had also insisted they stay for the trail and hanging.

He had left Molly and the rest of the crew aboard the ship, readying to sail out as soon as the events were over. He did not cherish the idea of leaving her on board for so long without him but knew the others would not allow anyone on the vessel without his permission and were being more cautious and vigilant than they typically would be, because of Banning being aboard. They had kept it secret that he was with them but would not take any chances.

Benjamin shuffled his feet uneasily beside him. "What is it, lad?"

"I dislike leaving Amara and the others aboard the vessel, so near the plantation." He admitted, looking nervously around at the crowd.

Alaric could not help but smile at their similar thoughts. "Aye, I agree, but the women will be quite safe. The crew will take good care of them, and I have no doubt the women are more than capable of handling themselves." He spoke with confidence. He did not relish Molly having to defend herself, but she had done so on a few occasions with rather impeccable success and would wager Amara was just as capable.

"I know you are right," he acknowledged, still looking unsure.

Alaric could not blame him. He had a similar feeling that he could not shake. He had caught a man looking their way and moving closer to them. He wondered if the man knew one of the men to be hanged and knew that they were the ones who had captured them. Keeping an eye on the man, he waited impatiently for the hanging to be over. The sound of the planks dropping from beneath their feet, the ropes snapping naught, turned his stomach. He doubted any of the men on the stand would have had any qualms about watching if situations had been reversed, but it did not make it any easier for him.

"Come, let's get going. I rather not linger." He spoke up,

waving Ethan and Benjamin on. They pushed through the crowd that was quickly dispersing and headed for the docks. Cutting through a side path that was clearly not as well kempt as the main pathway, they hoped to get to the ship quicker, rather than having to make their way through the folks that meandered around the streets, looking into the shops and chatting with their friends.

"You there," A voice called out from behind them, drawing closer. "Yeah, I recognize you, boy." He pointed a finger at Benjamin, a couple men coming up behind the first and several more coming up the path they had been headed down. "Ain't you the kid that escaped and freed all them slaves?" He snorted a laugh, "Don't look like much. Word is, you then commandeered a ship and stole off into the middle of the night." He waved a hand dramatically through the air.

"You must be mistaken. I am sorry to disappoint you." Benjamin began, glancing from the first group to the next and then to Alaric, who gave him a look to tell him there would be no getting out of it without a fight. He stood up straighter, resting his hand on the hilt of his sword and grinned, "It was not the middle of the night, more like early morning."

A deep snarl emanated from the first man's lips as he gestured for the others to draw closer. Alaric, Ethan, and Benjamin stood in a sort of triangle, their backs to each other, guarding one another. They came quickly, clearly wanting to capture Benjamin and claim the reward before anyone else could. The path between the buildings was narrow, not allowing much movement, making things even more dangerous. Alaric tightened the gap between himself and his friends. His sword drove deep into the leg of one of the man, dropping him instantly to the ground, clutching at his wound. He could feel Ethan against his back, struggling to fend off more men as they came. His body went limp against Alaric's. He felt him hit the ground. Stepping over his friend, he and Benjamin guarded him from further harm.

Another one of the men, a large knife in his hand, grabbed for Benjamin. The man stood about the same height as the lad, but his body was twice as large. He held fast, pulling Benjamin with him. The knife pressed dangerously close against his middle. "Put down your weapon and the boy will live. A partial reward be better than none at all."

"Aye, we have no qualms about killing you or the boy. Alive may be better than dead, but dead be better than nothing at all. Put down your sword." The first man demanded. His hair fell limply about his shoulders. Edging closer to Alaric, two others following closely behind, a look of smug victory upon their faces.

Alaric turned to Benjamin as he winced, the man's blade drawing a drop of blood that quickly seeped through his thin shirt. Tossing his sword down, it clanked against the side of the wooden building. He raised his hands, "Very well, you've won. I've given up my sword. Now what is it you plan to do?" He asked, his tone the same one he used when teaching the younger sailors, a lesson.

Confusion spread across the face of the burly man that held tight to Benjamin. His eyes widened, his knife falling from his hand as his body dropped to the ground. Without another thought, Alaric swung around, pulling the dirk from his boot. Slicing the hand of the first man, catching the sword as it fell. Blocking the blade that swung at him from yet another of the companions. He brought the sword down across the man's chest, knocking the last man in the face with the hilt of his dirk. Blood spurted from his mouth and nose as he clutched at his injury.

Benjamin stood rooted to the spot. A small laugh of surprise escaped him. Alaric grinned, nodding his thanks. "How did you find us? And what are you doing here?" Benjamin asked, clapping the trapper on the shoulder.

"I heard tell of the trial and hanging to come. They be saying *The Trinity* brought the pirates in. I came to see how Captain Stein and his friends be fairing. I met them not long after you left me, though I had not realized the connection." He explained, replacing the flintlock he had used to knock the other man on the head with.

"Let us return to the ship," Alaric said, helping Ethan up, who had begun to awaken. A gash had formed above his temple. "We can catch up there and have Doc take a look at your head, mate."

"What of them?" Benjamin jutted finger at the men lying on the ground, a couple of them still clutching their wounds.

"Leave them where they are. They can talk all they want to when they can walk again. We will be long gone." Alaric responded, moving towards the docks. Between the buildings, the sails and masts of the ships could be seen. It was much like any other port. It was busy, loud and reeked of fish, animals, grog, and unwashed bodies. The cobblestones and wooden planks did little to keep the mud and dirt away from the paths. A young boy stood at the corner of one of the nearer buildings, a spade in his hand. A wooden, wheeled barrel sat behind him. He was busy scooping up the droppings left behind by the horses that passed.

"Doc," Benjamin shouted as they walked up the plank.

Ethan groaned, trying to walk on his own. He swayed, grasping the railing next to them and closing his eyes once more.

"Quit trying to do it on your own, you'll only injure yourself more, mate." Alaric insisted, passing him off to Doc who had rushed on deck. "Seven, see to it *The Croga* is ready to weigh anchor. After what we just encountered, it's best we do not stay in port much longer. We will follow them as soon as we can. Tell them to meet us a few miles off the coast, just south of Savannah." He ordered, gesturing for Benjamin and Leon to follow him to his cabin.

They sat around the desk in Alaric's cabin. The gentle sway of the ship momentarily sending a feeling of peace through him. The familiarity of the motion and even the smell of the room soothed the edge he had felt. The room felt different than it had when he had begun the voyage. At first, he had to get used to calling the cabin his, and not Lucas's. He had always stayed in his hammock with the rest of the crew or made one of the other cabins his. He had finally settled into making it his own, when Molly had snuck aboard, throwing his senses off and making him feel as if he had to tip toe around his own cabin, and for more than one reason. Now though, he could not imagine the cabin without her. Her clothes rested in the chest with his and the scent she left behind that lingered on the sheets and pillows filled him.

Taking a sip from the cup he held, he shook his head and grinned. "You sure waited long enough to join us in that alley."

"Aye, I wanted to see just how good you were and if the rumors of your skills are true." Leon laughed, his gaze turning to Benjamin. "You, lad, are a courageous fool." He blurted out another laugh. "What were you thinking coming back? And with the ship in tow?"

"We had little choice. There were little to no goods aboard and damage had been done during the battle to bring Banning in." He looked between the two men. "How is it you two are acquainted?" His brow furrowed.

"I was about to ask the same of you two." Alaric sat back in his chair. It creaked but did not falter.

"I met him and the others sometime after I showed you the way to the town. I had headed o'er to the other towns to make some trades, stopping off at another cabin I have. A merchant had been askin' for dried meats, furs and the like. I needed to check in on my traps and the hides and furs I had strung up. That's when I ran into Thomas Banning, meetin' with a well to do man." Taking a quite drink, he continued. "I stopped o'er at the tavern and heard that lot," he pointed to Alaric, "Askin' 'bout Thomas Banning. I took them back upriver to tell 'em what I knew of the man. I had not known then that you were lookin' for him too or that you were the lad that had been taken from Captain Stein during battle." He said to Benjamin. "These lands may be big, bigger than we are sure to ever know, but word travels fast." He laughed, "When I heard tell *The Trinity* had returned to port and with a load of pirates in tow, I had to come see. I tell you though, I had not thought you would be in their company, lad." His voice disbelieving and proud.

"You showed him to town? From where?" Alaric asked, confused at the missing side of the story.

"He's the one that saved my life and stitched this up." He said, taking his shirt off, showing the long scar that ran along his torso. The brand marks on his side still an angry red, as if they had not stopped their burning. "I told you and the General of our escape, but never mentioned Leon's name. I would not want him in trouble for aiding us." He explained.

Alaric nodded in agreement. "It was a wise choice." He shifted his gaze to Leon, "And you have my thanks. We are both indebted to you. I owe you a great deal for saving the lad's life." He raised his cup to him. "You did a mighty fine job sewing him up." Gesturing towards the pink scar."

"It's a skill many a men should know. I've had to sew myself up on occasion." He lifted his leg onto the table, pulling up the hides, revealing his skin. A wide scar ran down the length of the meaty part of his leg. It indented slightly at a portion, indicating just how bad the cut had been and explaining the small limp that the trapper walked with. "I had not been in the mountains long when I came face to face with a wild boar. It charged me before I could pull my knife." Shaking his head at the memory and patting his leg. "I stitched myself up before seeing nothin' but blackness. The local tribe found me and took me in for a time." He drained what was left in his cup, accepting more when Alaric lifted the bottle in a silent offer. "What I be wanting to know, is how you ended up on the plantation in the first place."

15

"Git up there!" Skraag yelled, shoving Benjamin forward. His wrists and ankles had been shackled, with heavy chains, linking every slave to one another. They had been led off the ship and were being forced into metal cages. The metal was cold and covered in splintering rust. The cage barely allowed enough room for their group. Other cages had been brought forward, allowing the rest of them to be hauled up and taken down the path that led along the docks and to an area where a large crowd had gathered. Other cages, holding more men and women sat alongside the crowd. A stage of sorts had been erected in the middle. A man stood on it, a thick stick in one hand. The other grabbing tightly to a man whose eyes shone with a mixture of anger, fear, and shame.

Benjamin rolled his shoulder, shaking Skraag's meaty hand from him. "What's wrong with you, man?" He shook his head in disbelief and anger. "You know this isn't right." He paused, "I think you also know that this hasn't ended between us. You haven't won, and nor will you."

Skraag threw his head back, "I'm not the one in chains, boy. Nor am I the one that is to be bought and sold as a slave, just like the rest of 'em" He nodded to the group inside the cage. "Don't you worry, neither I'll come to the plantation you are sold at and," he smirked, "Make sure you are doing as you are told." He pushed Benjamin into the cage, "Oh," he grinned, the expression not showing in his eyes. Instead, they were dark and empty. "I will also be sticking around awhile to see how the girl is fairing." He looked pointedly at Amara. "I mean to make her feel most welcome, here in the colonies." Locking the cage against the look of anger that spread across Benjamin's face, Skraag took his position next to the captain who was leading the way through the group of people.

Benjamin watched, as men, women and children were brought forth from the cages and placed on the stage to be examined and shown to the crowd. Hands shot up, shouts erupted, calling out numbers, and names of plantations and their owners. Not a single person in the cage Benjamin was in, spoke or made a move. They simply stood and waited.

Benjamin's mind reeled. He had known he could not trust the captain and as their voyage to the colonies had continued, he knew he was less and less likely to make it to the Royal Navy as he had been promised. He had expected the captain to even kill him but had not thought he would enslave him with the rest. He needed to get word to the Royal Navy. If he could give even tell one of the men the name of *The Trinity* and its captain, he might have a chance. He had little doubt he would be sold to a taxing and dishonorable man. There would be no way Captain Stoll would allow him to be sold to a kind one. He would want to see to it that Benjamin suffered.

Benjamin felt a weary hand touch his arm. "There is no fighting back this time, I'm afraid. You've been brave, but we must face what comes next with just as much strength and bravery if we are to make it through." The older woman spoke softly. Her words heavy and weighed down with truth and wisdom. The lines on her face, showing her years, though, he suspected she was not as old as she appeared.

"Aye," he replied solemnly. He could not help but wonder if he had kept his head down those weeks, if he would have been handed over to the Royal Navy and getting word to Alaric and Lucas of his survival. Instead, he had not. He had tried doing what he thought they would have done, only difference was, he did not feel like he had succeeded. He had only, made matters worse for himself and the others. *How was he supposed to help them if he was a captive with them?*

His gaze shifted to Amara, Skraag's words repeating in his mind. His stomach turned at thought of what the man had in mind by making her feel welcome. Mayhap it was better this way. If he were to go to the same plantation as her, he may be able to protect her, at least he could try. Even if it cost him his life, he would do what he could. Amara's soft eyes fell on him, the gold flecks in them, shining bright, strength and determination wiping out the fear he knew she felt.

It was their turn. The cage was unlocked, and they were taken from their metal confines. The breeze felt cool, the trees on the outskirts of the town seemed to whisper with each movement. As if they were watching the proceedings in shock and disgust. The man on the platform spoke loudly, his voice echoing over the crowd. Men and women shouting comments back at him, then sending their foremen to claim their purchases. One by one they were brought up on the platform. A man, standing next to Captain Stoll, spoke with him. Waving a hand in the air with each slave that was brought up. He seemed to be claiming just about every man, woman and child that had been aboard *The Arbiter*. Another man, Benjamin suspected to be the foreman was scowling at the lot of them, his gaze repeatedly flicking to Amara. Benjamin shifted uncomfortably. He had to make sure he found himself on the same plantation as her. Amara was brought forth. The crowd had grown quieter. The foreman's eyes were fixated on her. The fear and anger were unmistakable now in the way she stood. There was nothing she could do. Nowhere she could hide. The eyes of the crowd bore into her. Whispers and shouts continued.

The man next to the captain, growing furious. He motioned for the foreman to take her to the others he had purchased, before anyone else could claim her. A man stepped forward, challenging the foreman. Offering an enormous amount for the girl. Benjamin swallowed, not one of those men seemed decent. He had a feeling she would be highly regarded, and any number of the plantation owners would want to own her. She was strong, healthy, young, and there was no doubting her beauty.

Benjamin pushed his way to the front of the line. The foreman grabbed Amara firmly by the arm, threatening any man that tried to get a closer look at her.

Benjamin was yanked from the line. It was his turn to stand before the crowd. He eyed the captain and plantation owner. They whispered amongst themselves. A few shouts from the crowd began the bidding. Several folks stared at him suspiciously, wondering what he had done to find himself on the platform.

The plantation owner raised a hand, calling out a bid. Benjamin did not hear how much the man said and did not rightly care. Keeping an eye on Amara and the foreman. Captain Stoll grinned, tipping his hat to Benjamin in mock farewell as Benjamin was brought down to join the others. Relief flooded him. He knew there was little he could do in that moment. He was only thankful the same plantation owner had agreed to take him. He vowed to himself in that moment, looking the others over, he would find a way to escape, and he would be taking Amara and anyone else that wished to go with him.

"Seems to me, you are more of the, how should I say it, sympathetic type." The plantation owner approached him. His face merely inches away. Benjamin scrunched his nose, he could smell the man's breath, his body and clothes wreaking of some sort of sickly-sweet smell that he could not place.

"And it seems to me, you are not." Benjamin shrugged as if he could not care less what the man had to say. In truth, he really did not care, but he wanted to hear what he had to say. Wanted to learn anything he could that may help them escape.

The plantation owner laughed, the sound nearly silencing the crowd around them. "Captain Stoll did not warn me of your sharp tongue. Not to worry, not to worry, lad. My fore-man," he said, gesturing to the approaching man, "Will teach you when to hold your tongue in place." He began to turn, a smirk on his face. "I just hope for your sake, you have no need of his services." He walked from the group, towards his carriage, a wooden cane in his hand.

Benjamin and the others were crammed into another cart, the splintering wood and rough, rusty metal that made up the floor of the cart, poked mercilessly through his thin and worn boots. He winced as he thought of the others that stood with him. Most of them only wore thin strips of animal hide on their feet, if anything at all. Horses pulled the container down that path. Each bump, jostling the men and women, making it hard to stand and driving the splintering metal and wood deeper into their feet. Looking back, Benjamin could still hear the bidding continuing, shouts and whistles from the crowd echoing around the buildings and down the paths. He could see the ships bobbing sleepily in the dock. *The Arbiter* seeming to stare back at him. A gull flew above the cart as if trying to call him back to the sea. Back to where he belonged.

He wracked his brain, trying to keep in mind certain odd-looking trees and houses, wanting to remember his way to the docks, should he need to. He needed to get word to Lucas and Alaric, let them know what had happened and where he was at.

"You are deep in your thoughts, no?" Amara whispered. Sadness filled her voice.

"I am, yes. I am sorry." He felt guilty for upsetting her. He had not realized she was watching him.

"These men, they are much like the captain, yes?"

Benjamin let out a long breath, "Yes, they are." He replied soberly. He wanted to say more, to tell her it would not be

111

terrible, that she would be safe. But he knew better. He knew things would only get a lot worse for them before long.

"What will they have us do?" She asked, lowering her voice even more when the foreman shot a look back at them.

"I imagine they will have us working in the fields. Managing whatever crops, they grow." He did wonder what was in store for him. Clearly the captain had spoken about him to the owner.

The path turned to a smoother one, as they rounded a corner and passed through an open gate. The sound of small stones ground under the wheels. A large estate came into view. Its grandeur matching that of the finest estates he had seen on the islands. Whispers spread through those around him. Despite their fear and heartache, they could not help but be stunned by such a sight.

The cart pulled past the estate, veering further away from it. The crops now in sight. Workers were spread out through the field, tending the crops. Several of them glanced up for the briefest of moments, meeting the saddened and fearful eyes of those amongst him. A shout rang out over the fields, a man with some sort of whip in his hand called out, ordering them to return to their duties, though many of them had already done so. A hedge of rose bushes spanned the length of the field, preventing anyone from attempting to climb the wall. Though, Benjamin doubted anyone would be able to scale such a height, even without the added prevention. The breeze shifted, causing his stomach to do a flip. The scent he now recognized. The scent that had coated the plantation owner's clothes and skin was that of the flowers that helped to secure his estate and keep his slaves in. He remembered Miss Catherine speaking of the flowers with great love, they brought her comforting thoughts of her mother. For him, though, he now feared they would forever remind him of the plantation and this moment.

16

He looked about the deck, the breeze blew steadily across it, giving him a strange sense of relief. He watched, as *The Croga* slowly faded from sight. They would not be far behind. Leon had retired from the ship and returned to the town, needing to get back to his lone cabin in the woods. Though Leon lived by himself and not with a crew always around him, he felt they lived a similar life. Doing what needed to be done, tasks that many would not relish or be able to stomach. Life on a ship was not an easy one, nor was living off the land the way the trapper did. Both though, had their freedoms, their excitements and many others relied on them doing what they did, to stay safe and receive the goods they needed.

The sails of *The Trinity* snapped down as the ship rocked in the water, pulling away from the docks. He was relieved to be setting out. He did not wish to stay any longer in port and was uneasy about what had happened. Clearly the plantation owner would not rest until Benjamin was returned to him and with word of his escape, gossip of the mutiny would begin to spread as well. Not to mention the fact that Ethan and himself had now been branded pirates by half the Royal Navy. Their connections may not be enough to save them, and certainly would do little to aid Benjamin's cause. He could only hope that taking down the *The Amity* and bringing in Thomas would rectify any misconceptions and clear their names.

Alaric turned, looking about the deck. Many of Benjamin's crew had returned to *The Croga* just before they set out, needing to tend to the women and children that had remained below and had not switched over. Amara however, had remained on *The Trinity*, not wanting to sail away from the ship Benjamin was on and Benjamin had heartily agreed. He could not fault them. They had been through a lot together. Circumstances he did not wish to dwell on. They had clearly grown very close, and Alaric admired how both of them were trying to put past events behind them. He knew it was not easy to do. When he had thought he had lost Benjamin, he knew moving forward was the only way, but it did not make things any easier.

He watched Molly show Amara how to mend the sails and where things were. Brushing away comments and jests from the crew who good naturally teased her often. She had grown used to their taunts and now made jests of her own. It had taken her a long while to feel comfortable, even still she feared angering him or the other men, despite knowing they would never lay a hand on her. Aiofe rolled around at the feet of the two women, grasping onto the thread they were stitching through the sail. She had yet to earn her keep, she filled up on the delights of Cooks dishes and slumbered about the ship as if it belonged solely to her. Molly brought her down with her, each time she tended the livestock, hoping she would find herself vermin to capture, instead, she would wrestle in the straw and bat away at the bottom of Molly's dress. He suspected she was still too young to know what more to do but doubted she would ever learn with the way she was being spoiled.

"You saw the burns." Doc came up behind Alaric. He rested his hands in his pockets, watching the docks disappear from sight.

"Aye," his jaw tightening. "I saw only one brand mark, the others appeared to be from a hot stick or bit of metal." He swallowed hard, his chest tightening. He had thought he could not loath himself anymore when he had believed he had failed Benjamin and the boy had died. Now, knowing what Ben had lived through made him realize just how badly he had failed. He should have looked harder that day. He should have scoured the waters and torn away every bit of debris and searched for the lad. If he had done that, instead of heading below and drowning himself in drink, Benjamin would never have met the fate he had. He would never have had to endure the pain he had experienced.

"You could not have done anything for the lad. We had believed the debris had pulled him under. And so, it had, just not as far down as we had reason to believe. Miss Catherine is a fine healer and she saw him get shot. She swore the ball had hit his chest. Not one of us could have suspected the lad would live." He let out a breath, desperate to prove Alaric's thoughts wrong. "As for the burn marks, you are correct, he does have a single brand. The others were made from a rod that a brand had previously been on. It had been heated and used so many times that the metal wore thin, and the brand broke off. The foreman continued to use it as a punishment."

He spoke softly, explaining the marks on the lad's side.

"And why was Benjamin punished so harshly?" He knew the lad could have a sharp tongue. He also knew he was young and acted without thinking at times. Alaric, however, could not think of any reason, someone should be punished in such a way, especially not a lad so young.

"He did not say." He laughed, though the expression did not sound genuine. "He claimed he probably had deserved it. Amara had walked in at that moment, and I do not think he wished to bring any memories back for the girl." Doc had turned, his gaze upon the two women now as well. Both of them seemed content, smiling up at Ol' Shorty who was telling one of his exaggerated tales. "You and I know the lad well. I suspect he was protecting the girl."

"Aye, you are probably right. I cannot blame him for that. You, I, or any of the other men would have done the same." Catching the eye of Molly, he smiled back at her. He was proud of Benjamin really, part of him even wished he had gotten the chance to see Benjamin stand up for the girl.

"He has been through much, most of which, you and I will not know all of, or understand why it happened. For now, just give him time. He is alive and despite his many scars, he is well." Doc assured. "And," he added cheerfully, "We are finally heading back to the islands. I am in want of seeing Captain Harding and Miss Catherine and discussing all she has done with the workers on their plantation. And I am sure it will do you good to be with the captain again."

"Aye, it will be good to see them. This voyage lacked

something, without Lucas." He admitted. He and Lucas had scarcely been apart since they were boys and had rarely sailed without the other. He was looking forward to seeing his brother again and to see how he was getting on with the plantation. When they had left, the fields were being burned and Lord Benedict was setting off to fetch the seeds they would need to replant the entirety of the fields.

Alaric let out a laugh, "And seeing his reaction when learning Benjamin is alive, will be a sight." Laughing again, he clapped Doc on the shoulder and strode over to the women. "I believe I saw Charlie take our tray in." Reaching a hand out, Molly gently placed hers in his and stood.

"Amara, I'm sure Cook has your tray ready as well. I had Henry clear out a cabin that had a few extra barrels and crates in it. It's not much but I'm sure you will be comfortable in there and that way you don't have to dine with the crew." She wrinkled her nose at the thought.

"Oh, thank you." She replied, her gratitude evident. She glanced up at Benjamin who smiled beside her.

"Come, I'll take you to the cabin and see what Cook has mustered up." Benjamin thanked Molly for her thoughtfulness and turned, walking Amara down the hatch to their cabin.

"That was very kind of you. I am glad you thought of that. It had not occurred to me." He led her to their own cabin, Aiofe in tow.

"They will be with us a night or two, I thought, so I imagined not only she would need a space of her own but that her and Benjamin would want some privacy." Meeting his gaze, she blushed.

Clearing his throat, he quickly opened the hatch for her. "It's rather hard for me to imagine the young boy I've known since he was a small child, having a lass of his own aboard this ship." He laughed again, shaking his head.

"He may still be a young lad, but he is no mere boy." She met his eyes again, as she poured each of them a generous scoop of stewed meat, carrots, and potatoes.

"No, I suppose you are right." He raised his brows.

"And, from what I've heard from the men on this ship, you and your Captain Harding had your share of fun and excitement at even a younger age." Molly tried hiding her grin with a long drink.

"Aye, I suppose you are again right." Clearing his throat once more, he quickly took a bite of his food, hoping to avoid further conversation on the topic of his past adventures. He felt Aiofe brushing against his leg, her purring growing louder with every moment. Letting out a sigh, he picked a chunk of stewed meat from his plate and tossed it on the ground for her. Through her purring, she quickly ate her share as if it would scurry away before she could finish.

"With you giving her all your scraps, she'll be too fat to catch the vermin below." Molly teased, waving fork in the air and pointing it accusingly at him, just as she tossed a small bit of meat from her own plate, down to the furry beggar.

Alaric frowned, causing Molly to burst into a fit of laughter that she quickly tried to get control over, clearly trying to spare him but unable to help herself.

Finally staunching her laughter, her face grew serious. "About Thomas Banning, I met him once, well, not met exactly, I did not know who he was at the time." She kept her gaze on her plate.

"You what? When?" He sat up straighter, his expression a mixture of anger and alarm. "Molly?" He softened.

"It was the day I ran away. The day I approached you at the docks. I was trying to find passage on a ship when a man grabbed me. I kicked him, he let go quick enough but I then all but collided with Thomas. He gripped me by the arms," she swallowed, she remembered the fear she felt when she had looked into his eyes in that moment. They had almost looked lifeless, they had contained no emotion, no feeling. Alaric shuffled in his chair, his face hardening as she continued. "He did not harm me. He also quickly let go. But I cannot help but think, how close you were to him those months ago."

Alaric shook his head, he placed his fork down, a bit harder than he had intended. "I had known we were close to him all the time but had not realized just how close we were so early on." He let out a sigh, looking her over, "You are sure he did not harm you?" He asked, moving his plate aside and leaning his arms on the table.

"I'm sure." She blushed, gathering the plates onto the tray to take them up.

"Leave them, Charlie will be back down in a bit to gather them. You do more than enough. You need to let the lads work. They'll grow soft if you keep doing their tasks for them." He teased, standing and moving to the water pitcher. Removing his shirt, he tossed it on the chest that sat at the end of the bed. Splashing water on his face, he wet his hair and scrubbed the dirt and sweat from the day off his body. The growing silence in the room had not gone unnoticed by him. Taking the towel that sat beside the pitcher and bowl, he dried the water droplets off, running it roughly over his hair. Stepping away from the cabinet and towards the bed, he stopped. He was aware of Molly's gaze upon him but had not realized that she had removed her dress and stood before him in only her shift. The sight was not wholly new to him, but something was different about it this time. Her brashness took him aback. In the past they avoided one another in an unspoken agreement. He tried his best to avoid her after their meals until he was sure she was tucked in the bed, fast asleep. His gaze rolled over her, the movement of the ship causing the gown to sway and pull against her. Taking a step forward, he reached his hand up, pulling her close to his own body. Tilting his head down, he gently placed his lips against hers. When she did not pull away, he deepened the kiss. He could feel her body relaxing and molding against his. A small sound escaped her mouth causing him to pull her in tighter. His hands running the length of her body, discovering every bit of her. He groaned, not willing to let the moment cease. They had not kissed since after the battle and the tension be-tween them had been growing with intensity. He had scarcely thought of anything else since their last kiss and had wanted no more than to have her in his arms again.

17

A loud blast sounded, breaking the near silence in the cold cabin. Alaric sat up, "Stay here, lass. I'll go see what is going on." He assured her, placing a quick kiss on her forehead. She nodded sleepily.

Throwing on his boots and a shirt, he reached for the hatch, just as a knock sounded on it. "Henry, what is it?" Alaric asked, a frown on his face at seeing Henry's shocked gaze.

"Tis the Royal Navy, Capt'n. They fired a warning shot." He explained.

"Tell me, why was I not alerted to a Royal Navy vessel nearing us?" Anger evident in his voice.

"The fog, Capt'n. It was mighty thick, and we did no see the ship until it were already upon us. Captain Clarke says, they be wanting to board us and to fetch ye." He awkwardly glanced passed Alaric, his gaze briefly landing on Molly who had rushed to pull a gown over her shift.

Alaric grunted, turning and grabbing his sword and flint-locks that lay on the desk. "Perhaps it is best you come with me, lass. I rather you remain by my side if they are to board us." Alaric placed a hand on her back, pulling her closer to him in a protective grip. He did not remember their last encounter with the Royal Navy with much fondness. He had not liked then, how the Lieutenant Mason had watched Molly and he had no doubt that is who was aboard the vessel that now approached.

"What do you suppose they want this time?" Molly asked. He could feel her body shaking under his hand.

"They have not come for you. Remember, all that happened with that man is over. You are not to blame and will not be tried." He stayed his steps, turning his full attention on her.

"It is not my fate I fear at the moment." She began, her eyes shifting between the vessel that was now pulling up alongside theirs. "You said yourself that Lieutenant Mason and Captain Hanes were spreading rumors of you being a pirate. What if they have come to arrest you?" Tears threatening to spill, she looked away, unable to meet the gaze of the two men waiting to board from the other ship.

"They could not hold us. There is no truth in their words, and we have Banning as proof of our innocence." He whispered, his face hardening at the thought of Captain Hanes and Mason taking over his ship and crew.

"Captain Hanes, what an…unpleasant surprise." Ethan

said, his arms crossed over his chest.

"Ah, Ethan, tis good to see you doing well." Hanes spoke, crossing over the plank that now joined the two ships, Lieutenant Mason and a couple other officers joining him.

Alaric did not miss the fact the captain had dropped the title from before speaking Ethan's name and judging by the look on his friend's face, Ethan had not missed the offence either.

"What is it we can do for you this time?" Alaric asked, a feeling of unease steadily rising. He caught sight of Benjamin. The lad clearly believed the Royal Navy to be there in that moment because of what he had done. If it had been any other Royal Navy vessel, Alaric would have suspected the same. He believed this had more to do with the altercations between Mason and Ethan than anything.

"Well, you see, that is just it. It is rather an awkward situation. You see," Captain Hanes began, looking around at *The Trinity's* crew, not one of the men appearing any more welcoming than Alaric had sounded.

"Get on with it, man!" Ethan said, exasperated.

"Very well, what the good captain is trying to say is, we've come to bring you in."

Benjamin took a step forward about to dispute the allegations. Alaric shook his head, just enough for the lad to notice.

"Ethan Clarke and Alaric Stein, you are being arrested for

piracy on His Majesty the King's waters and will be brought to justice. Your ship will be taken over by our men and any one of your crew members that chooses to go against our man's words will be locked in the brig along with your own prisoner." Lieutenant Mason rocked back on his heals, "Did I forget anything, Captain Hanes?"

"No, I think you said it all really rather well, Lieutenant." He snapped his fingers, his hand waving in the air, "Lock them in the brig of our ship. Lieutenant Commander, take control of this vessel." He waved one of the men that had followed them onto *The Trinity*, forward. See to it you bring the ship into port without any complications."

The other men that had come aboard stood behind Alaric and Ethan, ready to bring them over to the Royal vessel. "Take care of the crew, Captain. I'm sure I'll see you soon." Alaric's gaze looked onto Benjamin, who stood directly behind the Lieutenant Commander. The Lieutenant's brow furrowing in confusion. He quickly waved a few of his men to take their positions, aiding him in keeping *The Trinity's* crew in check, should they try and take their ship back.

"Miss Maclean, it is a great pleasure seeing you again. Do not fear, you will not have to go to the smelly brig with those ruffians. You may come and dine with us this evening." Mason said, gesturing for her to follow him.

"I should think I would prefer the smelly brig. At any rate, I would rather sleep in a cage with rats rather than dine with them." She looked at him pointedly. Alaric did not bother to hide his grin at her words.

Captain Hanes quickly raised his hand to the Lieutenant's chest, choking back a laugh, "If she would prefer to stay in the brig, let her."

The men behind Alaric shoved him and Ethan forward. Keeping one hand on Molly, they walked across the planks, to the Man o' War. The ship was much larger than *The Trinity*. Several windows spanned the stern. The fog closed in, thickening around the ships, encompassing them in a dark shadow.

"Come now, Captain," an officer came forward. "I really must protest. A beautiful thing like this should not be hidden away." His hand came up, stroking the hairs away from her face.

"Keep your hands off her, you bloody bastard." Alaric growled, grabbing the sailor behind the neck, driving the officer's head into the railing and letting him drop to the planks.

Captain Hanes grimaced for a moment at the sound of the sailor's head meeting the railing. Snickering as he helped the man up, he calmed the crew, "No one will go near the girl, or I will let the pirate have you." A roar of laughter erupted through the ranks, despite how many of them cautiously eyed Alaric.

The bars locked them into the brig below. Rats scurried along, just like on most ships, however a cat sat upon a crate in the far corner, tearing at a small, furry carcass. The planks on the floors of the cells were damp but at least they were not filled with an inch or more of water.

"Are you alright?" Alaric asked, pulling Molly close to

him. The brig was cold and though it had shelter from the elements outside, there was little warmth in there.

"I'll be just fine." She muttered, kicking at a rat that was sniffing a little too closely at her dress skirts.

Ethan grabbed hold of the bars of the cell, slamming his fist into them. Turning, he paced the small confines.

"It will be alright, mate. They cannot hold us, and I have faith we will be released very soon." Alaric shot Molly a wink. Ethan merely nodded, his jaw tight, his gaze locked onto the hatch as if it would spring open at any moment.

18

"Alrighty mates, you heard the captain." Benjamin whispered. "He's expecting us, and we won't be letting him down." Benjamin grinned. He had missed the crew from *The Trinity*, many of them had been aboard the vessel since Alaric had first brought him on board.

"Aye, lad, but how do you plan to take on an entire Royal Navy Man O' War?" Eddie asked, his voice filled with concern and disbelief.

"Easy," He shrugged, "We wait until dark. The fog will aid us as well. We will first take care of the men captaining *The Trinity*. Once done, Charlie, you'll climb the rigging and wave the lantern. Dowsing it and relighting it to catch their attention, signaling them. They will come up alongside us to be sure all is well with their men. From there, we'll board the Man O' War and release our captain and his mates." He explained, as if there was nothing to it. "Oh, one more thing. Try not to kill any of the men. We are all in enough hot water with the Navy as it is. There is no need for us to take on the entire vessel of men, just the ones that spot us." His grin broadened. He looked about the men, skeptical looks upon their faces. "Come now, mates. haven't you heard, I'm an expert at mutinies." A ripple of laughter travelled through the crew.

Benjamin crept down the companionway towards Doc's surgery. He needed to inform him and cook of the plans and wanted to make sure Doc would stay with Amara. She had been resting when the Royal Navy approached. He had told her to hide behind the crates in the cabin until he came for her.

"What are you doing, sailor?" A voice broke through the growing quiet as the evening light began to sink in. The fog already making difficult to see.

"Not but my duties, Officer." He replied simply, heading into the surgery. Mutinies did not typically involve the surgeon of the ship. He doubted the officer would question him even more. Leaving the door to the surgery a gape to prevent it appearing as if he had secretive plans, Benjamin greeted Doc, a look of understanding upon his face. Grabbing a piece of parchment, he quickly jotted down the plan and what he needed Doc to do.

Stay with Amara

We are getting our Captain back

Nodding in agreement, Doc set the parchment alight so it would not be accidentally discovered.

Emerging onto the deck, Benjamin kept an eye on the

officers, counting them, watching how they patrolled the deck. He knew there were two more below and one man in the captain's cabin. Five men walked the deck, cautiously watching the crew almost as if they expected there to be an uprising. Benjamin scoffed at the thought, he had no intent of disappointing them.

Benjamin's clothes were damp from the cold and foggy air. The night had set in, only allowing a few feet of visibility on the deck. The faint glow from the lights of the navy Man O' War shone distinctly through the dark. Catching the eye of a few of the crew, he moved forward, towards one of the officers. The man looked at him, guarded, clearly unnerved by the way Benjamin had suddenly approached him. "Sorry, mate." Benjamin said, knocking the officer over the head with a club they had used to break apart the crates. The confused look still formed on the man's face as he fell.

He heard the thud of the other officers being taken care of. Throwing a rope to Eddie, he gestured for him to tie the officers up, in case they woke too early. Charlie was already climbing the ringing, preparing to signal to the Man O' War. The light flickered in the top sails from the lantern that Charlie held. Benjamin watched, waiting, hoping they would be concerned enough about their men to stop. Hoping they would even see the light. The fog had grown even thicker and the glowing lights from the Man O' War had grown fainter by the moment. He caught sight of Ol' Shorty emerging from the cabin, having tied up the Lieutenant Commander.

The lights slowly and steadily began to brighten as they neared. Benjamin smiled. He only hoped the rest of his plan went just as smoothly. "I'm mighty glad you saw us signaling,

Officer," he began, "It's the others, they've been taken ill. It began with your Lieutenant Commander. His stomach is not right. Our Doc has the others below, trying to help them gain some control of their bowels again."

The officer scrunched his face in disgust. "Madison," he turned to the other man that stood beside him, "Go across, see what's going on with the Lieutenant Commander and report back." He ordered, taking a step back from the railing clearly wanting to keep his distance from the infected vessel.

"I won't be going aboard that pirate ship. What if it's catching?" Madison shook his head, keeping his feet firmly planted on the Man O' War. "Wake the Captain. See what he has to say about it."

"No," he replied firmly, "They were in their cups all evening, celebrating their capture. If you want to wake them, you can and risk their rath, but I won't be the one doing it." Shaking his head, he stumbled back as Benjamin and the others came rushing across the planks.

"I beg of you. You must help your fellow men." Benjamin proclaimed, feigning fear to be able to board the ship without the officers sounding the alarm. They had appeared too shocked at their sudden rush to even make a sound. Grabbing hold of the first officer, Benjamin spun him around, feeling his body grow slack in his grasp. He slowly laid him on the planks, making as little sound as possible, the rest of *The Trinity's* crew, now right behind him, sprawling across the deck, quickly dropping each man as they came upon them. The dark of the night and the dense fog, protecting them from being seen by any man in the rigging. Making their way below decks and towards the brig, they cautiously moved about, not wanting to wake any of the sleeping men or alerting any that were on duty.

Two men were posted at the hatch, one of them opened their mouth, ready to shout and alert the rest of the crew. The other man turned as white as the foam that lay upon the waves. Quickly placing his hand over the sailor's mouth, Benjamin shook his head. "Don't be doing that, mate." Slowly lowering his hand, he quietly grabbed the keys off the man's belt. "Many thanks." He grinned, patting the officer's cheek. The two men had to be no older than Benjamin himself, but clearly had far less experience than he did. Red quickly tying the two up, wrapping a cloth around their mouths so they could not call out once they regained their composure.

Opening the hatch, Benjamin peered into the big, unsure if there would be more guards. Taking a step in, he squinted in the darkness, "Alaric," he whispered.

"Aye, down here, lad." A reply came from further in the darkness.

Waving a hand forward, Benjamin led the men that had come down with him, towards Alaric's voice. The rest of the crew remained on deck in case there was trouble. "We must hurry. We took out as many men as we could, but it will not be long before the bell rings to change shifts." Benjamin explained, twisting the key in the lock.

"You did well. I couldn't have done better myself." Alaric said, squeezing Benjamin's shoulder, his other hand keeping a tight grasp on Molly.

"Aye, well done, lad." Ethan spoke up, "Let's get out of here before they realize what has happened. You lot, return to *The Trinity*. Alaric and I have to pay our compliments to the captain for such a lovey stay." He said, rushing up the stairs and out of the hatch.

Benjamin hesitated once on deck, catching Alaric's gesture to return to *The Trinity*.

"Take her with you," Alaric motioned to Molly, drawing her close for a brief moment and placing a kiss on her parted lips, before she could protest.

Nodding, he quickly led her across the planking and to the awaiting crew.

19

Ethan led the way to the captain's cabin. The deck was slippery from the fog and drizzle that had continued to fill the air around the ship, giving no signs of relenting or breaking up. Ethan placed his ear to the hatch, listening for voices or sounds the captain and the lieutenant may still be awake. Glancing at Alaric, he shook his head and grinned. Opening the hatch slowly, they quietly entered the large cabin. Ornate carvings decorated the frames of the windows and the hatch. A lavish desk and chairs sat in the middle of the room, a couple empty bottles of rum and whiskey sat atop it. The Lieutenant lay sprawled out in one of the chairs, his head falling back, his mouth agape. Foul smelling breath blew from between his lips, a loud snore escaping. The captain was draped halfway over his bed. The glass he had been holding lay forgotten beside his open hand, the contents spilling from it and onto the bedding.

Alaric walked over to the water basin. Lifting the jug, he stepped up to the lieutenant, splashing him with the chilly water. With a shriek, he sprang from the chair, fumbling for his sword that Ethan had already removed from his person.

"What do you think you are doing? How did you…" The captain bellowed, doing his best to stand.

"Oh, never mind that now." Ethan said, waving the lieutenant's sword through the air. "Well, I'd say, it's been a pleasure, but truth be told, until now, I haven't enjoyed one moment of this visit." He shrugged as Alaric threw a rope around the lieutenant, pulling him over to the bed where the captain had all but fallen back down onto. Tying the two men together and strapping the remaining rope to the post that held the bed firmly against the wall, Alaric backed away, grinning.

"Now, don't they look cozy?" He asked Ethan.

"They really do." Ethan tossed the sword down and bowed in mock salute. "Until we meet again."

The officers and crew on deck watched Alaric and Ethan emerge from the cabin, their faces of pure shock and uncertainty. The men on *The Trinity* held their guns at the ready. One of the young naval officers stepped forward, ready to speak, and more than likely try his best to stand up for his captain and scold the rogues. Ol' Shorty raised his hand, catching the young man's eye. Placing a single finger over his lips, indicating that for the officer's own sake, he should remain silent.

The Trinity pulled away from the large naval ship and sank into the thick fog.

"Let us catch up to *The Croga*. We will stop and make port for a short time. The naval ships will believe we made a run for the islands. With luck, they will not check into the colonies and once we've caught our breath, we can continue on our way." Alaric waved a hand in the air for them to let the sails out fully.

"You alright?" Alaric asked, walking up to Molly. He had been furious at the comments the sailors had made about her. The look on her face at the time had been a mix of fear, anger and desperation. He knew she was afraid for herself but also feared what would happen to him if the Navy had succeeded in bringing him back to the islands and branded a traitor and a pirate.

"Yes, just a bit cold." She replied, running her hands up and down her arms in an attempt to warm herself.

He looked her over, "Why don't you go in the cabin and check on Aiofe. I will join you in a bit." Pulling her closer to his own form, he wrapped his arms around her. "You are safe." He whispered against her ear. He could feel her body trembling.

"It's not myself I fear for." Looking up at him, her eyes filled with unshed tears. "When we reach the islands, what is going to stop them from arresting you as soon as you set foot on the shore? Won't they be awaiting your arrival?"

"They very well may be. They have nothing they can prove. We have more men speaking up for our characters than against. The Admiral is no fool. He may be furious at the gossip, but he knows the captain and lieutenant have it

136

in for Ethan. He is angrier that he lost his best man and is afraid another captain, not under his command will defeat the French fleet. If that happens, he will not get the Royal recognition he is wishing for. He simply wants Ethan back to do his bidding and since we are bringing in Thomas with us, he will have no reason to punish us." He reasoned, lifting her chin slightly. "Go get warm, I will be in, in a moment."

She nodded numbly, a slight smile of reassurance on her lips.

"Red, how's the prisoner?" Alaric asked. He had worried that in all the scuffle, Banning might have found a way of escape.

"Tis rottin' perfectly fine in there. Them rats be pestering him proper like." He let out a gruff laugh. "I had extra men stationed at the hatch to the brig once them naval bastards came aboard. I did not want them releasing him to make it out you be a liar or none. They did go on down too. Just as I had suspected. We kept them at bay though.

"Smart thinking, sailor. You saved our hide." Alaric acknowledged, dismissing Red to continue with his duties.

Bounding down the companionway, he went to Doc. It had always been the visit he and Lucas dreaded after every battle. Wandering how many men they had lost and how badly others were injured.

He would never forget the first year they had *The Trinity*. They had come across a Portuguese Brig that they had been following around the outer islands for weeks. It had kept evading them. The captain and the crew had clearly been well trained and knew what they were doing. Once they had finally caught up to her, they had fired the first shot. A warning. They had known she would not simply surrender though the hope was high. They needed to resupply, desperately and likely, the enemy had needed to as well. What they had not foreseen though, was the reason the Portuguese had been avoiding them. Not long after the first shot struck the enemy vessel, two more came into view. They barreled down on them at all sides, locking them in against one of the smaller islands. The sandbars around them making maneuvering even more treacherous. Alaric had never felt so vulnerable as he had in that moment. He could still recall the sounds of the crew, their cries and shouts of desperation. The battle lasted hours. Somehow Lucas had managed to steer *The Trinity* out of their watery prison. They had squeezed between two of the enemy vessels and just as both had fired another shot, *The Trinity* broke free. The cannons ripping into the Portuguese. The friendly fire hit just after *The Trinity* had fired. It crippled the two ships, leaving one remaining to steer around and try and capture.

In the end, they had suffered the greatest loss they ever had. The victory was bitter and washed down greatly by the loss of their crewmates. When they had returned to Barbados, Alaric and Lucas had personally seen to letting the families know of their losses. They provided the families with the sailor's earnings, even though they knew at the time, it meant very little.

"You can wipe the dismal look from your face, Captain Stein. Your crew is safe, this time round. No casualties, and aside from single bump on the head," he gestured to Colin who sat sheepishly on a bench, a bandage around his head. "No other injuries to report."

Alaric raised his brows, relief and surprise evident in his voice. Glancing back at Colin, he tried to look sympathetic. "May I ask what happened?" Judging by the look on the boy's face, he had not gotten the wound from defending the ship.

"I slipped while getting out of my hammock, just before the younger Captain Stein set the plan into motion." He confessed, "I tried to continue on the deck to help, but Doc spotted me and would not allow me to go any further." He bowed his head in embarrassment.

"It can happen to the best of us, lad." Alaric choked back the laugh. He knew the boy felt poorly and did not wish to make him feel worse. He went to step back through the hatch and paused, "You said, 'the younger Captain Stein,' who did you mean?" He looked from Colin to Doc, who simply smiled.

"Who do you think the lad means? That is what the crew calls Benjamin. They do not know his other name and you are the closest thing he has to kin." Doc explained.

Alaric felt his throat tighten, clearing it quickly, he turned and headed to his cabin and to Molly.

20

Molly sat upon the bed, the fur blanket warming her legs. Aoife curled up beside her. The kitten's soft and rhythmic purrs soothing what worry she still felt. Molly pulled the shawl tighter around her shoulders, the thin shift doing little to keep her warm. She had taken the dress she had been wearing, off. The stench from the brig clinging to the fibers. Flipping to the next page in the book Doc had given her a several weeks back, she ran her finger along the writing. The sketch showed the teeth of a horse. The text spoke of the debate of whether or not the madness of a horse was caused by the teeth or not and what could be done about it. A common practice seemed to be cauterizing the areas in the mouth that had become painful. A chisel, mallet and iron puncher were also shown. The writing spoke of a condition called, Lampas. According to what had been written, there was much debate amongst farriers of whether or not the wolf teeth should be removed and whether or not any treatment was even necessary, many believing the illness originated in the beast's mind rather than a physical condition.

Molly furrowed her brow. Running her finger along the drawing of the horse's teeth, she made a note in her mind to speak with Doc about the information on the page. She felt there had to be more to it and wondered why there was so much debate about what seemed like a straightforward diagnosis. The next page went on to show the parts of a horse's body, labeling each one. Over the next few pages, the writing and sketches spoke of a horse's legs, hooves and the tools used to treat various ailments.

"You seem really absorbed in that book." Alaric's voice broke the silence in the cabin.

"I am rather." She voiced, skimming over the page with the horse's teeth once more. "I can't figure this one out though." She tapped the page with her finger, glancing over her shoulder at him.

Alaric opened the hatch, taking the tray from Henry who had just knocked, and quickly shut it again. Setting the tray on the table, he strode over to her, a slice of bread in his hand. "Aye, back home we had a horse that we used to pull the carts and plow the fields. She was strong and gentle at the same time," He laughed, brushing her hair over her shoulder, his meaning clear. "One day though, we woke to her kicking at the stable door. She was obviously uncomfortable, and something had been bothering her. We tried looking her over to see what was ailing her. Gave Lucas a rather bad kick to his thigh."

"And it was this, Lampas, that was causing the discomfort?" She moved over a bit, giving him room to sit on the bed.

Alaric shrugged, "Never truly found out. The farrier, he said the horse had gone mad. He claimed he could not find anything physically wrong with her and said we could either shoot her and end her suffering or try and pull her teeth and see if it ends her madness." Lucas's father ended up shooting her. She got so angry that we couldn't hardly enter her stall without lashing out at us."

Molly pulled her brows together, looking the sketch over. "Poor beast must have been in real discomfort."

"Aye, she was, though I could not say from what. At the time we believed pulling her teeth would have only caused her more pain."

"And so, it would have, I am sure of it." Shaking her head, she closed the heavy book. "If the teeth were the problem, I am sure the farrier would have seen an obvious sign. If no obvious sign was there to see though, I do not understand why he would have wished to take the teeth."

"I cannot answer that, except to say, it is normal practice." He beckoned her over to the table that he had returned to.

"Aagh!" Ol' Shorty exclaimed, kicking his foot and flinging a retched and fowl smelling substance through the air. "Mangey beasts are all over the streets. It's as bad as on the

142

islands." Waving his arms in the air, he shooed a scraggly looking dog away from the group.

"Come now, Shorty. You should feel something akin to those animals." Ethan began, "After all, you smell as about as bad as they do." Chuckling at the other man's scowl.

Molly walked closely next to Alaric, her arm brushing against his. The warm fur vest covering the coat and dress he had purchased her. The air was getting colder the longer they remained in the colonies, though the further south they got, the temperatures around them seemed to even out. The rain, however, was relentless, causing the streets to be several inches deep in thick mud. The carriages passing by, splashing the brown and dirty water high. They had found and met up with *The Croga*. They had agreed the best course of action would be to once again head into the colonies, believing Captain Hanes would not search for them there.

Molly spotted a small and quaint tearoom. It was not nearly as extravagant as the one they had met Mrs. Banning in. Instead, it had a modest sign hanging above the door, it read, The Singing Bee. Flowers surrounded the building, engulfing it in a sweet aroma of petals, tea leaves, and freshly baked biscuits, and cakes.

"We will catch up to you lot." Alaric spoke up. "Keep a close watch out and be back at the ship before sundown." He added.

"Oui, Oui," Cook responded, waving a hand in the air and flashing a knowing smile at them. The others nodding in acknowledgement, continuing on their way. Even if new supplies were not needed, each port added a new adventure, new discoveries for all onboard.

"Care to go in?" Alaric asked, gesturing towards the tearoom.

Molly's mouth fell open, "Truly?"

"Aye, of course. I saw you gazing at it." He said, stepping toward the building. "We have no pressing matters at the moment. Why not enjoy ourselves a bit?"

Molly looked about nervously, her hands running along her skirts. She plucked at the vest she wore. "I'm not sure… that is, I'd love to, but…"

"Tis only a tearoom. You will not look amiss." He reached up, gently brushing a stray strand of her hair back. "You look lovely, as usual." He assured, "Now come, you know you are aching to have a look inside." He grinned, wrapping her hand around the crook of his arm, guiding them over to the building and through the bell.

The scent of herbs and sweet cakes wafted over to them. "Please, do come in." A tall woman approached them. Her movements were so graceful, it looked as if she were gliding.

"Thank you, may we sit anywhere?" Alaric asked, eyeing a window on the opposite side of the room. It had a stunning view of the gardens behind the building.

"By all means," Her smile widened, "Tis my preferred spot as well." She led the way to the table. "My name is

Mistress Cameron and I will be back in a moment with your refreshments." Helping Molly remove her vest and coat, she quickly hung them up on a hook near the entrance before disappearing behind a door that led to the kitchen.

"I don't believe I've ever been in such a sweet room before." Molly whispered, looking about the place. A framed sketch hung on the wall here and there throughout the room. The glow in the room was dim but the large window in the back let in a brighter, welcoming light. The wallpaper was a soft green that complimented the array of colors that sat in the garden.

"Tis a fine place." He relaxed in the chair. "It reminds me of a tearoom back home. An aunt of mine had owned it."

"In Ireland or in Barbados?" Molly asked, curious to know more of his past.

"In Ireland. The small village we grew up in was not much, mostly farmers and that such. My aunt though, she kept a tea-room much like this, close to the coast. Her tearoom was the last place Lucas, and I had a good cup of Irish tea at, before we were signed onto the Royal Navy." He chuckled, gazing out the window, his face clouded with memories.

"Do you wish to go back?" She asked, placing her hand on his briefly before pulling it away again, her face flushing.

"Aye, in time, I suppose. For now, though, I enjoy the ship," leaning forward, his gaze heating, "And your company onboard."

Molly's lips parted. She wished to reply but the words were stemmed as Mistress Cameron returned with a tray of cakes and tea. Molly felt her face flush.

"There you are," Mistress Cameron beamed, "Now, if you should need anything else, just holler." Sweeping over to another table, she gathered the cups and tea pot up. Putting them back on the tray and stacking the plates carefully. Crumbs from the sweat cake, still clinging to the dishes. The two women that had been seated there had left, shortly after Molly and Alaric had arrived. Their heads pressed closely together, whispering about whatever gossip they could think of and eyeing Molly with suspicion and scrutiny. Molly could not blame them, though the colonies seemed to host an abundance of folks from all over, but Molly's hair seemed to draw in attention wherever she went. The color matching that of the autumn leaves that filled the mountains further north.

"Your tea will grow cold if you sit their daydreaming." Alaric whispered, drawing her gaze to his.

"I'm sorry," smiling sheepishly, she took a sip, savoring the warm, floral taste. "Thank you for this." Taking a small bite of the cake, she licked her lips, not wanting to waste a crumb. "Mmm, 'tis as good as Cook's."

"Perhaps even better," Alaric teased, "Though if you tell him I said as much, I will deny every word of it."

Molly let out a giggle, quickly covering her mouth to stifle the sound. "I wouldn't dream of it."

"Good," he replied, covering up his own laugh with another sip of tea.

The door to the tearoom opened, a naval officer, accompanied by a beautiful young woman, entered. The woman's hair was done up in an elaborate mass of curls and twists. Her gown was lavished in tiny flowers that had delicately been sewn on. Lace framing the edges, adding a rich touch to it. The naval officer glanced in their direction, nodding politely, before returning his attention back to the young woman.

Molly took a shaky breath in, "Do you not fear they will see your ship in the docks and arrest you again?"

"No, I do not fear that, because it will not happen. No other naval officer will arrest us or even take a second glance at me or my ship. Lieutenant Mason and his cronies will have seen to that. They made sure to spread the word of our, endeavors, enough to cause suspicion and a buzzing of rumors but no more. They will have made sure it was not talked of to the point that any other officer would wish to bring us in to claim the rewards. They are playing a game to get their own gains, we must simply, outmaneuver them for as long as we can, until we can clear our names for the Admiral's benefit." He assured her, finishing the last of his tea and cake.

"I see," smiling in relief at the explanation. She had not thought of the circumstances in that light, only that the Royal Navy was after him.

Stacking the dishes back on the tray for Mistress Cameron, Molly looked up at Alaric who had risen from his seat. "I would like to see what more the town has to offer. Would you care to join me, or would you prefer to return to the ship?"

He asked, holding his hand out to her.

"I'd love to see more of the town too," she beamed, taking his hand and avoiding his gaze. She was afraid if he looked at her too closely, he would be able to see exactly how he made her feel.

"Excellent," Alaric placed a few coins on the table and followed Molly outside.

The town was smaller and much less established than the other colony towns they had been in. Near the outer edge, further from the docks, logs and trees were being stacked and pulled by large teams of horses. They were being placed near the mill so they could be cut into more manageable sizes.

Alaric led them up the small steps and into a building that doubled as a mercantile and trading post with a livery and blacksmith attached to the side of the building. "Have a look around." Alaric encouraged, stepping over to a shelf that held maps, spyglasses, ledger books and a rather intricate sextant.

Molly hesitated, looking about the place slowly. The back shelf behind the counter held sacks and crates of food and dried good. A shelf near the end of the counter lay a stack of books. Jars filled with candies sat on the counter, just at the perfect level for small eyes to spy. A woman stood over at the other end of the store, folding long stretches of fabric. Some of them plainer, more subtle patterns and colors, others of richer, more vibrant shades. Molly slowly made her way over to the fabric and ribbons.

"Good afternoon, my dear, can I help you with finding

anything?" The storekeeper asked, placing the pile of fabric on the shelf where it belonged.

"I couldn't say," Molly replied, touching a bundle of fabric, the color was a dark yellow.

"If you do not mind me saying, this green will go lovely with your complexion. It would pair better with your hair than the yellow, I believe." She offered, pulling the green fabric forward.

"Thank you, I would probably agree with you on that, however I was not thinking of myself when looking at the yellow." Molly ventured a smile. She knew the shopkeeper had meant well.

"See something you like?" Alaric asked, coming up behind the women.

Molly wrang her hands together. She did not know if she should say what she had in mind. It was not Alaric's responsibility to pay for more items for her. He had already treated her to the tearoom and had bought her more than enough items during their time on the ship together and she had no way of repaying him for any of it. "It is only," she paused hoping he would not be angered at her idea. "Amara and the other women, their dresses are old and torn and could use mending." She began, looking back at the yellow fabric. She thought of the women on *The Croga*, the children and how their garments hardly stayed on their bodies. A bit of fabric could go a long way for mending and patching their clothes and the babe could use a warmer wrap.

"You've a kind and generous heart, lass. You pick the fabrics you think necessary. I am sure Amara and the others will greatly appreciate it." He ran a hand over the same fabric. "Besides, I believe we owe them for saving us the other day. Wouldn't you agree?" He winked.

"Well, in that case," the shopkeeper quickly moved forward, pulling the yellow fabric from the shelf and showing Molly the others she had in store, as if she were afraid Alaric would change his mind, eager to sell as much of the fabric as she could.

The two of them left the store, shortly after. Alaric had requested the boxes be brought to the ship by a delivery boy. Chewing on a sticky, maple candy, they slowly made their way back in the direction of the docks. Alaric had purchased some dried meat he said had been made from the large bison that roamed the plains further north.

"Oh!" Molly exclaimed, a dog, its fur scraggly and matted in places, began to limp towards them. Its back leg hung oddly from the body. Patches of missing fur revealed cuts and wounds. Slinking down low, it sniffed the air, approaching them slowing and cautiously. Clearly it was not entirely comfortable or trusting of people. Molly raised a hand, causing the dog to halt. "It's alright, you poor creature." She took a step towards it. A low growl emanating from its muzzle.

"Molly, perhaps this one should be left alone." Alaric advised, his hand wrapping around her arm in an attempt to stop her.

"I can't possibly leave it like this. It needs helps." She

whispered, glancing back at Alaric. "It is scared, hurt and starving," she explained, seeing the dried meat in his hand and realizing why the dog had begun to approach them in such hope. Grabbing the meat from Alaric's stunned form, she crouched low, holding the meat out and talking softly to the dog.

Molly heard Alaric let out an exasperated sigh. The dog's eyes widened at her approach, but it did not back away. Another growl sounded, this time a little more assertive. "Molly," Alaric stepped forward, his hand ready to pull the sword from its place on his hip.

Continuing her approach, she reached the meat out towards its nose so it could know her intentions. The dog's tongue flicked out, swiping around its wet nose. Whimpering, it gingerly began licking at the meat she held firm in her hand. She did not want the dog snatching the meat from her and running off. Stroking a hand on the beast's head, she soothed it, allowing it to calm and trust her. An occasional grow still sounding a small and helpless warning. Alaric now crouched beside her. As she fed the rest of the dried meat to the animal, he secured a strap he had pulled off from around his waist.

"Just to be safe," his voice low. "I'll hold her, you look her over and see what can be done." He relented, allowing the dog to rest her head in his lap in defeat and trust.

Nodding, Molly worked as quickly as she could, looking over each cut and mark that spanned her body. Feeling the bone and joints around the leg and hip, she quickly found the problem. She had seen this very thing on a couple of the men after a storm or battle. Doc had explained how a finger or arm could be pulled out of place and how it needed to be set right. She had aided him in doing so on a couple occasions. Feeling around the area more, she looked up at Alaric. The dog was whimpering and moving around, wanting to escape the pain but not wanting to leave the hands that had fed her. "Hold her as steady as you can. She'll not be liking this." Placing a hand of the animal's hip, she rotated the leg slowing, feeling the limb slip back into place. The dog yelped, seeming to relax quickly after. Molly let out a small laugh of victory. "There you are lass. Tis much better, is it not?" Looking over the wounds, her smile quickly faded, "I wish I had a bag like Doc's. To be able to tend animals anywhere I find them." She breathed out, stroking the dog's fur. The animal was a little smaller than the goats on the ship, its fur a mixture of browns and greys.

"You stay here. I'll fetch her some water." Alaric said, standing quickly and moving off towards the livery.

"It is not much, but at least you can walk now." She ran a hand along the dog's belly, it was clear she had pups at some point and either they had not made it or they were now weaned, as her milk had recently dried up.

"Here you go." Alaric said, as much to the dog as to Molly. He set a bowl on the ground at her nose and handed Molly a wet bit of fabric. "Much to the livery owner's dismay, I poured a bit of his whiskey on the fabric." He explained, patting his pocket of coins. "I tossed him a few in exchange for the whiskey."

Smiling up at him, she quickly set to work once again. Squeezing drops of the liquid onto each cut and clearing the

152

dried blood from the wounds.

"I reckon the man at the livery thought I had gone mad, wasting his whiskey by pouring it onto a cloth." Alaric chuckled, "I've seen Doc do it many times though. He says it cleans the wounds and helps prevent fever." He smiled sheepishly.

"Aye, t'was a good thought. It will help clean the wounds and hopefully help her to heal properly." She replied, focusing on the last and biggest of the cuts. It was a deep one and Molly wished she had a needle and thread to stitch it up. "Tis all we can do for her now." Stroking the dog's head once more, she gingerly removed the strap from its muzzle. "You stay out of trouble now." She said, coaxing the dog to stand. She carefully placed weight on her back leg. Licking at the limb that had been giving her such pain. Scampering a ways down the path, she looked back at them, as if to thank them for their kindness.

"You did very well." Pride evident in his voice.

"Aye, we make quite the team." She beamed, pleased at being able to help the animal. Blushing, she placed her hand back in the crook of his arm. "Thank you for allowing me to do that."

"I do not believe I could have stopped you even if I had wished to." He laughed, "In truth, I was a little worried the beast might attack at any moment, but you calmed her with remarkable swiftness." They stepped up the plank that led on deck of *The Trinity*. "You do owe me some more of that delicious, dried meat though." He said, winking and leaving her to tend to the animals below.

21

"I was right, this fabric looks wonderful on you." Molly exclaimed, holding the fabric up to Amara.

"You and your captain shouldn't have. We make do with what we've got." Amara replied, uncomfortable at the generosity.

"I am not sure he is *my* captain," Molly blushed, "And I am the same. I have always made do with what I have, but I've also found, that it is ok to accept the help and kindness of others." Molly smiled down at the young girl that sat next to them. "Now, for you, let's see what we can find." Molly suggested, looking to the small girl that sat beside them. Molly rummaged through the fabric, unraveling a long strip that would make a beautiful wrap for the young girl's head and help to keep her hair from her face. The girl's eyes lit up at the browns, reds and yellow on the fabric.

"What is it like, where you are from?" Amara asked, spreading a bit of fabric out to size it up next to the dress she was mending.

"Green, very green. With lots of rolling hills and rocks. The cliffs over the ocean are steep and very dangerous. The water is colder than it is in these parts." She explained, "When I would wash my clothes in the stream that flowed passed my uncle's farm, my hands would turn an angry red and grow painful for a time, until I warmed them in the straw in the barn or by the fire in the lamp." Molly shook her head at the memory. "In the warmer months, the flowers would fill the hillsides. They smelled so sweet, like honey." She smiled at the women that sat around her. "I remember once, when I was young, my mother and I lived in a cave under the cliffs, at the edge of the sea. We had a fire going to keep us warm and keep the damp from our clothes and skin. My mother was telling me a story of the creatures that live in the waters. The ocean seemed to be listening in that moment. A large whale came up, blowing water from the top of his head." Molly laughed at the surprised expression on the young girl's face. "I had never seen the like before." She pulled a needle and thread through a bit of fabric on the dress of one of the other women. The red fabric nearly matched the woman's old dress perfectly. "And what of you? What is it like where you are from?" She asked Amara.

"Not green," She laughed, causing a ripple of the joyous sound to travel amongst the women. "We too lived by the ocean, but the waters we were near were warm. We lived in a village with many others. Our homes were made of the muds and there were many children in every home." Amara continued, helping the girl to wrap the fabric correctly about her head. "I have brothers and sisters. My father is a *saltige*, a great hunter for our village." She spoke of her family with great pride, explaining what her life had been like.

"How is it that you came to be on the slave ship?" Molly could not help but wonder how the course of events had played out. Like her, these people were a long way from their homelands, had been bought and sold as if they were not but goods.

"The chief was angry. He had wished me to marry one of his sons, but I had been promised to another." Her voice solemn.

"Did you love either of these men?" Her brow furrowed.

"No, I did not, but I would have had no say in the matter." She explained, "The ship came. They traded weapons and lavish goods for slaves. My people wanted and needed them to fight their own wars. The chief chose me and others to be amongst those that would be traded. My father was away with my brothers and there was not that my mother could do."

"I am sorry," Molly sympathized, the memory of arriving at her uncle's was masked by the terror of arriving at the plantation he had sold her too.

"But now, we are free, and we can smile once more." Amara looked at the others who nodded in agreement. "How about a story?" She asked the children, eagerness in their expressions. Amara began a tale as she sewed and mended her dress, pulling the thread through the warm fabric. Her voice softly flitted about the large cabin, not one person spoke, all listening to her story of a baboon and tortoise. The baboon was the trickster. His cunning and deceiving nature making him a foe rather than the friend tortoise thought him to be. "It was tortoise's turn. The baboon needed to be taught a lesson. The trick he had played on the poor old tortoise was unkind. Tortoise invited baboon to share a meal with him…" She continued, the eyes of the children were fixed on her, excited to hear how tortoise would get his revenge on the baboon. As she spoke, Molly realized Amara's words changed, she spoke in different tongues, one, Molly recognized as French, the other a tongue she did not know or understand but guested it to be the language of Amara's village.

"That was lovely," Molly said, raising the fabric she had been sewing up, checking it for size.

"Thank you, it was a favorite of mine as a child." Her voice was soft, and her skin had paled.

"Are you quite alright?" Molly moved closer to her, concerned for the young woman. "Perhaps you should go back to your cabin and lay down for a bit. I will have some bread and cheese brought it." Molly stood, helping Amara up who now looked to be in discomfort rather than distress.

"Tis fine. I will do as you suggest, however." Squeezing Imani's hand briefly, giving the older woman reassurance, she headed for the hatch and towards the cabin.

Molly's brow furrowed as she watched Amara enter the captain's cabin on *The Croga*. The girl had clearly become upset and was in discomfort but from what, Molly could not guess. Crossing the plank that joined the two ships, she headed for Cook's. The ships had anchored briefly when Benjamin had signaled. One of the children had taken a turn and he needed Doc. After examining the boy, he assured the mother, the child would be fine, that his body was simply not used to the steady amounts of rich foods. The boy had all but starved on the plantation and his body had been very weak. Doc requested that the mother and boy be brought aboard *The Trinity* for a few days, for monitoring. The boy had a fever, and his body was having a hard time recovering. A few days under Doc's watchful eyes would see him right.

When they had anchored together, Molly had taken the opportunity to help the women on *The Croga* with their mending and she had been eager to speak with them all again. She enjoyed their company and, in a way, felt akin to them.

"Cook," Molly began, as she entered the small cabin. The smells of the vegetables and meat roasting made her mouth water. A thick pot of stew sat steaming in the corner and a fresh loaf of bread was wrapped in a cloth to keep it warm and soft. "Amara is feeling a little unwell, I wonder if we can have some bread and cheese brought over to her. I'll find Benjamin and let him know."

"Oui, of course," he nodded, gathering the bread and cheese into a bowl to be taken to Amara.

Molly rushed off to find Benjamin. She did not wish to bother Doc just yet, knowing he was busy with the child and perhaps Benjamin would know what was ailing Amara. Approaching the hatch to Alaric's cabin, she could hear voices inside. Knocking quickly to let them know she was there. She opened the hatch. "Excuse me, I am sorry to interrupt," she began, suddenly feeling uncomfortable about barging in on their conversation. "Uh, its only," she stammered. "Amara is feeling a little unwell. I sent her to have a lie down and Cook is having some refreshments sent over." She breathed out, glancing from Benjamin and Ethan to Alaric.

Alarm registered on Benjamin's face, "Is Doc in his surgery?" He asked, heading straight for the hatch.

"Aye, but he is still tending the child." Molly placed a hand gently on his arm to slow him. "I will accompany you if you wish until Doc can see to her." She suggested, knowing there was not much she could do for the girl but wanted to be there to at least comfort the two of them for a time.

"Aye, mayhap that would be best. I will come over as well in case you should need anything. Ethan, please, see to it that Doc comes over when he is able." Alaric said, giving Benjamin's shoulder a squeeze before leading him out of the hatch.

"I'll fetch some water and a cloth. It may make her feel better." Molly offered, turning back for the pitcher and cloth that sat next to it.

As they approached the cabin Amara was in, her soft cries could be heard from inside. Benjamin quickened his steps, throwing the hatch open and rushing in. "It's alright. It will be just fine." His voice was filled with desperation as he looked back at Alaric, his eyes pleading for him to help.

"Amara, tell me where it hurts," Molly asked, quickly looking the girl over. She wrung out the cloth from the pitcher, dabbing it gently on Amara's cheeks and head.

"Tis my middle." Closing her eyes tight against the

pain, her hand not leaving the lower part of her stomach.

"She's," Benjamin began, "she's with child." He stood, staring down at Amara, his face filled with anguish.

"She's what?" Alaric blurted out, his voice not hiding the shock. His eyes searched Benjamin's face, "Ben?"

"Aye, the babe's mine." Benjamin released a breath, kneeling next to Amara and gripping her hand in his.

The hatch flew open, allowing Doc entrance, "You lot, clear out so I can examine my patient. Molly, I ask you stay, though, in case I should need assistance." He paused, looking about the cabin. No one moved, shock and fear showing in all their eyes. He looked back down at Amara, her hands still upon her stomach. A moan escaping her lips. "I see," he sighed, "All will be well in a bit." He spoke softly. Molly was not sure who he was speaking more to, Amara or Benjamin. "Captain, why don't you take the lad back with you. There is no more he can do now, and we require privacy."

Stepping forward, Alaric placed his hand on Benjamin's shoulder, "Come," he whispered. Nodding numbly, the lad did as he was bit. Allowing Alaric to lead him back through the hatch.

Removing the covers, Molly's breath caught. Amara's gown and the bedding was saturated, the sheets now stained a light red. Molly glanced up at Doc, who shook his head. "I'll need warm water, rum and a bowl. Once you return, I'll have a list made up of the herbs I'll need you to make into a tea." He stood above the desk, jotting down the names of the herbs he had in his surgery. "There is not that we can do now for the babe, it is coming too soon. We must make the mother comfortable and wait until the time passes. The tea will aid in speeding her time along."

Returning to *The Trinity*, Molly gathered the items Doc had instructed her to. Rushing into the cabin, she tried to ignore the concerned look on Alaric and Benjamin's faces as they watched her rifle through the chest of clothes. Pulling out an extra night gown she headed for the hatch once more, pausing, "Doc is taking good care of her. Amara will be alright, I'm sure of it."

"And the babe?" He asked, his voice cracking slightly.

"I'm very sorry. Her time came too soon. She still had approximately a month or two to go." She whispered in reply, shooting Alaric a sympathetic look.

"Here you are, Doc." Molly said quietly, entering the cabin again.

"I will revise the list of herbs on the paper. The first batch will not be needed now. The babe came very quickly. I suspect she had been laboring awhile but had been ignoring the pain, hoping it would pass." He spoke quietly, covering Amara back up with the blankets. She had calmed and no longer seemed in discomfort. "I will have the bowl now, and you can begin to clean her up with the warm water, if you do not mind."

Molly moved forward, handing Doc the bowl and bringing the pitcher of warm water over to the side of the bed. "I brought her a shift as well. She'll need a new gown." Ringing out the water from the cloth, she set to work, not baring to look at the bowl where Doc had placed the bundled cloth. She had helped on the plantation from time to time with the slaves when their time had come. She would fetch cloths and water then too. She had always tried to gather clean linens from the storeroom in the big house, unable to face the idea of placing a new babe in one of the filthy cloths that remained in the slave's quarters. "Shhh, it's over now." She stroked Amara's forehead, covering her up once more with the blankets. She would be warm and comfortable in the clean shift and could rest as long as she needed. The room now smelt of herbs and steeping tea that Doc had made to aid her recovery. He had said the herbs in the tea would help with pain and replenish the strength she had lost, but there was not they could do to mend her mind or heart. That would be between her and the lad.

22

"Care to talk about it?" Alaric asked, sliding the cup of rum over to Benjamin. The lad sat at the table, unmoving. Alaric turned, unable to face the pain and confusion in the boy's eyes. Looking out at the dark waters through the window, he wished he could do more for the lad.

"I made Doc swear not to say a word. I asked him to examine her when we first met up. I thought you'd be angry, and I couldn't bear the look of disappointment on your face that was sure to be there. Doc tried to reason with me. He isn't to blame. He told me you would likely understand more than I expected."

"And he was right." Alaric interrupted. His voice came out a bit harsher than he had intended. He ran a hand through his hair, hearing Benjamin's shaky breath.

"In the end though, Doc promised not to say a word. To allow me a chance to tell you." He waited, "I'm sorry." He sighed.

"You've nothing to be sorry for." Alaric admitted. He had wished circumstances had been different. Amara's body had been weak, and half starved. The gown had hidden her growing belly well.

"At first," he began, "I would stay with her in the hut to keep her safe from Skraag. He wanted her something fierce. That is one of the reasons he stayed on at the plantation for so long. He was waiting for the right opportunity, and he got his chance more than once." He took a sip, his hand shaking. "After a time though, it became more than that." He confessed. "We witnessed things no one should ever have to see or be a part of. I did what I could for them, but it was never enough, but I knew, no matter what, I had to keep her safe and out of his reach."

Alaric stood silent, listening. His admiration and pain for the boy, growing with every word the boy spoke.

"She has bad dreams. Dreams of what happened and what might happen. I'd lay next to her at night to try and keep them at bay and to help her get through them when they would wake her." He went on, "We were out in the fields and a ruckus had begun. A fight had broken out between a couple of the slaves and one of the guards. I went to go and stop it, when I caught sight of Skraag slinking off towards where Amara was working in the field further away." He shook his head, swallowing. "I had to walk away from the fight. In truth, I do not even know why it began or what ended up happening with it. All I could think about was getting to her before he did." He sat back in the chair, "I was almost too late that time. He had her pinned against the wall of one of the farthest huts. I went right for him. He had dropped his club on the ground, and I picked it up. He was too distracted to notice me. I thought I had killed him then, but I didn't. Amara's voice was calling my name, telling me to stop, that I could not kill him, or I'd be hung or worse."

Alaric's eyes were on him now, "I am surprised you were not, even having not killed him in that moment. An attack on a foreman is a death sentence."

"Aye, it is and likely that is what happened to the men that attacked the guard. Not me though, they chose to merely punish me. The foreman chose that over death because he feared an uprising if he killed me. I had helped too many of the workers and had earned their gratitude. Plus, the foreman couldn't stand Skraag, he was jealous of him and hated him strutting around the plantation as if it were his duty to do so. He undermined and countered him on more occasions than I can count. The foreman hoped that if I remained alive, I would eventually kill Skraag myself, ridding him of the thorn in his side, and so I did."

"What was the punishment?" Alaric asked, the look on his face, showing he had already guessed the answer.

"The burns on my sides." He put a hand over his ribs. "There was a branding iron that had been used on the slaves so many times, being heated and cooled too often that the brand eventually broke off and it was a mere poker in the end. It was in the fire and red hot and the quickest and most painful punishment the foreman could perform in that moment. He had drug me away from Skraag and over to the fire where the guards held me firm." Benjamin shrugged. "It's that very day that gives Amara the bad dreams. She blames herself, says she should have been stronger, fight him off harder." He looked up at Alaric. "It was not her fault. She did all she could and had fought him off and avoided him on other days. He was just particularly ruthless that time."

Alaric nodded, taking it all in. Benjamin could feel his eyes on him, watching him. "And now she is in there, fighting for her life and when she wakes, she will be mourning the loss of our child." He took a shaky breath in, now having said the words out loud, he had no more to say.

"I wish I had been there. Been there for you when you needed me most. I would have taken every one of those punishments for you, you know that, right?" He swallowed hard, his hands on the desk.

"Don't you see?" Benjamin smiled, "It is exactly those thoughts that led me to do all I did. From the moment I was pulled from the waters and onto that ship, I kept thinking, *what would Alaric do?*" He let out a half laugh, "I took the punishments for others and did what I could to save them because that is exactly what you would have done for me, and for them, had you been there."

"I could not have done better." Alaric said, "You have shown more strength than I could ever imagine." He looked down at his cup. "You love her a great deal?"

Benjamin grinned, "Aye, I do, and the truth is, all I went through, I would endure it all over again for her."

"Luckily, that will not be necessary, but very nobly said." Alaric acknowledged, a knock on the hatch drawing their attention away from one another.

"She is awake now and asking for you," Doc gestured towards Benjamin. "She is very weak and will need to rest." He added, glancing at Alaric, "We are nearing many small islands, perhaps we should anchor at one of them for a time being. The fresh air and change of scenery would do her good, and the others for that matter."

"Very well, we will choose one to rest at, I would not wish to push them too hard." He answered, "I'll ready the ships to weigh anchor. You tend to Amara."

Benjamin did not hesitate, striding quickly out of the cabin and across the deck. He felt his stomach tighten as he neared his own cabin. Slowly opening the hatch, he stepped in, gently closing the hatch behind him. Smiling lightly when both women looked over at him.

"I'll leave you two," Molly took the cup Amara had been sipping from and placed it on the table before leaving.

"Did they tell you?" Amara whispered. A tear ran down her cheek. She quickly wiped it away, placing her hand on her belly.

"Yes," Benjamin choked out. He had no idea what he could say. Never had he been in a position like this one and never had he witnessed the crew face a moment such as the one he now had to face. He remembered once when he had just been old enough to join the crew. Eddie had come aboard, his face stricken and pale. Not once that entire voyage did he play his violin. Benjamin had felt as if that had been the longest voyage they had ever been on. They were gone a couple of months, no longer, but without the joyous sound of his violin in the evenings, it felt strange and Eddie and seemed but a shell of a man. Alaric had explained to Benjamin that Eddie's wife and child had died during the birth while they had been gone. That when they had returned to Barbados, he heard the news. "You don't deserve this." He shook his head, bringing her hand to his lips. "I wish I could take this pain from you. Both what your body and your heart suffer from."

"You cannot save me from all." She smiled weakly at him. "This is one trial, one moment you cannot take the pain for me."

"You are right of course, and we both know you are stronger than you look." He said, returning the smile.

"What will happen to the babe?" She asked, her other hand still upon her middle.

"We are still a few days from land," he watched her expression, unsure of what her thoughts would be. When someone had passed on at the plantation, they would simply be buried in the cemetery that was at the far end of the estate grounds. The workers were not to attend the funeral, except for the immediate family and no singing or words could be spoken.

"I should prefer a sea burial for the child, that way, the waters can take the babe back to our homeland." Amara murmured, the tears beginning to flow once more.

"Aye, and it will." Clearing his throat, "I will leave you

to rest. Doc said you'll need lots of it. I'm going to see to the crew." Standing, he headed for the hatch, turning before going on deck. Amara's eyes were closed. He knew she was not yet asleep, but he needed air and wanted to give her the time she needed.

"How she be doing?" Ajani asked, approaching Benjamin.

"She'll be well soon enough, I'm sure of it." He forced a smile. As much as he was trying to reassure the others of her current condition, he knew he also spoke the words for himself.

"That she will be, Cap." He replied exuberantly, not letting the current mood aboard bring down his own spirits. Even on the plantation, Ajani had done his best to keep the others smiling.

"I will be back aboard shortly," Benjamin began. "I need to speak with Captain Stein and Doc." Crossing over the boards once again, he headed for Alaric who was mending a line.

"I wonder if I could speak with you a moment?" He had seen Alaric watching him and knew he was worried. Benjamin felt as if the past year's events were all finely catching up with him. As if they were a large wave that was crashing down on him and threatening to drown him. When it was just himself, when he had just been pulled from the waters, he had no other thoughts, but to get back to *The Trinity*. Now, all that had changed. He did not know where his place was or how he was going to escape this wave.

"Of course. You know you needn't ask." Alaric passed the line off to Amos. "Let's go to my cabin." He motioned for Benjamin to lead the way.

Pouring them each a cup full of Rum once more, Alaric stat down at the desk. A map of the region lay open upon it. It showed the small islands that dotted the areas. Benjamin had known they were closing in on the islands. They would be stopping at one of them, but he could not think which would be of most benefit to them. He would not say no to fresh meat.

"How are you holding up, lad?" He asked, his eyes also fixed on the map. It made Benjamin wonder if Alaric was pondering the same thoughts as himself, regarding the scrape with the Navy.

"I suppose, as one might expect." He shrugged. "To be honest, I do not know what I feel." He twisted the cup around in his hands. Sorrow and confusion at what just transpired. Anger," He shook his head. "She didn't deserve this. None of it." He took a long drink trying to calm himself. Alaric remained silent, just listening. He went on, telling him what Amara had said about the burial and how he wanted nothing more than to take the pain away but did not know how. Running a hand through his hair, he finished, pouring every last emotion he had building inside him, out. Alaric had merely sat, drinking from his cup, and refreshing both of theirs when they had drained them. Benjamin had not realized how much he had needed to say. How much he had needed to let out and explain. Finally, he began again, "I'll see what Doc can do for the burial ceremony. I know it will mean a lot to Amara if she can say a proper goodbye." He looked down, "It would mean a lot to both of us." He murmured. Meeting Alaric's gaze again, "Perhaps, Molly wouldn't mind helping Amara prepare?"

"Of course, I have no doubt, she'll be happy to assist." Alaric assured him, "There is one other thing I believe you should think on." He stood, "You and the girl should be married. I know it will be a bit unconventional, but if it is what you wish, I believe it is for the best." Alaric said, his voice casual. "Besides, I think we could all use such a joyous occasion to lift our spirits."

Benjamin could scarce breathe. The idea had occurred to him many times, but he had not thought it would be possible and was worried Alaric would have been furious at the notion. "Do you mean it? Truly?" The surprise evident on his face.

"I will marry you myself as soon as we reach the nearest island." He clapped him on the shoulder. "Now, we best get back to our posts, Captain." He grinned, "I'll go speak with Molly and you should go speak with your bride."

23

He stood at the entrance to the large hold, leaning against the wall. He watched Molly as she brushed down the cow. Never had he ever seen livestock so spoiled or being shown so much affection. The sound of her voice floated to his ears. The words in the song were soft and gentle. Soothing the animals around her.

"How long you planning to just stand there and stare, Captain?" She asked, drawing him from his thoughts. Her eyes still on the beast in front of her as she continued her task.

Letting out a loud laugh, he pushed himself off the wall. The smell in the cabin had always reminded him of home, of the farms he had grown up on, but now it held a new meaning. "That cow is one lucky beast." He said, coming up beside her.

"Oh? Why is that?" She asked, trying to hide her smile.

"She gets your undivided attention as often as she likes." He placed a hand on the animal, his eyes on Molly. "Where is

I have to be contented with an hour or two a day at mealtime."

"Mmm, tis only right. They are merely poor beasts. They cannot help their manners. You, however, are a scoundrel, Captain Stein." She squealed, leaping out of his reach.

Alaric tried again, grabbing her around the waist, he pulled her down into the fresh straw. "And you my love, wouldn't have me any other way." He whispered, pulling her tighter against his form and drawing her lips to his.

"Tis not appropriate," she grinned, her eyes alight. "We should be aiding Benjamin and Amara." Her voice turned more serious, despite the fire that remained in her eyes.

"That is precisely why I came to fetch you. He asks that you help to prepare Amara." He propped himself up on his arm, rolling to his side to face her better. "I wish there was more we could do for the wee one. Some white linen perhaps and I'll see what more I can find."

"Aye, t'would be better if there were flowers to be found and a basket." Molly stood, brushing the straw from her gown.

"And after, there will be happier announcements for the lad and the girl." Alaric hinted, now standing in front of Molly, his hands on each of her arms. Giving her one last quick kiss, he retreated up the companionway.

Alaric opened compartment after compartment in his cabin. Most of them he had never even rummaged through, having no need to. Maps, parchment, fine clothes that he and Lucas had rarely worn, flags and miscellaneous tools a captain may need but hardly found himself in want of were stored in the compartments. Opening one of the smaller ones, he found an array of small treasures, some rather insignificant, others of more value. Picking up a small, silver broch, inlaid with green gems circling the perimeter of it. He and Lucas had received it in thanks for saving the life of Countess Degress. They had come upon a Portuguese vessel that had attacked a fellow privateer ship. The privateer captain had been killed during the battle and it was clear the enemy ship was going to take the victory. *The Trinity* fired their shots, letting the enemy know they were there and preventing them from boarding the other privateer ship. By the time they took down the Portuguese Brig, the other vessel was beginning to sink due to the damage and lack of men to save it. Alaric and Lucas had not hesitated. They quickly made their way across to the other ship, helping any survivors a chance of escape. Locked away in a cabin, stood the Countess. The ship was tilting precariously, the water rising faster and faster through the companionway. The countess was frozen in fear, Lucas had no choice but to pick the woman up and all but drag her across to *The Trinity*. Once they reached port and had safely deposited her at her intended destination, she rewarded them with a promise of high praise to His Majesty the King and the small, jeweled broch.

Placing the token of gratitude back in its place, he found an assortment of beautiful shells. Gathering them up, he smiled.

"Amara," Alaric began, drawing the attention of Benjamin and her, who stood soberly at the railing of *The Trinity*, awaiting the burial to begin. "I found these in one of the compartments of the ship. Miss Catherine, a woman who sailed a time on this ship and wed its other captain, collected these on a beach not far from here. I know she would have liked your wee one to have them on the journey back to your homeland. She is a healer and was very fond of Benjamin," he gestured to the lad. Alaric placed a steadying hand on Benjamin's shoulder, while placing the shells in Amara's hands.

"I thank you, Captain Stein." She said, speaking quietly in an attempt to control her shattering emotions. Picking one, she placed it in the folds of her dress. Leading Benjamin over to the basket, she placed the rest of the shells around the white cloth that lay inside, protecting the small child within. "There," she smiled sadly back at Alaric and Molly. "I'm sure you didn't know, Captain Stein, but my people bury those that pass on, with shells." She explained, touching the shells gently with a finger, "So you see, they are perfect."

Benjamin and Amara climbed into the skiff, basket in hand. Pulling the lines, Eddie and Amos lowered them down so they could place the basket on the rolling waters. Amara spoke softly, her words unable to be heard over the lapping of the waves against the hull of the ship. The chanting began aboard *The Croga*. The sound of the song being sung was mournful yet held a sense of peace. The words were unknown to Alaric, but the meaning was clear. Alaric placed an arm around Molly, as she buried her face into his chest. Her tears flowing freely.

Benjamin gave the signal to raise the skiff. The songs from the other ship still being sung.

24

"Amara," Molly tapped on the hatch to the cabin. "I brought you some vitals. You'll want to keep your strength up." She entered the cabin. "Captain Stein assures me that there will be much celebrating and likely to continue into the wee hours." Molly smiled at her, putting the tray on the desk. "Oh, you look that lovely." Molly exclaimed, stepping up to Amara.

"Tis beautiful fabric. I'm grateful to you and Captain Stein." The gown her and Imani made was rich in yellow and green and suited the occasion perfectly. "I never imagined…" her words strained, falling short.

"I understand completely. There was a time, and not too long ago that I felt very much the same." She let out a small laugh. "It has taken me a time to trust in myself. To believe I could indeed be so fortunate. To believe I am worthy of such happiness." She tucked a strand of hair into the wrap Amara wore. "Give it time. You will feel the safety and happiness come."

"I've begun to see it." She smiled weakly, "But 'tis true, to feel the uncertainty." She gripped Molly's hands in her own. "You've been that kind to me. I have not the words to say how grateful I am."

"It has been nice having a friend to confide in, I must admit." Molly returned the smile. "Come, the skiffs will be ready shortly." Leading her through the hatch, she watched Amara's face as she saw the island they had stopped at.

Amara gasped at the site. The skiffs rowed between the island and the ships, dropping off the crews and supplies. The island was studded with tall trees. Green bushes thickened the island. The white sands looked soft and warm in the light of the sun. Birds flitted amongst the trees, their bright colors adding to the beauty of the scene. The children from *The Croga* splashed and played in the clear waters, squealing each time the small, gentle waves washed over the sand. Crew members gathered scraps of wood, cut branches from lower hanging trees and piled what they had gathered into several different spots on the beach.

"I haven't seen such a place before." She murmured.

"You wait until the sun has fallen a wee bit. The fires are a sight." She helped Amara into a skiff where Imani waited for them to join. The skiff bobbed in the waters, against the hull of the ship. "And Cook, he be preparing a fine feast. A few of the crew have gone off to see what meat they can find."

"Where is Benjamin?" Amara asked, looking around for him, seeming suddenly unnerved.

"Do not fear. He's with Alaric, Doc, and Captain Clarke in the other cabin." She answered. "He will join you on the beach shortly."

Their feet splashed in the shallow water that led up to the sand. Molly slipped the boots from her feet, placing them, on the soft beach. Walking along the warmed sand, she closed her eyes, listening to the sounds around her. It felt as if for just a small moment, time had slowed. For just a brief pause, they were not being chased or looking over their shoulders to find enemy gazing at them.

"You are not like the other women I have met since coming to the colonies."

"No? How so do I differ?" Molly asked curiously. Digging her toes deeper into the sand as they walked.

"You are kind. The woman on the plantation was not kind." She began. "She treated us ill, especially me."

"Why was that?" Molly asked, perplexed at the thought of anyone wanting to treat Amara with dislike or contempt.

"Skraag was the man she sought. He did not see her so. He wished to have me, instead." Her brows scrunched, trying to find the words. "But not in a kind way. Not to care for me like Benjamin." She looked down.

"I quite understand." Molly bid her continue. Her voice soft and empathetic. Knowing all too well how Amara felt. She swallowed as her own memories flooded her mind. Closing her eyes against the sound of the flintlock firing. His body lay still on the planks of his cabin. Unable to harm her any longer, yet still threatening to haunt her mind.

"The foreman often left me alone. Afeared of Skraag, but his wife, the young mistress, was vicious, and cruel. She did beat me often. She'd be awful cross if I did not wait on her when she bid me, even if I already be called to the big house to help. I could not defy the Master. He knew me to be close with the others and Ben. If I were to defy him. He would beat them instead." Her voice was strained.

"The Master, did he lay a hand on you?" Choking back the emotion she felt.

"No, he too was afeared of Skraag." Amara replied. "It's their fear and his wanting that spared me more grief." She let out a half laugh at the irony. "Once, the young mistress, she spotted me walking into the fields from the big house. I was to continue the pickin', with the others, but she stepped in front of me. She claimed she needed to teach me the proper way to pour tea." Amara scoffed at the memory.

Molly shook her head. It was not uncommon for a foreman's wife to teach the women of the plantation. The more the women knew of cooking, mending, healing and general edict, the more successful and healthier the slaves would be. This would save the master from having to pay for more.

"The tea was ready to pour. The water has been heating over the fire." She lifted her hand. Showing a thin white scar along her fingers and palm. Molly gasped, looking from her hand to Amara's eyes. "She would not give me a cloth to lift the handle with. I knew what she wanted." Amara shrugged and smiled. "I lifted the handle, walked to the table and poured the tea. The pain of the burn did not bother me, for I saw the anger and defeat in her eyes in that moment." She laughed again. "Oh, she beat me sorely for my contempt, but she rarely challenged me after."

Molly was silent, her shock evident. "You are braver than I." She confessed.

"I think not. We've heard of your past and what you did. I think you would have done much the same as I. I only wish I too had a bucket to hit over my master's head. Or better yet the young mistress's." Laughing, they turned around to be sure they were still in sight of the others.

"We should head back, I believe." She could see Benjamin standing next to Alaric. The music from Eddie's violin floated along the beach. The fires had all now been lit.

"Yes," Amara's face alight with excitement.

Molly could not help but feel the joy she knew Amara was now feeling.

"You look incredible." Alaric whispered in her ear. Everyone had gathered on the beach. The fire was glowing steadily in the dimming light.

"I would say the same for you, Captain Stein, but I shouldn't wish to encourage you." Molly replied, trying in vain to hide her smile.

25

"Case, load up those crates first. Set them outside Cook's. He'll do what he wishes with them. Then, begin with the last set." He ordered the young sailor. The others rowed the skiffs back to the ships, returning the others to them so they could prepare to weigh anchor.

Looking up at the trees, Alaric listened a moment. Each island he anchored at, each town in the colonies seemed to have their own breath, own rhythm and own sounds. The night before had proven a great success. Everyone from both ships had enjoyed themselves greatly and Benjamin and Amara had been happier than he could ever have wished for the two of them. He performed the initial ceremony, his words being translated as he spoke them, to the others that stood around. The dancing and music began immediately after, some he and his crew knew well, others were sung by the men and women from *The Croga*. The music reverberated along the sand, the words, though he did not understand, were joyous and upbeat. As the fires on the beach grew, the smell of the fair Cook was preparing, filled their senses. A few of the sailors had found and killed a large turtle, providing a luxurious and delightful addition to the meal. Though the attractions on the beach did not cease until near dawn, Alaric and Molly had returned to *The Trinity*, while the rest of the crew found spots on the beach to rest their heads.

"The last of the crates are aboard, Capt'n. We are ready to weigh anchor." Ol' Shorty shouted from the waiting skiff.

Turning from the island, Alaric hopped into the small boat, eager to inch their way closer to Barbados. As the sails unfurled, the trees and white sand faded steadily in the distance.

"How's the goat's leg?" Alaric announced his presence as he entered the large hull.

"Fairing up. He still limps from the discomfort of the injury, as well as the bandage." I am glad you came down actually, I need to put a new wrap and salve on the wound. You can assist." She gestured for him to grab hold of the still rambunctious kid. It had gotten a leg stuck in the gate and caused a nasty looking cut. Molly did her best to stitch the wound up but there was not much of the tight skin to pull together.

Unwrapping the bandage, she looked the wound over. It appeared to be healing just fine, though some of the skin still appeared puffy around the site. The swelling had gone down drastically and there was no fresh blood. "Aye, I'd say that its looking masses better." His hand stroked the little goat's head, keeping it as calm as he could, though it voiced its discontent loud enough for the entire ship to hear.

"Tis even better than last time I had a look. I do not think the new wrap is necessary." She beamed, gently kissing the goat and allowing it to scamper off to the others. Standing, she brushed the straw off of her skirt and Alaric's vest. "What is it?" She questioned, taking a step back and looking him over.

He gave her a halfhearted smile, gently running a hand along her jaw. "The ship feels different, as if we've slowed and the water is quieter." He looked about the hull, spotting Aoife, practicing her stalking by sneaking up on the cow's swishing tail. Quickly picking the kitten up, he gave it to Molly. "I'm going to have a look on deck. You take this one back to the cabin." His smile lacking slightly.

"Aye, I'll meet you on deck in a bit." She responded, stroking Aoife's fur and taking her to the cabin as directed.

Striding across the deck, Alaric looked up at the sails. They were pulling very little wind.

"It don't be feeling' right, Capt'n." Shorty came up beside Alaric.

"I couldn't agree more." He answered, tugging on a line. "Tell Gray and Cook to meet me in my cabin and inform me at once if there is any change in the wind" Making his way to his cabin, he flung the hatch open and headed for his desk. A map lay open upon it. Running his hand along the lines, he set a small flag marker on the spot they were at. Shaking his head, he beckoned the two men enter. "We are here," he began, tapping his finger near the marker.

"Aye, 'Tis no wonder we be headin' for the doldrums." Gray spoke up.

"We've seen it before, though we've been fortunate to've missed them the last few times we've traveled his area. We are several days from the next group of islands." He pointed to a cluster of rough looking spots on the map. "You know what to do. Put the crew on half rations and make preparations," Alaric looked at the two men in front of him. "And pray it is not long lasting." Nodding to the men to prepare the ship and crew for a possibly long sitting. The winds had not died completely as of yet. He could still feel the slow movements of the vessel skimming the waters below. It could still be a few days before the winds stopped all together, or with luck they may pick up strongly once more.

"What will you have me do, Captain?" Molly asked, breaking the silence in the cabin.

He looked up at her. Her hair framing her face perfectly. She looked equally strong and innocent all at once. "I'll have you come and give me kiss." Holding his hand out, he gestured for her to come to him. Drawing her to himself, he kissed her, allowing her body to soften against his.

The Trinity bobbed solemnly in the water, *The Croga* not far to the right. The sky as blue and still as the waters below, save for the occasional ripple caused by a sailor dropping a fishing line in the water. There was little chance of catching anything, especially not enough to feed two ships worth of crew mates, but it was something to occupy the mind. On deck and in the hull, the men played chess, dice, read books and conversed, trying to pass the time.

Alaric clipped his spy glass closed. No sails on the horizon. No seabirds soaring above, hoping for a morsel. Walking to the edge, he waited to help Amara and Benjamin aboard. They had rowed a skiff over. Alaric felt uneasy. Their provisions had already been growing low. Now with being sitting on the waters, unmoving for over a week already, they would be getting dangerously close to running out altogether.

"Alaric," Benjamin greeted, his voice solemn.

"Ben, Amara, glad to see you holding up." He smiled politely. "I believe Molly is in the surgery with Doc if you'd like to speak with her. I'm sure she will be pleased to see you." He pointed a hand in the direction.

"Oh, I'd enjoy that." Amara nodded eagerly, glancing up at Benjamin who nodded, smiling in response to her excitement.

"How are your rations?" He asked, his hands on the railing. It was hard enough, knowing his own men were growing hungry, but they were hardened sailors and had been through tough moments before. It was the thought of Molly and the other women and children aboard *The Croga* that made his stomach turn. Not the hunger he knew he himself would soon be feeling. The thought of Molly's words those months ago, not long after she first came aboard his ship. How she had said she was used to not eating much or well, echoed in his mind. He had made sure to stop more often, to keep their provisions higher than they usually would. He had vowed to himself that she would not want for anything while aboard his vessel.

"Not good, I'm afraid." He began, "Truth is, Alaric, I don't think they will last much longer." His face paled. Hitting the railing with his fist, "I was supposed to help them. Save them. They looked to me to keep them fed, their kids fed and well. Now, look what I've done. I entered them into a ship battle, nearly got them sent back or hung by the Royal Navy and now they are back to nearly starving to death." He turned around, staring at the deck, rather than *The Croga*.

"You've given them the best and likely the only chance for freedom and a life of their own, that they will ever get. Several families chose to depart back in the colonies, to try and build their lives there, so you cannot be too hard on yourself. As for the ones aboard your ship now. You've looked after them better than they've been taken care of since they set sail from their homelands." He sighed, knowing the words were all falling on deaf ears. He understood all too well how the lad felt. "The still winds are always a risk, same as the storms, and there is absolutely nothing a captain can do to avoid them." His hand rested on Benjamin's shoulder. "Together, we will make a decision."

Waving a hand at Ethan, he and Benjamin entered the cabin. "We do not know how long this will last. It may end in a couple hours, or last a week or two more. By then, we will have no more food at all and will be exceedingly low on grog.

"Do you have spare sponges?" Benjamin asked, "I was going to have the women boiling the sea water and collect the vapors in the sponges to drink, but I could not find any." Benjamin asked.

"Aye, Cook'll have plenty. I too have men preparing sea water." He beamed over and the young man. "Twas good thinking. Your mind is sharp." He encouraged.

"He's right," Ethan acknowledged, nodding his agreement.

Alaric's face turned grim once more, "I'll appreciate it if the two of you will not say a word of what must be done. Not until I've had a chance to discuss it with Molly." He breathed out. He had no doubt she would understand, but wondered if her trust and comfort in him that she had finally begun to feel and even seek, would change.

"Aye," they replied in unison, leaving him to go speak with Molly.

Amara and Doc now stood on deck, walking the length of it and talking quietly to one another. Hesitating only a moment, Alaric headed down through the hatch. His footsteps slowing as he entered the large hull, the musky smell of the animals filling his senses. The bucket of dank and used straw sitting in a corner, ready to be taken out and dumped. Molly sat. Chickens clucked contentedly about her. The goats milled about, nudging Molly occasionally for attention. Her soft song filled the room. A sole hen rested in her lap as she stroked its feathers.

"That's a new one." He spoke up, announcing himself.

"I've not heard you sing it before."

"Oh, aye," she looked up at him. "Tis a bit mournful, I suppose, but I always felt it be a bit hopeful in the end."

Alaric took a tentative step forward, trying to find the words. "I need…" he stammered. Before Molly, he would not have thought twice about using the animals for meat, in fact, this would not be the first time they had to be used. Just the first time since Molly had been aboard. They had used a hen or two for meat but those, Molly had been prepared to depart with and had not grown attached. The goats would be even harder to part with for her.

"Our provisions are low." She finished for him. "I understand and I've known it could happen all along." She smiled weakly at him. Gently touching his face, she nodded to the edge of the gate. I set out the cages for a couple of the hens. Slowly handing him the one in her lap, she continued. "Her and the one just there," she pointed to a speckled hen that pecked at the straw. "Are the poorest of layers we have." She reached for the other hen. "They will serve their new purpose well." Standing, she placed the bird in one of the cages. "As for the goats," she paused, holding out her hand, drawing them near to her, eager for her endless affection. "That is your choice."

Alaric stepped up to her, his hand resting on the small of her back. "You are brave, lass. Brave and incredible," he whispered. Grabbing hold of the crates, he carried them up to the deck. Returning to the animals to choose the goats, he found Molly gone. Swallowing, he knew it was harder on her than she wanted him to know. Looking around, he saw Aoife gone from the hull as well. When she returned to the cabin, she always brought the cat with her.

The goats pulled tight against the ropes as he led them above, as if they knew what awaited them. He felt his blade slide cleanly and effortlessly against the fur. The animal unmoving. Closing his eyes briefly, he glanced at the hatch that led to the cabin. Grateful that it remained closed tight. Returning his gaze to the task in hand, he worked quickly, not wanting the process to take any longer than it needed to.

Alaric stepped up to the hatch. A few of the men finished up the last of the task by scrubbing the deck clean, removing all traces of what had happened. Stepping into the cabin, he removed his shirt, tossing it directly into the bucket of sea water. Pulling his boots off, he looked over at the bed. Molly sat, her hair falling to the side, hiding her face. Aoife lay, purring against her leg. A paper rested on her book, a light sketch upon it. The cabin was warm as the sun shone in through the window in the back.

"Molly, that is incredible." His fingers going out, lightly touching the edge of the paper. The sketch was of the kitten, the likeness nearly identical. "I had no idea," his sentence fading.

Blushing, she pulled a small stack of papers from the inside of the book and handed them to him. Looking from her to the pages, he blew out a breath of admiration. "How long have you been doing these?"

"Since Doc gave me the book." She shrugged, the blush still upon her cheeks.

Slowly flipping through the pages, he examined each one. Sketches of the cow, the goats and chickens, covered the parchments. Small sketches of the injuries she had worked on and the process of each remedy, as well as the ingredients to salves, mixtures and poultices were listed below. A separate page had notes written upon it of treatments for various ailments that animals might experience and how to care for them.

"Why have you not shown these to me before?" He asked, returning the parchments to her, to which she tucked away safely in the book, her fingers brushing the sketch of a goat.

"I was unsure and embarrassed, I suppose." She looked up at him, her eyes meeting his. "Do you like them, truly?" Her voice hesitant and hopeful.

"Lass, they are remarkable." He assured, looking at the sketch that sat atop the others, once more. "I am truly sorry about what had to happen." The sincerity in his voice unmistakable.

"I understand and always knew it was a possibility." She rested her hand on his.

26

"Eddie, what do you make of that?" Alaric asked, handing his spyglass to the man. It had not even been a fortnight since the winds had picked up again. They were nowhere near any ports and were once again growing very low on provisions. The meat from the animals had held over well and the water supply they had been able to increase over the last few days, but it was the other foods they were now almost out of, and the fresh water and meat would not last much longer.

"Looks to be them Royal Navy, again." Eddie frowned, "Can't rightly tell if it's the same vessel, but I'd wager it be."

"Aye, that's what I feared you'd say." Alaric cursed under his breath. The voyage back to Barbados was already a long one and the last few weeks had put them behind greatly. The last thing he wished for was to have to fight off the Royal Navy once more, risking the lives of the women and children aboard *The Croga*, not to mention his own men and Molly. On top of that, any further confrontation would only fire the rumors further. "Ring the bells. Signal to *The Croga*." Hopping down the steps and away from the helm, he bellowed, "To your posts, lads!" The bells rang out. The sound seeming to reverberate off of each wave, caring the call to beat to quarters across the waters. "Molly, see to it that Doc is prepared." He placed a quick kiss on her forehead, brushing a lock of hair out of her face.

"Keep safe." She whispered into his chest.

"Have no fear. I do not intend to enter into a fight with those men. With luck, we will outrun them." He assured her. Taking up position at the railing, he kept a close eye on the sails in the distance. If his men had to be alert and on guard, he would be too.

"How's it looking?" Ethan asked, bringing Alaric a tray of dried meat and various vegetables that had been soaking in a jar of sour brine to keep it from spoiling. Taking a bite of the fare, he quickly took a swig of the grog to soften the meat.

"They've not gained on us, but nor have they slowed." He sighed, bringing a crate over to set between them, each of them sat as Ethan unrolled his chess set out. The crew was still alert, though Alaric had allowed them to return to their regular shifts until further notice. The sun had begun to settle on the horizon, creating an incredible vision. The oranges and golden yellows met the deep blue of the waters, "We cannot simply hope to outrun them. Though I have little doubt we can, one false move, one simple need to anchor or any other unforeseen circumstances and they'll be upon us." Alaric voiced, his gaze concentrating heavily on the game board.

Ethan laughed, "Sorry, mate. I am not used to running

from or avoiding the Royal Navy. I have no sound advice to give." Ethan moved his Rook forward.

Alaric shook his head, his own half smile showing, "Nor I." Glancing back at the distant sails. "How quickly alliances can shift." He scoffed.

Ethan's hand paused over his Knight. "Maybe that is our answer."

"What is?" Alaric looked over at him.

"Who do we know that is notorious for evading the Royal Navy?"

"You can't possibly mean we ask Banning for his aid?"

"And why not?" He shrugged, moving his player. "We are precariously low on supplies, need to avoid and lose the Naval ship, and come up with a solid plan for when we reach Barbados. As we get closer, I suspect the Navy will be waiting for us. We will not stand a chance. Handing Banning over will not be enough, I fear."

Alaric let out a slow breath. He knew Ethan's concerns to be just and very likely exact. The Admiral had already been reluctant to allow Ethan further leave and had let his feelings be known about him not seeing to the French fleet. There was little doubt the Admiral would be furious and possibly unforgiving about the rumors. He ran a hand over his face. "I suppose we have little choice, though it will be a gamble. We cannot trust Banning and how do we know he won't lead us into a trap of some kind?"

"We don't. We find a way to gain leverage over him. Sparing him from the noose will not be enough."

"I suspect not. What of his wife? We can threaten to expose her, ruin her. We spared her that mercy before, when the crew was taken and hanged. We can say we do not owe her that mercy again." Alaric suggested, wincing at how harsh it sounded. In truth, he did not think he would do it. He just hoped Banning would believe the threat.

Ethan nodded, "Tis a sound plan, well, sound enough."

"Aye," Alaric moved a pawn into place. "Check". He announced, grinning.

"Wake up, Banning." Alaric kicked the bars on the brig. "Brought you an extra ration." He slid the tray under the bars. Leaning against them, he gestured for Ethan to begin.

"We find ourselves in need of your cunning and elusive nature." He picked at a bit of fabric on his shirt.

"Ah, so once again, the mighty hunters become the hunted." Standing, he paced the cell.

"So, it would seem." Alaric drawled.

"And now you ask for the aid of the man you finally captured. Help from a pirate." Thomas looked him over. "Bit ironic don't you think?" Seeing no emotion from the two men he continued. "Careful, Stein. Some might say you are turning pirate yourself." His eyes widened in mock disbelief.

"Oh, don't you worry about my reputation, mate. It's your wife's you should fear for." His eyes locked with the man on the other side of the bars.

"How the hell do you know of her, you bastard?" Thomas raged, as he gripped the cell door.

"Don't be unfriendly, now." Ethan began. "She invited us to dine with you after we all but shared a cup of tea together."

The stunned silence in the brig was nearly too much to bear. "Stay away from my family, you rotten bastard." His voice ice and alarming quiet.

"I intend to. However, my final move will depend on your aid and trust." Alaric's words leaving Banning little choice.

"Tis simple, really. You aid us until we say we no longer need your services." Ethan stepped closer to Thomas. "Or your wife be ruined."

"Her fate and that of anyone close to her lays in your hands alone." Alaric waved a hand in the air. "We will give you a minute." He turned, heading for the hatch, closing it behind Ethan. "Edward, see to it we are summoned when our Prisoner has made his decision."

The sailor replied quickly returning to his post just outside the hatch that led down to the brig.

"I don't suspect it will take long for him to decide." Alaric clapped Ethan on the shoulder. Stepping up to the helm he released Eddie from his tasks. Taking a firm grasp of the helm. He felt the tug and sway of the ship, pulling gently against the waves.

"You are sure we will not regret asking for his aid?" Molly asked, coming up the stairs. The light from the moon now shone brightly, reflecting off the water and lighting the way. Though it still stirred a chill in the body. The air had grown warmer the further south they sailed.

"We will have to hope his loyalty to his wife is stronger than his greed and revenge." She wrapped her cloak tighter around herself and stepped closer to him.

Pulling her to him, he held her close. He did not realize when she first began to seek comfort in him, but never wished to ever give her reason to regret her placing her trust in him. He could not think what he even did to deserve the sentiment. Placing a kiss on her hand, he whispered, "Do not fret."

With his arms around her, he moved back to stand behind her. The heat from her body could be felt even through her gown and cloak. He placed his hands over hers, allowing her to feel the sway and pull of the helm. Over the last few months, he had been showing her the movements of the ship, how to handle her in the heavy winds that could whip through above the sea and teaching her the commands and meaning of the orders that would be shouted on deck. She had proven to be a worthy pupil, so much so, he had let her man the helm on her own on more than one occasion.

"Cap'n," Edward stood at the base of the steps. Banning be ready to talk, Capt'n." He announced, quickly returning to his post to unlock the hatch to the brig for Ethan and Alaric.

"Show me the map." Leaning against the cell wall he raised his eyes. "And I'll need a rum."

Alaric let out a laugh, the sound echoing in the dank room. "The map you can have. The rum, I'm afraid is lacking." He shrugged "How about a grog?"

He scoffed, "That'll do if it must."

27

"We have speed on our side." Thomas informed the other two men. Though both Alaric and Ethan knew this already, they did not say as much, giving Banning a moment to examine the map. "You say we are here?" He asked, looking briefly at Alaric before returning his gaze to the map.

"Aye," Alaric replied, leaning against the cell bars, his arms crossed over his chest. The smell of the brig was rank, the air around them heavy and sticky. Save for a couple cautious rats, the brig was cleaner than most, but in no way as cared for as the rest of the ship.

"We are but about a few days journey from La Louisiane. We can hide out there." He raised the cup, scrunching his face. "And resupply." He leaned back against the wall, taking a long drink of grog. "I know of a particular spot. Your ship, and your son's will not be registered. The Naval vessel will not go past their jurisdiction, nor will they be able to find the spot if they did choose to follow. It will be backtracking some, but I doubt the Naval vessel will guess you going there."

"Alright," Alaric eyed Thomas cautiously. He did not like the idea of having to put their trust in the man. He also did not like that they would be heading into more dangerous waters. Over the years, he and Lucas had dared, even explored the waters around the particular area they were heading to, but the circumstances had been far different.

Reaching a hand out, Alaric took the map back from Thomas. "Many thanks, mate." He raised the cup in the air, "I was a might parched."

Without another word, Alaric and Ethan made their way on deck. "Give the coordinates." He ordered. "Red!" Shouting out the crewman's name as he headed below the hatch.

"Aye, Cap," he paused his task, "What be my orders?"

"See to it all of the men are prepared for battle and not just the ship." He reached into a chest with flintlocks and another with knifes and swords. "We are headed to an unknown area. I do not wish to be caught unawares if this be a trap." He explained.

"Aye, of course. I just cleaned 'em all and filled the powder pouches." He opened a crate filled with prepared powder, balls and cut cloth. "We be well in order, Cap." He explained eagerly. "When we gets closer to this place, I'll help Edward guard that Banning."

"Thank you, I was going to suggest the very thing." Alaric agreed.

Returning to the deck, Alaric spied Molly. She was toying

with a line that had come loose. "What is the meaning of this?" He asked, raising a brow at the sight before him.

"Seven went to fetch a new line for the one that frayed. Then this one went and came undone. I had but no choice but to reattach it." She reasoned, working quickly to tie the line back in place. It snapped with the sail in the wind. Molly's grip was tight, pulling it taught once more and finishing the tie.

"Well done, sailor." He winked, "I don't believe any of these useless dogs could have done it better." Saying it loud enough for the men around him to hear. A chorus of grumbles and jests were heard in reply. "Come," he urged, "You remember how to reload the flintlock, yes?" He asked, kicking himself at the half insulted look she shot him. He cleared his throat, "Right, uh, well, that's good then. No need for another lesson." He handed her a smaller bladed sword and a pair of flintlocks. "Turn, I'll fit the straps to you so you do not have to hold them, and your hands will be free." Adjusting the straps to her shoulders and chest, he gestured for her to reach for a pistol, being sure she could pull it from the strap quickly. "How does it feel?" he looked her over, hiding the smile he knew would only encourage a fiery response. He looked the woman in front of him over. Her hair framing her face perfectly. Her eyes shown with excitement and something more that made him want to do nothing but pull her close to him and bring his lips down on hers.

"Tis nice," she started, "But are you sure you wish to trust me with such an armory?" A teasing smile on her face.

With a smirk, he replied, "I'll take my chances." She

raised a brow in response. "I'll be sure to keep a very close eye on you, don't you worry." He winked, stepping closer to her, sliding his hand along her back. Leaning in, he gently brushed her lips with his.

"I'll go make sure Cook and Doc are not in need of any assistance." Blushing, she pulled away.

"Ethan, be sure the men are ready for any possibility. I do not think Thomas will risk his wife, but we cannot be sure." By Banning's reaction, he was surprised to realize the man might actually have a conscious and given how Mrs. Banning had spoken so proudly and fondly of Thomas, led him to believe the two might very well care for each other.

"Come get me when we near French waters." Alaric told Ol' Shorty, who waved a hand in response, his focus on repairing a part of the railing.

28

"Capt'n," there was a banging at the hatch. "We be nearing them waters now," Ol' Shorty called from behind the door.

Alaric grumbled. He had hardly slept the night before, going over their dwindling provisions and writing a letter to Lucas that he hoped he could get to him before the Navy got them in the port. He had racked his brain, going over every possibility that may save his crew. He knew that whatever happened though, Molly, Benjamin, and Amara needed to be hidden. He would do whatever it took to keep them from the gallows.

"You best wake, lass," Alaric gently nudged Molly. Her head and arm resting on his chest.

"Mmm," She buried herself deeper into the covers and closer to him. "Do you speak much French?" She asked, rolling from the bed and pulling the gown she had worn the day before, from the chest and slipping it on.

"As much as I need to." Truth was, he and Lucas spoke it fairly well. They had become rather fluent during their stay in France. He strapped his sword and flintlocks to him. Looking back at Molly, he grinned. She had her own sword and flintlock strapped to the belt he had fitted to her. She looked every part the dangerous she-pirate. "You are an intimidating sight, I must say, Miss Maclean." He reached for the small dagger she had first brought aboard with her. He watched her tuck it safely away in the front of her gown. She wrapped the cloak about her, hiding her small armory.

Leading her on deck, he looked up the mast, being sure they had switched the ship's flag to a French one. The more they could blend in, the better. The coast was becoming visible. The green of the trees, nearly matching the vibrant green of Ireland. Turning his head in the direction of Banning's voice, he listened to the man give orders on where to sail to.

As they neared the shoreline, having angled the ship as if they were to head far up the coast, only to turn abruptly. The ship now faced an inlet that had been all but invisible when heading for the coast head on. The port sat a couple miles walk from the beach they landed just off of. The ship was surrounded by a tall portion of land, covered in thick trees. Only a narrow strip of water revealed the mouth leading to the ocean. Eddie had done an impeccable job. Steering the vessel into such a secluded area. He had to hand it to Banning, he knew what he was doing and did it well.

"Now that I've shown you a spot secret to all but me, I think you may stop sending me such glances, Captain Stein." He shot a wink at Molly, causing Alaric's gaze to harden more.

Giving the orders to lower the skiffs, they made their way into them and rowed them silently to the shore where only a narrow strip of beach lay, before halting at the thick vegetation line. Benjamin and Amara followed in their own skiff. Once they were all ashore, they followed closely behind Thomas. Red and Ol' Shorty keeping a close watch on Banning, their flintlocks in hand. The path Thomas led them on was thick, not unlike that of the hidden ones on the islands. The trees reached high. Birds flitting from branch to branch, giving the illusion the trees were sparking with color.

Alaric led the way behind Banning and his guards, Ethan and Benjamin bringing up the rear. It did not take long for them to break through the shrubbery covered path. The port was not as busy as the others they had recently been to but was just as lively.

"I reckon we will find my friend over by the tavern there. He enjoys the drink and women." He grinned at Ethan, "What of you, Captain? Do you partake from time to time?"

"As much as any man, I wager." Ethan admitted.

"Good," he clapped Ethan on the shoulder, "Time to see what you are made of Captain Clarke." Banning chuckled, leading them over to a shack rather than an actual building. It contained a back wall, roof of sorts and had an open deck with tables scattered about it. The shack looked out over the beach. Small fishing boats and skiffs were just out of the reach of the small waves that brushed against the sand. Fires dotted the beach. Sailors gathered around, drinking and singing.

"Ah," Banning spread his arms wide, above his form. "And there he be!" His voice rose, drawing the focus of the crowd.

"Ha ha," a man staggered forward, "We've got trouble now," the man yelled, causing a chorus of cheers to raise. "What brings you back so soon?" He asked, shoving a man off of a stump that sat around the fire. He grabbed the jug of ale the man had just put down and handed it to Banning.

"What do you think, mate?" Avoiding those that want to see me hanged," he glanced back at Alaric, "Or at least trying to," he smirked. "Listen," he leaned closer to the man, Claude owes me a favor," he looked pointedly at Laurent.

Laurent straightened, looking around to be sure none of the other sailors were listening. His eyes locked with Alaric's. "Who be they?" His voice suspicious and guarded. "Where be your old crew."

"Dead," Banning relied simply.

"They don't be lookin' like your normal kind." Laurent eyed Thomas.

"Ha, no, they aren't." he admitted, "They be privateers."

Laurent adjusted his stance, "What are you thinking, bringing the likes of them here?" He asked, anger evident. He looked about again, clearly unnerved.

"Relax, mate. I'm sure you've heard the rumors." He began, "This bunch turned Rogue. Best lot of privateers the

Governor of Barbados had." Alaric nearly choked at Thomas's words. "What better way to hide from the privateers and Navy than to be aboard one of their vessels, I ask ye?" He shrugged, "Alas though, we got stuck in still waters and have exhausted our goods." Thomas explained.

Laurent's body relaxed, "I can take you to 'im." He pointed a boney finger at Thomas, "But I warn ye, he ain't gonna like that lot," pausing, his gaze roamed over Molly's body. "'Cept perhaps that one." He nodded his head in her direction.

"Ah, yes, well, any man would." He turned toward Alaric who had stepped in front of her protectively. "Unfortunately, they'd have to go through that brute to get her."

Laurent scoffed, avoiding Alaric's gaze. "We best leave this area if we are to speak more of this." He held out an arm, allowing Thomas to lead the way off of the beach and into the town.

"You alright?" Alaric asked, putting an arm around Molly's waist.

"Aye," She shrugged, "We can't expect Banning's friends to have very many manners. Besides, you forget, I'm well armed." She grinned, patting her cloak that hid the weapons. Alaric laughed under his breath in response.

"Too many of ye to take them horses this time. We'll be needing the boat," Laurent looked over his shoulder at the group. "It'll be a tight squeeze, right enough."

Alaric breathed a sigh of relief as they approached the

edge of the town. They had attracted more notice than he felt comfortable with. French officers had eyed them suspiciously. Laurent had waved a hand at them, shrugging off their gazes. As they had passed another tavern and inn of sorts, a woman and her friends approached them. One of which clearly knowing Thomas from previous occasions.

"Be sure to stop in for a time, before sailing off again, love." She ran a hand down Banning's arm, her accent thick and sensual.

"And be sure to bring your friends with you." Another sidled up beside Ethan. "Your crew is looking far more handsome these days, Captain." She ran a finger through a strand of Ethan's hair, giving it a small twist.

Thomas laughed, "Aye, a right sight better looking than the last bunch." He pulled the woman next to him, close to his side, giving her a long kiss. "I'm afraid we are not in a position to stop and enjoy the local fair this time." His gaze traveling her body, "Much to my regret."

The woman that stood beside Ethan stuck out her lip in an exaggerated pout. Her dress was rich in color, the blues and purples, making her eyes shine brighter, her hair a striking sleek, black.

"A pity to be sure." Ethan whispered, hardly loud enough for the others to hear. Alaric bit back his grin. Ethan gently removed the woman from his form. Clearing his throat when he caught the look on Alaric's face. Thomas let out a loud laugh, excusing them so they could be on their way.

"Well, if we lose you along the way, I think we can all safely wager a guess at where we would find you in the end." Alaric jested.

The commotion from the town faded as they neared the edge of the river. Boats sat on the banks. A man stood at the edge of the river, a long stick with sharp, curved tines on the end. Waiting patiently, he suddenly jabbed the stick into the water. Bringing up a large and wriggling fish.

"This here be the bateaus." Laurent jutted his thumb at a rough looking boat. The cypress appeared to be wearing precariously thin on one of them, the other two were a bit sturdier, made from hallowed logs. "We will need to take two of them." He gestured for all of them to pick their boat. Laurent hopped in with Banning, casting Red and Shorty a look of annoyance.

Alaric's hands gripped the paddle tightly. They steered the boat through the shallow waters. Thick beds of tall grasses could be seen under the water. Trees reached tall, the branches beginning several feet up the trunks. Long strips of light green moss hung from them like lace.

They were very soon deep into the swamps. Plants clung to the tops of the water. A tall pink and white bird flushed from the grasses, its beak an odd, rounded shape at the end. All around them, the sounds of the birds, frogs and other animals created a chorus along their path.

"Mind you don't bump the gators. They're none too friendly and some being bigger than the pirogues." Laurent chuckled at Red's cursing and muttering.

Alaric nudged Molly, "Look there," he whispered, pointing to a ripple a few feet from the boat. A pair of beady eyes and a scaled snout poked above the water, slowly dipping below again.

The pirogue swayed, as another set of ripples appeared, closer this time. A scraping could be heard. The boat jolted suddenly, tipping dangerously to the side. Alaric's hand shot out gripping Molly's arm and preventing her from falling out of the shallow pirogue.

"Ha, reckon them gators be extra hungry today." Laurent laughed.

"You won't be finding it so funny when I toss ye o'er," Shorty grunted at him.

The shallow, grassy waters wound through the tall trees for miles. The scenes around them were relentless. They were surrounded by birds of all sizes. Alligators lay on the small island banks, soaking in the sun. Even a snake had slithered a top the water, moving out of the path of the boats.

"Not long now," Thomas spoke up, his voice sounding out of place amidst the chorus of the nature around them.

Alaric adjusted the flintlocks strapped to him, glancing at Benjamin who sat behind him. A knowing look passed between them. Both feeling equally uneasy.

Rounding around a small island, they approached a section of land, an old wooden bridge connecting it to a path that continued in both directions and was likely the same path Laurent would have taken them on if they had come by way of the horses he had mentioned earlier. A building of such stood on the large island that sat in the middle of the bayou. Another half rundown shack sat just off to the side. Shards of wood stuck out in all directions from the side of the shack, making it appear abandoned. A steady ribbon of smoke came from the cabin, giving the island a sense of life and inhabitants, though an eerie one. The cabin sat on long posts, keeping it off of the island and out of reach of the water. They pulled the long boats onto the island.

"Claude!" Laurent called out. "Banning be back and he be askin' to cash in on that debt you owe him."

"Aye?" A man emerged from the cabin. A large brimmed hat pulled low, making his eyes nearly impossible to see. His voice was deep and rough. Paired with his thick accent, it made it difficult to understand him. "I thought I tasted the air souring." A croaking laugh escaped him. "Back so soon, hey?" The man shrugged, coming down the steps that led off the wide deck. "Non!" he shouted, raising his arms, causing an egret to spring from the bank and take flight. "Then I will no longer be indebted to you." He laughed again, this time it ended in a gravelly cough.

"Fair enough." Thomas drawled, clearly unamused at having to call in the debt. "We be needin' supplies." Thomas said, watching Claude look the group over suspiciously. "Laurent can fill you in on the crew," he waved an arm in the air, dismissing Claude's questions before he had a chance to ask them. He stepped forward, "So, when can we expect the goods to be delivered to my ship?" Thomas asked, now leaning against a barrel at the base of the stairs.

Claude raised a brow, spitting on the ground, looking the group over. Alaric adjusted his stance, not liking the way the man watched them, particularly how his eyes hovered momentarily over the two women. "Couple days' time." He turned to go back up the steps. "You be wanting to stay here the night." Stopping on the deck, he turned back to the group, "The bayou ain't no place to be paddling around at night. That be when the gators get hungry. You wouldn't even see 'em coming." He scowled down at them. Red grumble, mumbling low curses.

"Ah, don't be so down hearted, mate." Thomas beamed, slapping Red on the back. "We're all in for a treat." He nodded up to the cabin, "Claude makes the best snake and gator stew."

Laurent rubbed a hand on his middle, "That he does," he gestured for the group to lead the way up the stairs. A few crates and barrels lined the deck. A single chair sat at the railing, a rifle leaning up against it.

The inside of the cabin was not much. A bed sat in one corner, a table and a chair were placed in the middle. Animal skins and pelts hung drying both on the deck and inside the cabin. A fire was going strong, with a large, heavy pot swaying above it as Claude stirred the contents. The aroma from the stew was surprisingly pleasant. Claude turned to face his guests. His hat still pulled low, Alaric could see no more of his face than the jagged, rough scar that angled down across it. He could sense his eyes roaming over Molly's form. She must have felt it too, as she stiffened next to him, adjusting the cloak she wore, slightly revealing a flintlock and blade. Claude smirked, turning his attention back to the stew.

"Come, let us wait outside," Ethan suggested.

"Aye," Shorty replied, scrunching his nose and ushering Benjamin and Amara out.

Alaric waited, catching Thomas's gaze, who grinned in mock innocence, leaving the cabin obligingly. Alaric did not wish to give him any opportunity to try anything untoward.

Red and Benjamin set to work building a fire as best they could. The smoke from it was thick and the fire burned low. The moss and branches they could find were nearly too wet to light at all. Setting a pile near the flames, they let it dry the rest as much as the small fire could.

"You be hiding from the Royal Navy still?" Claude asked, coming out. "And what of them relentless brothers you was escaping?"

Alaric placed a hand gingerly on the hilt of his sword, careful to not catch anyone's eye with the subtle movement. Ethan doing the same.

"Ah, 'twas all, but an honest mistake." Thomas gave his knee a slap. "Tis the Royal Navy I must now find a way to be forgiven of my sins, by."

Claude scoffed, "I may have news for you that might prove useful, then."

"Oh? And what may I ask would that be?" Banning broke a small stick, tossing half in the fire that now steadily grew.

"That information is highly sought after and comes with a hefty price." Claude tilted his head towards Molly.

Thomas's eyes grew serious, raising to meet Alaric's. A clear warning in them, telling him to remain still. "You'll not go near her." Alaric growled, his grip tighter on the hilt of his sword now.

"Then you'll not get the information you seek." Claude stepped closer, ignoring the threat.

"That'll do," Thomas had come to his feet, now standing beside Claude, his back to Alaric and Molly. "You don't want to be doing that, mate." He jutted a thumb at the two of them. "If he didn't get you, she would. She'd as soon as cut you down before you had a chance to loose yer belt." Thomas gave him a light shove. "Go get the stew and we can discuss payment."

29

"What do you suppose the information is?" Benjamin asked Alaric who sat next to him on another crate.

"He's a spy." Alaric confirmed. "He's loyal to only the highest payer at that moment. Loyal to anyone who can prove to be a profitable ally." He explained, "Much like his friend." He nodded in the direction of Thomas.

"I can take the first watch tonight." He offered.

"Aye, alright," he nodded, keeping an eye on Claude, who was now bringing out the pot of stew.

"Five shillings and you tells us what it is you know," Thomas began, scooping up a generous portion of stew into a cracked, wooden bowl, he had been handed.

Claude spat in disgust, "I have others that pay more."

"Very well, eight shillings." Alaric retorted.

"Twenty, and no a mite less." Claude leaned against a barrel, folding his arms across his chest. "If it were discovered I be telling you what I know, I'd swing or have my head on a pike."

"Or thrown to the gators you're so fond of." Alaric shrugged, "In fact, what's stopping us from doing that very thing to you now?" He raised brow, a murmur of "Ayes," from the others, strengthening the threat.

"Then you would never know what it is I've to say, now would you?" His voice dark. The scar on his face and shadowed eyes only added to his sinister appearance.

"Suppose not, that is, unless we feed you to them bit by bit," Ethan voiced, pointing to the dirk Alaric now twisted round in his hands.

"Banning," Claude growled. Laurent remained silent, unmoving as Red held a flintlock to his side. "Call your men down."

"My deepest apologies, mate. Unfortunately, I cannot, see, Captain Stein here," he cocked his head at Alaric, "Actually be the captain of the ship I be hiding out on, if I wish to leave with me own neck intact, I cannot give him the orders." Thomas stepped up to the man. "Plus, I be a trifle curious to the information you possess, be it that valuable to you."

Laurent's lips twisted in a horrid way. "Ye've changed," he snarled.

"Perhaps," he threw the other half of the stick he had been

holding, into the fire, "Or perhaps not. I couldn't really say."

Claude took a step back, halting suddenly. Benjamin held a small knife against Claude's back. Benjamin had stepped behind him to prevent him from fleeing to his rifle on the deck. "So, tell us, what is it you know?" Benjamin asked, twisting the tip of the blade against the man's back, just enough for it to be uncomfortable, but not yet enough to break the skin.

"You all are goin' a rot in hell." Claude spat out.

"Aye, most likely, but we already knew that. What do your French allies tell you?" Alaric demanded.

"Agh," Claude arched his back away from Benjamin's blade. "There is a fleet of French ships in the water, just a few days from Barbados. They be hiding around some islands. There be a secret alcove, much like the one you anchor at here." Claude shifted his eyes to Thomas, his voice tight. "There be five of 'em. They be waiting to attack the islands."

"Which island?" Ethan demanded.

"I couldn't say. I heard tell, they awaiting a second fleet before attacking. If the first is destroyed, the second will no stand a chance and will retreat. Take the first fleet out and you be pardoned, Banning."

"These islands, where about are they? Do you have more precise coordinates? There are many islands between here and Barbados."

"He knows 'em." He shoved a finger at Thomas's chest. "Hides there himself from time to time," He shifted his eyes from Thomas to Alaric. "Hid out there when he was running from the likes of you." Claude laughed at their expressions. "Aye, ye have changed, Banning."

"Enough," Alaric silenced him. "Tie him up. We'll wait until first light and make our way out of this god forsaken place." He pointed his blade at Claude. "Where will we find the goods you owe him?"

"A man in port. He holds them. He'll no give 'em to you unless I give the word, though." His lips turned, forming what could almost be called a grin. A few teeth missing, others cracked and yellow, making the expression look more like a wild animal snarling.

"What of him?" Benjamin asked, nodding to Laurent who had not moved or said a word under Shorty's watchful stare.

Thomas clapped the man on the back, sweat beaded across Laurent's forehead. "We don't have to worry much about him. Do we, mate? You won't go doing nothing stupid." Banning wrapped an arm around the man's shoulders, leading him to a crate and pushing him down on it.

"You've my word." The sincerity of the statement not matching the look in his eyes.

Benjamin watched the exchange. It was amiss. He did not trust Banning and his betraying the men so suddenly. Nor did he trust Laurent. The man did not appear happy at the situation or at Banning.

"Try and get some rest." He said to Amara, his voice low. The others had settled down around the fire, leaning against crates. Molly rested her head on Alaric, who's arm was tight around her. Laurent lay still, his own hat pulled over his face. Shorty and Red remained on either side of the two French men.

Moving closer to him, he could feel her warmth. The night had grown cooler, the damp air and ground around them setting off the chill.

"Look," Amara sat up, raising her head from his shoulder. Small spots of lights danced and flashed in the darkness all around them.

"Do you recall the first time we saw them, on the plantation?" He looked down at her as she rested her head on his shoulder again.

"I couldn't forget." She let out a shaky breath. "I was terrified. They had unloaded us from the cart and lined us up. One by one they set the hot iron upon us." She put a hand on her shoulder where her mark remained. "You had spotted a bee fluttering over the flowers and when the foreman and Skraag had left, you followed that bee." She smiled up at him.

"Aye," he laughed, the sound low and deep in his chest. "I was so relieved when it led me directly to it's hive. I had a time of it getting the honey from it though."

"You returned nearly unrecognizable." She giggled.

"It was worth it, no?" He asked. "It certainly took the

burning away from the iron."

"Aye, that it did." She gave him a small kiss on the cheek. "We sat by a fire like this one, outside the huts that night. The field suddenly was alight with the bitty lights.

"Aye, if it were not the honey that took the pain away, it were those lights flying about." Kissing her on the head, he pulled her closer, feeling her steady breathing. He allowed himself to relax but made sure to remain awake. He would rouse one of the others in a couple hours to change shifts.

A splash sounded in the darkness. He listened closer, making sure it was not but a gator.

"So, how did you get the honey?" Alaric's voice was low in the darkness. Benjamin could hear the curious grin upon his lips. The flames danced, lighting his face briefly before casting it in shadows once more.

Benjamin let out a subtle laugh, trying not to wake Amara. "It was rather high in a tree at the edge of the plantation. I had followed the bee closely for quite some time before finding the hives. I had remembered what Doc and Miss Catherine had said about honey and how it helps with many ailments." He stared into the fire, watching the branches slowly shifting from red to grey, only to glow bright once again. "I could've knocked the hive down, but I didn't wish to destroy it. I knew we'd need the honey on more than one occasion and so we did." Raising his head, he looked over at Alaric. "I managed to climb a ways up but the branch the hive was on was not strong enough for me to be on and there was not a closer one above it. I stood up against the trunk, holding onto the branch with the hive. Like I said, it was not a strong one and was already baring a lot of weight from the hive. I used the branch to balance myself as I walked along the lower, stronger one. By the time I reached the hive, the bees were swarming. I reckon the swaying of their branch unease'd them. I broke a twig from the branch and used it to pry a generous chunk from the hive. The honey dripped down my arm and the side of my body." His chest rumbled with laughter, remembering trying to cradle the slippery and sticky mass, while trying not to fall from the tree. "The years of climbing the rigging likely aided me." He laughed again, hearing Alaric do the same. "I did my best to ignore the swarm around me. Somehow, I reached the ground, but when I finally got to the others, I was covered from head to toe in honey and bee stings.

Alaric's laugh filled the night. "I'm not sure which I would have liked to see more. You in the process of retrieving the honey or you on the return."

"It took most the day to scrape and wash the honey from my person." He admitted, stifling his laugh so he did not wake the others. "One of the women retrieved a bowl. We kept the mass of honeycomb in there for when we'd need it next." He explained.

Over the next few hours, Alaric and Benjamin continued to talk, Benjamin was curious of all they had done and gone through to find Banning. They had not talked much of Alaric's time when they were apart, in the past, mostly of Benjamin's time on the plantation. He enjoyed it, listening to Alaric tell of his adventures like they had before he was old enough to sail with them.

A dull light began to slice through the moss and tree branches. The water was nearly still. The birds were beginning to wake, flying low above the water, picking at bugs or small fish that came to the surface.

"You two done and talked all night. Damn hard to get any sleep with your blathering." Red grumbled.

Benjamin shot him a mock, sympathetic look. He knew Red was not truly upset. He had always been coarse and gruff, but the first to offer his hand to help. He had been the one that taught him to properly load a cannon.

"Git up!" Shorty kicked at Claude. Laurent, already on his feet and standing by the boats.

"Let's get going," Alaric commanded, kicking a pile of dirt onto the last smoldering embers.

Benjamin held the long, wooden boat steady as Amara and Molly climbed in. Pushing it into the shallow water, he and Alaric jumped in.

Making their way through the swampy bayou seemed to go quicker on the return. The commotion in the town could be clearly heard, long before being seen. Pulling the boats onto the shore, they got out. Benjamin stepped up to Laurent and Claude, allowing Ethan to move his attention on Banning.

"My man be up there at the port." He told the group. "After I give 'im the orders to the goods, you best be letting me go." He glared at Benjamin, who once again had his knife to him.

"Let's see about that." Benjamin replied.

"Monsieur Claude," The man gave a mock bow. "And how may I be of assistance?" He asked, adjusting the velvet coat he wore. It was obvious the clothes had not been tailored to him. There were even a few poorly patched marks about the garment. It was clear he wanted to give the appearance he was well stationed.

"Don't be toying with me, Louis. I've come to give orders about a shipment." He jerked his head at Banning.

"Ah," Louis rolled back on his heals. "Very well, very well. I'll see it's done with most swiftness." Louis scurried off, snapping his fingers and calling to his men to do as he commanded.

"There," Claude turned, shoving Benjamin away from him. "I did what you wanted." He raised his arms, dramatically turning in a circle.

"That's enough, Claude." Banning seethed.

Claude's hat remained low on his head, still shadowing his face. "I don't think it is, you traitorous bastard."

Claude's fist flew up hitting Shorty in the face, with a loud crack. Shorty swung back at the snarling man, his hit falling short. Spitting the blood from his mouth, he reached for his blade, but Red already had a hold of Claude. One hand tightened around the French man's shoulder, the other held a sword to his throat.

Ethan, keeping a flintlock pointed at Thomas, allowing Alaric and Benjamin to take care of Laurent. The confrontation causing the sailors and folks in the port to cease what they were doing. A group of guards came around a corner, heading from the center of the town.

"We need to be going, lads." Ethan raised his voice, loud enough to be heard over the skirmish.

Benjamin leapt back as Laurent swung out with a fist, a knife had appeared in his hand. He heard the intake of Amara's breath. Molly had pulled her from the fray, their own weapons drawn in preparation, but to Benjamin's relief, staying out of the fight.

Alaric tapped Laurent on the shoulder, drawing his attention to him and away from Benjamin. With a brief moment to breathe, he spun around to check on the others.

Ethan had a firm grasp on Banning, a flintlock against his side. Banning obediently keeping his arms raised, a blank expression on his face, his eyes watching the brawl between Alaric and Laurent.

Ol' Shorty rushed forward, knocking Claude to the ground, his sword through the man's side. A thud and gasp sounded from behind Benjamin. He turned to see Laurent fall to the ground as well, a pool of blood gathering where he now lay.

"Red!" Molly rushed forward with Amara, both trying to hold the sailor steady. A small knife protruded from his middle. With a shaky hand, Red removed it. Molly quickly unwound the cloth he kept tied about his neck and pressed it to the wound.

"It's goin' be fine, mate," Shorty breathed out, grabbing his arm and putting it around him. "Walk with me. We'll get ye back to Doc and fixed right up."

"Quit yer fussin, man." Red grumbled, a chocked laugh rumbling his chest. "I've had worse, no need to go worryin' the women folk." He replied, his face paling slightly as they made their way into the thick cover of trees.

Benjamin looked back. The group of soldiers had quickened their pace toward them. He hoped they would be able to lose them in the forest. With luck, Louis's men would already have the goods loaded.

Keeping a tight hold on Amara's hand, they ran between the trees and long hanging moss. The group followed close behind Thomas. The path being disregarded in an attempt to throw the soldiers off their tracks if they had chosen to follow.

Breaking through the trees, they came to the shore. Banning hopped in and helped to pull Red in, who's eyes kept fluttering closed. His face was now as pale as his shirt.

The men that had been loading the supplies had not finished, but they had little choice and could not remain. They would have to make do with the little they had loaded. Ordering the skiffs to be raised, Benjamin and Amara stood at the railing of *The Croga*. Alaric had told him they would flash the lantern if Red did not make it.

He heard Alaric's orders to weigh anchor, his own men

following suit. The ships were nearing the mouth of the alcove. Shouts could be heard from the shoreline now. The soldiers had pursued them. A shot rang out from a musket, trying to draw their attention to them, but their orders to turn back were ignored.

Benjamin stood at the helm, Amara by his side. He kept his eyes fixed on *The Trinity*. He had wanted to be on deck in case they signaled.

Amara rested her hand on his arm. Looking down at her, he gave her a weak smile, placing his hand over hers. His gaze shifted back to *The Trinity*. The sunset on the horizon still lighting the sky in a soft glow. A last remembrance before giving way to the night.

A flash caught his attention. He pulled out his spyglass and peered through it. Alaric stood at the bow, a lantern in hand. Flashing it slowly, he gave a silent nod and doused the lantern.

Benjamin drew in a long breath, letting it out slowly.

"I'm very sorry." Amara whispered.

Benjamin wrapped his arm around her and called for Archer to take his place at the helm.

30

Molly held a small mirror, just inside of Charlie's mouth.

"Go ahead and give the lad a minute." Doc instructed, placing a reassuring hand on the young sailor's shoulder.

Charlie gave a painful swallow, "Get it over with, Doc." Closing his eyes, he leaned his head back and opened his mouth.

Holding his head firmly, Molly watched Doc grab the expulser. A bowl sat at the ready for Molly to hand to Charlie to spit into, another smaller bowl was on the table beside Doc. Working at the tooth, it came free with a slight tug. Charlie shut his eyes tighter and groaned. "Well done, go ahead and rinse your mouth out with a swig of this. It'll help numb the area."

Molly held the bowl out for him while Doc handed him a cup of rum. He held the tooth between two fingers. "No wonder you were in pain and hardly able to do your tasks accordingly. It's nearly all grey and you've a piece missing from it." He dropped the tooth in Charlie's hand.

Charlie moved his mouth, feeling with his tongue, the empty space where his tooth once was. "Aside from the dull ache, tis already feeling better." He beamed.

Molly laughed, "That'd be the rum doing that. I reckon you'll feel the pain of it soon."

Doc grinned in agreement, clearing the area and tossing the tool in a bucket of vinegar water. "She's right, but no need to look so downcast. It will cease with its aching in a couple days. Until then, I'll have you marked down for an extra ration of rum." Looking slightly more cheerful with the thought of an extra ration, Charlie left the surgery to continue his tasks on deck.

"I've cut more cloth for you and cleaned as many larger ones as I could." She began. "I will clean and scrub that for you, too." Molly pointed to the expulser in the bucket. "Will there be anything else you be needing before we approach the fleet?" She asked. She wished to keep her mind busy. She was terrified of what the battle could bring. Alaric and the others had agreed to search out the ships and possibly, most likely, engage them. They had agreed it would be the most effective way to clear all of their names, though they had all admitted their dislike of Thomas playing a part in it. After all they had been through to capture him. After all he had done, they did not fancy the idea of aiding in his pardon.

"Thank you for your assistance. I have ground up more herbs and prepared some oils and salves." He said, pointing to a shelf with small glass files and bottles that sat securely and ready to be used. "You might see to it Cook isn't in need of any aid. Case will be preparing and running through drills with the others and will not have much time to help Cook prepare." He suggested, taking the cleansed expulser from her.

"Very good, then." She replied, stepping from the surgery and into the companionway, Aoife quick on her heels.

The aroma from the galley traveled through the ship, following it with a comforting sense of calm.

"How can I help?" She reached for the spare apron that hung from a single iron hook. Slipping it over her head, she tied it as tight as she could, the fabric still hanging large and loose about her.

"Oui, the pastry for the fish pies needs to be rolled out. Dried and salted fish had been amongst the provisions that had been brought to the ship and Cook's pies were the most delicious way to eat the dried fish. "After you be done with that, go right on to chopping and peeling the potatoes. I be working on the sauce. The corn'll need to be put in with the rest." He spoke as he mixed and heated a creamy sauce.

Molly pulled her sleeves up her forearms, tossing a pinch of flour onto the board and beginning to roll the pastry out, big enough to stuff with the many ingredients. Flour puffed up as she tossed another pinch down, preventing the pastry from sticking to the round, wooden pin. Careful not to roll the pastry too thin. She let it lay flat, gathering the rest of the filling in a bowl. Grabbing a sharp, tiny knife, she set to work peeling and chopping the potatoes. Once the corn, potatoes and fish were ready, Cook helped her raise the sides of the pastry, holding it up with her hands, he carefully filled it with the ingredients, pouring the creamy sauce over all of it. Sealing the pie with a pastry top, he put it in the stove to cook and pulled out a small bag of brown powder.

"What is that?" She came forward, breathing in a whiff of the ingredient. "Mmm, I've never smelled anything like it."

"Oui, Tis a true treat!" He exclaimed, excitement filling his eyes. "Tis cocoa powder and we be making a chocolate pudding." He brought out a large bowl and the sack of sugar. "Grab the eggs and the bucket of milk. We'll be needing them." Pouring in the milk, he then sifted the cocoa and sugar into a pot that sat on the stove. He combined the ingredients until it was smooth and near to boiling. "You crack them eggs and add a bit of salt to that there bowl." He handed her the large bowl. Adding in a couple other ingredients Molly did not know. Cook removed the hot pan and gently poured the chocolate into the bowl. He then transferred it back to the pot to set to boil. "It'll be just the thing." He responded cheerfully, finishing the pudding. "You git yours and the Captain's trays. I'll have the pudding brought down after a bit."

Molly filled their tray, balancing the foods on it carefully as she made her way up the stairs and into the cabin. "Oh, I did not realize you were already in here." She looked at him apologetically. "I am sorry I kept you waiting on your meal." She looked him over, his brows pulled together in thought. He was holding a piece of parchment, a silhouette of a woman on it. Molly's stomach tightened. Still holding the tray in hand, not knowing where to put it. A small, wooden box sat open on the desk in front of Alaric. A couple small jewels, a swatch of delicate fabric and several letters lay spread over it. "I've no seen that box before." She began, unsure of what more to say. She did not wish to pry but felt uncomfortable intruding. "Shall I leave you to your thoughts?" She asked, her eyes returning to the silhouette in his hand.

"Certainly not," he looked up, a bit surprised at her offer. He handed her the silhouette. "I was simply gathering Red's possessions. He was one of the men that joined the first year that Lucas and I had *The Trinity*. When we return to Barbados, I'll need to pay his wife a visit." His voice somber. "And after the battle to come, I fear there will be a few others that I will need to see to." Running a hand through his hair, he placed the belongings back in the box and set it aside. Taking the tray from Molly, he apologized for making her wait and sat it between them.

Molly felt her face flush at allowing her thoughts to stray to such assumptions as they had, especially since his mind had been so occupied with far more distressing notions.

As if reading her thoughts, he stared at her, he eyes searching hers, a grin showing on his lips. "You've nothing to fear, love. There's no other woman I want."

Blushing again, she pulled a bit of food onto her plate from the tray. "I fear the battle to come." She confessed, unable to look into his eyes.

He leaned over the table a bit, tilting his head so she would look at him. "We've seen worse odds. Perhaps not while you were aboard, but I have and most of the crew has." He winked, "It'll be thrilling."

"Oh, aye," she huffed, "That be one way of looking at it." She nodded to his plate. "You best eat your fill, Captain. You'll need to keep your strength up."

Obediently taking a bite of his food, he studied her. "Promise me, lass, you will stay with Doc."

She knew that if she were one deck, it would only serve to distract him, but she could not promise to stay below if he were in need of help. "I'll do my best, but in return, you must make it through unscathed."

"I'll do my best," he grinned. "Once we finish here, why don't you make the rounds with me and make sure all preparations have been seen to?" He suggested. A knock sounding on the hatch, announcing Case with a bowl of pudding.

Alaric gestured for her to take the first bite. Cook had made and served some delicious cakes and other deserts, but never had she tasted chocolate. It was smooth, rich and unlike any flavor she had experienced before.

"So, what do you think? Quite terrible really, isn't it?"

Molly looked up at him in shocked, disbelief, causing a deep laugh to pour from him. "On the contrary, I'd be more than happy to finish the bowl by myself, Captain." Giggles rippled from her lips.

Molly licked the last bit of pudding from her spoon. "How can we possibly hope to defeat five French Naval vessels with only our two?" She asked, heading out the hatch and onto the deck.

231

The men were singing a song about a whaling ship. One of going into battle with the beast. Of how the fight went on, until the beast concurred. "I rather hope that is not a glimpse into the future." Molly looked up at him skeptically.

"Depends on who you see as the whaler and who the beast." He smiled, looking up the rigging at the men pulling lines and adjusting them.

Fresh paint had been put on the ship, making her appear bright, the name shown boldly, and the figurehead had been done with a new coat of polish. The woman and seal entwined together, fierceness, a courage in their eyes. Molly had grown up hearing the tales of the selkies. Of reading books of them as a little girl, curled up by the fire with her mother. After she had gone to live with her uncle and knew she would never see her mother again. She often imagined that her mother was one of them. That had found her skin buried somewhere near the cliffs on which they lived under and had returned to her rightful place in the sea.

Coming from her thoughts, she felt Alaric's fingers gently brushing a strand of hair from her face. She looked down at her feet, embarrassed she had been caught in such deep thought.

"Let's go below. I'd like to be sure the guns are in order."

Ethan could be heard shouting commands and running another drill with Jim and the gun crew. They were training Clayton to lead the gundeck in case Jim is wounded or worse. Ethan would be needed above deck and would be leading them once they boarded the other ships.

"You feel ready, Clayton?" Alaric asked, putting a hand on the young man's shoulder.

"Aye, Capt'n," he looked between Ethan and Jim. "They says I be ready for the task."

"He is, though, let's hope it don't come to that. I'd rather not be found on Doc's tables." Jim gave Clayton a friendly nudge.

"They are all ready." Ethan nodded to the crew." The guns are cleaned, and all the materials are sitting and waiting to be used." Ethan said, pleased.

"Very good." Alaric acknowledged, moving around the guns and peering through the holes that the cannons sat in. In the distance, islands could be seen. "Ethan, I'll have you come with me. We are nearing the islands and will need to bring Thomas on deck. Clayton, lead your men in another drill. Jim, you may get your ration of rum and meal. Get some rest before we reach the fleet." He ordered.

Molly followed him back on deck as he commanded other sailors to take their meal and rest. They did not want to ring the bell for crew changes, as the sound could be carried on the waters for miles, and they did not wish the fleet to know they approached.

"Why don't you go see to your beasts. After, I'll meet you in the cabin." Alaric suggested.

Reluctantly stepping away from him, she headed down the companionway. The smell and sounds from the animals wafted through the lower decks, filling her with excitement and calm, clearing her senses of the nerves and fear that had been consuming her. Reaching a hand up, she stroked the cow's soft nose and giving her gentle scratches along her neck. A low sound came from the cow, as if telling her all would be right. There still remained three kids from the last litter of goats and two adults. The kids scampered about the pen. Unaware of what was to come. Scooping one of the squirming kids up in her arms, she planted a kiss on his head. Molly whispered a lullaby she had learned in the colonies. The rhythmic melody calming the wee beast in her arms. "Aye, you'll be just fine." She cooed, saying the words more for her own benefit, rather than the animal's. Returning the kid to its pen, she tossed in a bit more straw and turned from the pens and headed back up the companionway.

"I was beginning to think you preferred to spend your last hours before the battle with your friends below." Alaric grinned, stepping around the table and coming up to her. He ran a hand down her arm. "Here," he pulled a sealed letter from his vest. "If I do not make it," he began. His words being cut off by Molly's sharp intake of breath.

She stepped back and turned away from him. She could not bear to hear him speak of her greatest fear. She wrapped her arms around her middle, trying desperately to find the smallest ounce of control. She felt him move closer. Spinning around, she pointed a finger at him. She felt a tear slip out. "You will make it. You must!" Her voice unsteady. She hated how she had come to trust him, to care about him, to love him.

He pinched her finger between his and slowly lowered her hand. "I promise I will do my very best. You have my word.

I have no intention of letting this battle be the one to take me." He reached a hand up, wiping another tear away. "You must listen, love. This letter, it's important and will possibly be the only thing that can save you and the others. You must find a way to get it to Lucas and Catherine. They will know what to do and you will be safe." He tilted his head, searching her face.

She nodded in silent reply. Taking the letter and tucking it safely in the folds of her dress. He pulled her against him. Lifting her chin, he lowered his mouth to hers. Hesitating only a moment, she allowed herself to melt against him, letting her lips move with his. It was not that she did not want to kiss him, but she felt in doing so, she was almost saying farewell.

31

Alaric pulled a clean shirt on. His sword and flintlocks lay on the table, ready to be strapped to his person. There had been a knock at the hatch. Shorty informed them they were but an hour from the alcove. Alaric turned to face Molly. Her hair was pulled back with a strip of fabric. Her own sword and flintlock were now strapped in position on her waist. His mind went to the last few hours they had spent together. Her kisses still fresh on his lips. He had not wanted to worry her with the letter but knew he had no choice but to give it to her. He also knew he had to do everything he could to survive, not only to ensure the safety of his crew, as well as Benjamin, but he dreaded to think of what would happen to Molly if the French won.

Swallowing back the tightening he now felt in his chest, he gave her one last kiss. "You best get to Doc." He suggested.

"I'll see you after." Molly responded, a determined and fierce look in her eyes.

"I reckon you will." He winked, releasing her and grabbing the weapons from the table.

He stared at the hatch that led down to the companionway and where Molly was. He ran a hand over his face, pinching the bridge of his nose. On any other given day, under any other circumstances he would have felt ready and even possibly eager for the battle but having Molly aboard and at a greater risk than she had been in with any other battle they had encountered thus far. He felt uneasy, the memory of the young Lady he once had to protect and failed, refused to be erased from his mind. Molly's eyes, bright and filled with courage and a trust he had done all he could to gain, filled his thoughts. Her smile, her lips and accent that had reminded him so much of Ireland.

"She'll be safe." Ethan commented, coming up beside him. "And I have great faith in the Captain of *The Croga*." He grinned. "You taught him well. He may even be a more skilled a fighter than yourself."

"I dare say he is." Alaric responded. Benjamin had certainly proved his ability to take care of himself, as well as his crew.

"Look alive, lads," Thomas called out from the bow, hopping off the stepping and heading towards them. "We be making ready to enter the alcove. It be a bit tricky maneuvering. The inlet leads a good deal further in that the last one we were in." He looked hard at them. "I hope you and your crew are up for this. Once in that alcove, there will be no escaping until the battle be over." Banning shook his head, chuckling. "You lot be as crazy as myself." He started to walk off. "Best call your men to their stations and tell 'em to keep it quiet." Banning called over his shoulder to them.

"Right," Alaric breathed out, clenching his jaw.

"You'll keep him on deck?" Ethan asked, watching the man's back.

"He's a skilled fighter and with so much at stake, we can use all the help we can get. I do not think he will turn on us. This is his chance at freedom as well. Not to mention his wife and how she would suffer."

"I hope you're right." Ethan sighed, clearly unsettled.

"Alright lads, times come. Put on your most warn clothes. Idea is to look grungy, unkempt, like a pirate." He cast a glance at Banning. The men around them laughing in response. "Shouldn't be hard for you." He cocked a brow at Thomas.

"I aim to please," He stretched his arms wide and gave an exaggerated bow.

"Keep your voices low and give the Frenchies no reason to believe we are anything other than the pirates they claim we now are." He walked amongst his crew, being sure of their readiness, of their courage. "Strap that a notch tighter, Key." He tapped the lad's leather belt that hung too loose. "You go to pull that, and the belt'll go with it. You'll not be able to defend yourself in time."

Alaric scanned the deck. The men looked warn and ratty.

Their appearances and the looks in their eyes and upon their faces entirely contrary to one another. They were alight with daring eagerness. Fear flashed here and there but even then; the men stood tall, ready and courageous.

Alaric stood at the back railing, looking over his shoulder, he caught Benjamin's eyes as he stood proud at the bow of *The Croga*. Nodding to each other, Alaric grinned. It almost felt like times before.

Rounding another section of the alcove, sails became visible over a small bit of land. A pirate flag flew on the mast of *The Trinity*. With luck, it'd buy them time and trick the French into believing the pirates were merely hiding out too.

Coming about the bend, the quiet and low sounds coming from the French ships ceased. There was no more scraping of boots against the wooden decks and the sails on the ships furrowed, raising like the hackles of a wild animal.

"Steady men," Alaric voiced. He looked over at Benjamin. Both he and Benjamin stood at the helm of their ship. Catching his gaze, he flicked a hand low in the air, indicating Benjamin angle towards the left.

The French had conveniently been lined up beside one another. With a Frigate and Brig in the back and two Frigates and Brig in the front.

Thomas stood at the bow, waving his arms franticly. His words slurred in French, telling them they could not slow, to stay clear, as if they had lost control of the vessel.

Both *The Trinity* and *The Croga* began to slide between the French vessels. Their sides lining up perfectly. Just before the canons came to life, a French man yelled out. He had realized their mistake and had spotted the slight movement of the guns below deck taking aim. His shout alerted the rest of the fleet, but only moments before the canons splintered through their hulls and rigging.

Pulling in their sails, *The Croga* and *The Trinity* reloaded, taking aim once more. The men on deck raising their rifles. The ships were close in the tight alcove.

"Fire!" Ethan bellowed, not wasting a moment while the canons were reloaded. Once more, the shots from the guns below, rocked the ship. The waters splashed, turning a foaming white at the disturbance.

The French Frigate that had taken the shots from both *The Croga* and *The Trinity* was already near to sinking, and aside from being an inconvenient obstacle, was now of no concern to them. It could no longer aid its allies and merely sat helpless in the canvas and splintered plank, filled waters.

The Brig that had been hit had lost control of its rudder and could not move or maneuver out of the way of the next wave of shot from *The Trinity*. Letting out the sails again, the vessel lurched forward.

Alaric yelled for the men to get down as a blast came at them. Skimming across the deck.

"Get any wounded, below!" Ethan commanded, helping Charlie back on his feet, blood streaming down the side of his face. "Get yourself to Doc." He ordered.

Alaric spun the helm, putting his ship in line with *The Croga*. Each of them protecting the other as they cut the Brig off from the rest of the fleet. Pulling in the sails once more, they came up beside the Brig. This time on the starboard side. He heard Jim's order to fire. *The Croga* coming around on the Port side, once again, blocking the vessel in.

Leaving Benjamin to fire again on the Brig. Alaric steered *The Trinity* about, protecting *The Croga* from the oncoming Frigate.

Canon shot ripped across *The Trinity*. A deafening crack sounded from the main mast. "Benjamin!" Alaric shouted. The mast crashed down across both his ship and Benjamin's.

"Cut us free, lads," Ethan yelled, as sailors rushed forward. The men aboard *The Croga* doing the same. Without the mainsail, they would not be able to maneuver as well or as quickly.

The Croga was protected, trapped between the destroyed Brig and Alaric's ship. Once they freed themselves, they would be able to pull out from between them, but that still left *The Trinity* near to disabled.

Alaric watched his men push the torn canvas and end of the mast, over the shattered railing and into the water below. "Prepare another round!" Alaric ordered. "We aren't finished yet, lads." The crew responded with yells of thrilled bravery and encouragement.

241

The Trinity's canons tore through the Frigate as it passed, followed directly by the remaining Frigate. He heard Ethan and Benjamin's orders to remain low, as they took the shot from the second Frigate. Alaric praised the French Captains of the fleet for their high shots. It had been a good plan to take out their mast with *The Croga* directly on the other side and he could not be more grateful they aimed high, for it meant those below were safe.

The canons blasted from *The Trinity*, hitting their target directly, causing wood to shatter and fly about. Screams could be heard from the enemy ship, as the sailors were hit by the shot or debris.

Alaric turned around, hearing swords clanking together and flintlocks going off. The crew from the French Brig had taken advantage of the mast falling upon *The Croga* and chose to board them.

Knowing his ship was no help to Benjamin in that moment, he ordered the sail to be let out as best they could. The remaining French vessels would not fire upon *The Croga* as it would risk too many of their own men.

The ship lurched forward with an exhausted groan. The two Frigates came at *The Trinity*, clearly hoping to do as they had done to the first of the French vessels. Alaric called for the sails to be brought in. His muscles felt tight and strained, the wheel was heavy and difficult at best of times, but with a battered vessel, it was made far harder. Pulling against the helm, the ship began to turn. It would take on far less damage at that angle and be a much narrower target. "Sharp Shooters, take aim and fire when ready!" He ordered. His command being followed by Ethan's for everyone to stay low.

Alaric's mind went to Molly. Thankful she was not in the cabin or with the animals at the moment. If the French timed their shots just right, a blast would be sure to go through his cabin.

Alaric held fast to the helm, peering over the wheel just enough to catch a quick glimpse of Benjamin. He was holding his own against a much larger French sailor. Archer stood behind him, their backs together, watching each other's angles. Alaric smiled, despite the situation. Watching Benjamin and Archer in that moment was like looking through time and seeing himself and Lucas.

Bringing him out of the memory, the canons sounded. The timing had been precise. A few shots hit their marks well. Even with the precision, the way *The Trinity* had been angled, it took on little damage, though he cringed when he thought of what his cabin must look like.

As the two ships had passed, his men that had been stationed in the rigging with their rifles, had aimed true. The man that had been maneuvering one of the Frigates had been shot and the men aboard had been preoccupied with the rest of the vessel that they had not noticed. The Frigate was headed directly for the steep walls of the alcove.

The remaining Frigate and Brig were now separated and sat at opposite sides of the alcove. The Frigate was coming about but the Brig had all but remained out of the battle. Alaric searched the deck for Ethan. Spotting him, he waved an arm for him to join him at the helm.

"What are your thoughts?" Alaric asked.

"That Brig, it is the head of the fleet. We take it and its captain. We take the fleet." Ethan said, his shirt stained with blood.

"Aye, that was my thinking as well. I say we ram 'em. *The Trinity* has taken a right beating and we need to end this." He looked Ethan over. "And you should see Doc."

"I agree with the former. The ladder is not an issue. Tis not my blood." Ethan peeled the shirt from his body and tossed it aside. "It belongs to Amos. He didn't make it. A canon hit near him and sent a piece of railing through him. I'm sorry, mate."

Alaric nodded in solemn response. He did not want to think of the injured or dying. He also did not wish to think of Molly having to witness it. He had no doubt she could handle it but knew very well it took all she had to remain unemotional and focused while she watched the crew in pain or dying.

"Raise those sails, boys!" Alaric yelled. *The Trinity* was aimed directly at the Brig. "Prepare for impact!"

The Trinity was equipped with a sturdy ram, however, they rarely chose to use it, as it was always a risk and was always, only used as a last resort.

Shots behind them splashed in the waters. Falling short of their mark. The Frigate was trying in vain to halt their progress. The impact of hitting the Brig with such force and speed, rattled Alaric's teeth. A shout from above sounded,

Edward hung from the rigging, desperately trying to regain his hold.

"Prepare to board!" Ethan pulled his sword from its strap, holding it above his head. The crew followed suit. The ships were pulled closer together, the planks lay across where the railing used to be. Now bits of sharp and torn wood stuck up in its place.

The sharper shooters remained in the rigging as men boarded the ship, taking out the front line of sailors that awaited them. Alaric released the helm and pulled a flintlock and his sword from the strap that held them secure. Firing a shot, smoke billowed up, blocking his view momentarily. The French sailor that he had aimed at, crumpled to the ground, giving Alaric a chance to board the ship. Returning his flintlock to its place in the belt, he met the blade of another sailor. Driving himself forward, he did not give the Frenchman a moment to gain the ground. Alaric swept his leg out, tripping the sailor, his head hitting the planks with a hard crack.

The smoke from the flintlocks filled the air. The smell of the powder burned his lungs. The deck was crowded, making it difficult to fight on. The planks slippery with the spray from the disturbed waters below and a fresh mix of blood mingled with it. The clanging of the swords made his ears ring. In the thick fray it was nearly impossible to keep an eye on his crew. He could feel the presence of Eddie at his back. An occasional shove or bump from him, reassured Alaric he was still fighting.

Alaric swung his sword down, blocking the blow from a sailor. The man growled in frustration, shooting a dark glare at him. Alaric moved his sword to the side, purposely exposing himself and awaiting the next move. A groan sounding behind him, Alaric felt Eddie fall against his back. Whirling around, he tried catching Eddie as he fell at the same time as blocking the blade from the sailor. He winced, the tip of the French man's sword, going into his side. Holding onto Eddie with one arm, his sword in that hand, he reached into his boot and pulled his dirk from it, driving it deep into the sailor's middle. He felt the tip of the sword pull from his side and the warm blood begin trickling down, soaking his shirt.

"Eddie, mate. Hang in there, I'll get you to Doc." Alaric said, putting Eddie over his shoulder and rushing across the plank. "Doc!" Alaric yelled, alerting the man and allowing him time to clear a space on a table as he came down through the hatch. Alaric laid Eddie on the table, his face pale, his eyes staring far away, as if he were looking out at the horizon. Alaric panted, shaking his head, seeing the look on Doc's face and knowing the answer before Doc voiced it.

"Remove your shirt," Molly ordered, distracting him for a moment from the sight before him. Doc pulled a large fabric over Eddie's still form, gesturing for two younger sailors to lay him at the side of the cabin, allowing the table to be used for the next injured sailor that came stumbling in, his arm bleeding fiercely. Alaric did as Molly bid him. His eyes fixed on the six sheets that lay at the edge of the cabin. "You promised me you'd do your best to remain unscathed." Molly whispered, drawing his attention to her.

He huffed out a light laugh, "Tis but a small scrape, lass." He said, sucking in a breath when the needle poked through the tender flesh.

"Serves you right, Captain Stein." She replied, refusing to look him in the eyes. Her hand that held the torn flesh together as she sewed the wound up, slightly shook.

Placing a finger under her chin, he gently raised her head, so their gazes met. Giving her a wink, he nodded to the stitching. "You do that well."

"Captain, *The Croga* be joining us now." Key said, returning his sword to the strap as he entered the cabin. "Captain Clarke sent me to tell you."

"Aye, thank you Key. I'll be finished here in a moment." Alaric cleared his throat, looking over the men that lay in hammocks or sat on the tables, awaiting their turn to be treated. "How are you holding up, lad?" Alaric asked Henry, who sat on the table opposite him, his face near to a green color.

"Alright, Cap." His eyes shifted to Doyle whose forearm had been too badly injured to save. A thick set of bandages were wrapped neatly around the end, just at the elbow. Sweat poured from his forehead, dampening his hair. "Better than some." He looked back at Alaric who could not help but feel a pang of guilt. It was never easy seeing crewmates injured or dead, but witnessing friends lose their lives or having to help hold them down when a limb is removed were not easy moments to recover from.

Alaric lifted his arm a little higher so Molly could finish washing off the bits of blood that had dried around the wound, before hopping off the table with a wince that he tried desperately to hide from Molly. "You did the right thing. It may not seem like it now. It may not seem like it, even when he wakes, but you did what was needed to save your friend's life and there is no greater courage." He looked at the young man pointedly. He sympathized with the lad. The memory of when he and Lucas had to hold down a friend that had needed his leg removed after a battle, would forever stay with him.

The surgeon had placed a thick piece of rolled cloth in his mouth for him to bite down on. The instruments were laid out. They had been no older than twenty years of age and had seen men come from battles with missing limbs before but having to be involved in the process was a far different story. The battle had lasted hours, the three of them had been anticipating the fight to come with great enthusiasm. It was not long after the Portuguese vessel had boarded them that their friend had been shot at close range by a blunderbuss. His leg had been all but removed from his body in that moment. Lucas and Alaric pulled him below and had been told to hold him. The doctor gave their friend an ample amount of whiskey before proceeding. Alaric remembered Lucas picking the bottle up and taking a generous amount of the amber liquid, before handing it to Alaric, who did the same.

Alaric looked over at Molly. She was firmly pulling a sailor's arm, resetting the bone. He caught her gaze. Giving her a wink, he followed Key on deck and into the fray that had now spread onto the deck of *The Trinity*. Sword in hand, he scanned the decks for Benjamin. *The Croga* had pulled up beside them and had joined the fight. Rushing forward, Alaric brought his sword down upon the flintlock of a French sailor that was aiming at Ol' Shorty. The gun discharged, the ball firing and burying itself in the planking. Bringing his arm up, he sent the pommel of his sword into the man's face, causing him to howl in pain and retreat. The blood from his mouth and nose, clearly hindering his vision.

Alaric moved forward, desperate to find Benjamin, pushing the memories from before to the back of his mind. He could not dwell on them now. Driving his blade through another sailor that came at him, he blocked another blow with his dirk. Kicking the man back with his boot and over the edge of the ship. With very little railing remaining, it made it far easier to slip overboard.

More men moved toward them. Key fired his flintlock, hitting the first man. The other two did not stop. They did not even falter at the dispatchment of their crewmate in front of them. Alaric moved to the side, the French sailor's sword narrowly missing Alaric's shoulder. He twisted, bringing his blade down on the man's back, only to have to dive out of the way of another attack. A flash of bright, russet hair caught his attention. The man advanced once more. Readying to bring his sword down upon Alaric. Expecting to feel the force of the sailor's blade against his own, his brow furrowed as he cocked his head to see another blade intwined with the man's instead of his own.

"You promised you would stay below," He frowned at Molly as she pulled her blade from the man's chest.

"Correction, I had promised to do my best." She stepped closer to him. "And so, I did." She raised a brow at him, "For most of the time anyway. I knew you would be worried about Ben, and I wanted to help." She pointed the tip of her sword at the man that now lay on the planks. "Looks like I was just in time too."

"So, it would appear," Alaric's frown deepened. He did not relish the idea of Molly being on deck and in the middle of the fight but could not hide the pride and desire he felt for her.

Standing, he turned around. He no longer saw Key fighting. Instead, Shorty knelt over the young man's body, blood seeped from a wound in his chest.

Shorty shook his head. "The lad couldn't pull his sword in time."

Alaric growled, his fist meeting the face of another oncoming sailor, his dirk plunging deep into the man's side. He shoved the lifeless body aside. Looking back down at Ol' Shorty, he shook his head. "I told the lad to tighten the strap. I should have made sure he did it correctly."

"Twasn't your fault. He'd been in enough fights now to know better." Shorty rested a hand on the young man's chest briefly, before standing. His eyes narrowed and looked passed Alaric, over his shoulder. Alaric followed his gaze.

"Release him!" He ordered. Swallowing back the fear he felt. He had caught a glimpse of Benjamin's hair from behind. A French sailor held him tight, a blade against his throat. Blood steadily streamed from the side of Benjamin's face. The sailor had turned, still gripping Benjamin tightly. Bodies lay about the decks of all three of the ships. Blood turning the bright blue water below, a dark and menacing color.

The man looked between Alaric and Thomas, laughing. "I know you, Capitaine." He laughed louder, "Le Capitaine with the compass tattoo. Oui, we've heard much of you and your exploits." He tilted his head, glancing from Alaric to Thomas.

Thomas's flintlock was raised, the look in his eyes making Alaric feel uneasy. The memory of Thomas aiming at Benjamin once before, flashed through his mind. He took a step forward. His only flintlocks were empty and useless in that moment. Banning's gaze flicked to Alaric, along with his flintlock, a look of debate on his face as if he was weighing his options. As if he were contemplating whose side to be on and who could offer him more… or ruin him.

"Not a step further, Capitaine." The French man commanded, giving Benjamin a slight shake to emphasize his threat. "This has gone far enough. You'll take what's left of your men and retreat." He ordered.

Banning roared with laughter, his flintlock returning to point at who, Alaric could not tell. Whether he aimed at Benjamin or at the French Captain. Alaric's body was numb. He felt sealed to the very spot. If he moved forward, he risked the French Captain slicing Ben's throat and in not making a move, he was putting Benjamin's fate, in the very same hands that tried to kill him before. Thomas's gaze narrowed his eyes hardening. He shifted his flintlock slightly.

Alaric lunged forward, fear and anger taking over. Halting suddenly, his sword at the ready, smoke billowed from Thomas's pistol. The French captain dropped his blade and stumbled back, only to crumple suddenly. Alaric and Benjamin stared blankly at Thomas, surprise and shock evident upon their faces.

Banning shrugged, lowering his flintlock. "I hate to be predictable."

The silence seemed unreal and almost louder than the battle had been. Ol' Shorty chuckled, breaking the silence. "Down to the depths go them frogs." This caused a ripple of cheers.

32

Molly stood, hands on her hips, staring at the splintered stump that sat in the center of the ship. Once stretching up tall, carrying that billowing sail that drove the vessel forward. "How will you replace it? Fix it?" Molly asked, shifting her gaze to Alaric. His shirt removed, the fresh wound on his side looking angry and painful.

Alaric raised his brows, blowing out a breath. "Not easily. Our best bet will be to take one from the French Brig. Their mast is still in good shape and they will not be needing it." He cocked his head, "Still, not easily done. They are heavy and cumbersome, as you can imagine."

"Aye," Dropping her hands, she gently touched his side, careful not to make contact with the wound. "You should be taking it easier. You are stretching the torn flesh too much and will loosen the stitches." She warned.

Alaric looked down at the wound, "You are probably right, but I've little choice and it does not hurt much, now." He tried assuring her. "Besides," placing his hand one her cheek. "If it worsens or causes fever, it'll mean I finally get your undivided attentions." He winked, placing a slow kiss on her lips.

Blushing at the display, whoops and whistles coming from the sailors nearby, Molly stepped back, gathering a torn sail in her arms. Flashing Alaric, a playful smile, she turned, joining Amara and the other women in mending the sails.

"Right," Alaric waved the men around him, over. "Let's take the mast from the Brig," he began, pointing to the brig they had rammed. "You lot, cut it down and prepare to have it brought over. I will be over to join you in a moment. Henry, you and Shorty can begin sawing the splintered wood away from what's left of ours. It will help the mast to fit to it better." He ran a hand through his hair, hoping the mast would hold long enough for them to get to Barbados. Stepping across the board and onto the Brig, Alaric looked into the rigging. Sailors wrapped a rope around the foremast, their legs draped on either side of the yardarm, holding tight to the rope. As the mast was cut down, they slowly loosened their grip on the rope, lowing the mast to the deck of the ship.

"I'll help," Thomas came up beside him, his gaze on the lowering mast.

"Very well," Alaric replied. If their plan worked and they were able to get word to Lucas and Catherine in time, they would be pardoned. It was a gamble, but taking the French fleet was their only hope at clearing their names and Benjamin's. It also meant though, if their slates could be wiped clean, especially Ben's, then Thomas's would be as well. Alaric's mind flashed to the young man aboard the merchant ship they had come upon. Banning had run it aground and left none alive, or so he had thought. Young Mackay had hidden well. All Banning had done was inexcusable, unforgivable, yet, in order for Ben to be spared, Thomas would have to be as well. Shaking the thoughts from his mind and the feeling of uneasiness, he took his spot at the end of the mast, shouting the order for it to be lifted. The men resting it on their shoulders, carefully carrying it across the planks to *The Trinity*.

"Mind you watch your footing," Alaric called out. His warning answered by a yelp and a splash. Alaric's chest rumbled with laughter. Looking over his shoulder as best he could, while holding the mast. He saw Case's head bob up from the water, between the two ships. He had slipped from the narrow planks, having been unable to see where he stepped. His vision hindered by the large mast. "Fetch the lad a rope," Alaric called out to one of the sailors aboard *The Trinity*, unable to hold back a grin.

Pulling the new mast up the same way they had lowered it, they worked quickly. Chants and songs filled the inlet. Hammering a plank, attaching the mast and the stump together, sweat beaded down Alaric's back. Just weeks ago, the air further north was filled with the chill of ice crystals. Now, he stood, the beating sun harshly, relentlessly, heating the planks beneath their feet. Passing the hammer off to Henry, he took a step back. The mast was holding tight and firm. The true test would be when the sails billowed with the strong winds on the open ocean. They had mended the mast many times after battles. This one had been particularly destructive upon the ship. Wiping the sweat the dripped from his forehead, he headed into his cabin, the air inside being just as sticky, the only relief was the sun was no longer scorching him. Splashing water on his face and back from the basin, he washed the sweat from his body as best he could. He looked around the cabin. Shot had blasted through the room, nearly destroying the desk entirely. The window had been shattered. Broken glass and splintered wood had littered the cabin. Molly had done her best to clear it, but the repairs would have to wait until they reached Barbados. Grabbing a bottle of wine that sat beside the bed, he took a long drink. One of the many benefits of defeating the French fleet, was that the ships had been well stocked and supplied. Cook had been extremely pleased and was preparing a grand feast in celebration. The aromas all but filled the cabin and rest of the ship. Roasting meat in savory sauces and sweet desserts waited to be savored. The crew had mended the railing as best it could be and patched all of the holes in the hull. The sea water had begun to pour in, flooding the lower decks. The crew had worked all night, mending the holes and pumping the water from the hull. They had even carried buckets back and forth, trying to complete the task faster. The entire crew deserved the feast and celebrations to come, Alaric's only sorrow and regret was that Eddie would not be there to play his violin for them. To hear the joyous and calming sounds of it. As much as they would celebrate, the mood would be dampened by the sorrow of their losses and of the proceedings from the morning, when they had held the ceremony. Taking another drink, Alaric did his best to clear his mind and let his body relax. It would not be long before Molly came in with their tray and he wanted to clean up and be settled before she came in, not wanting to burden her with his dismal thoughts or worry of what they were to face in Barbados.

33

Molly swallowed the hard lump forming in her throat. It had been quite some time since she had seen the islands. The memories from her time on the plantation she had worked hard to burry. Now, seeing the islands made the memories and fear return with a greater intensity she had not prepared herself for. In fact, she had done her best to put returning out of her mind. It was not the same island, but they all were closely tied together. Even with the man dead and knowing she would not be condemned for what had transpired at the plantation, there was now an even greater risk awaiting them. They had taken the French Fleet down and were bringing in the Brig as proof, along with the captain's journals, letters and logbooks, but it did not guarantee Alaric's safety or the safety of the rest of the crew. She felt in her gown for the letter, her and Amara were to take to Lucas and Catherine if Alaric and the others were to be arrested. The smell of the salty air, the fish and trees from the island blew across the deck as they pulled into the port.

"You remember what I told you? You remember the directions to get to the plantation?" Alaric asked, stepping up beside her. His eyes on the town in front of them. Soldiers patrolled the docks, a group of them watching the ships coming in, closely.

"Aye," her voice low, she looked up at him. Gripping his vest, she tilted her head and reached up, pressing her lips hard against his.

"Hmm, perhaps I should put my life at risk more often," he grinned. He looked back at the docks. A larger group of soldiers were now walking up to the ships. "Best leave the very same way you once boarded this ship." He nodded to the opposite railing, indicating she slip from the ship as the soldiers made their way up the ramp.

"Good day to you men," Molly heard Ethan greet the soldiers and could now hear the sound of the boots scraping across the deck of the ship. She clung tightly to the side of the ship. She feared her grip would fail her and she would land in the water below, then alerting the guards of her presence.

"Captain Alaric Stein and Captain Ethan Clarke, you are under arrest for treason and piracy. You are to be taken directly to your rightful place in the jail, where you are to await your time with the gallows." The soldier's voice rang out across the deck. Molly bit her lip to prevent her from crying out at the soldier's words. "Your crew and all aboard this vessel will be taken to the jail under the same charges." Molly bit back the tears. She could feel her fingers growing tired and slippery. The sound of the men being taken from the ship was nearly too much to bear. She suddenly felt alone. A feeling she had put behind her months ago. A feeling she had feared more than she had realized. Pulling herself up, she peered over the railing. The crew had been ready and did not fight back. They did not challenge the sentencing and knew it would only cause trouble for themselves and their captain if they did.

Climbing back on deck, she adjusted the sack she had tied about her and peered in. "Ach, quit your squirming," She whispered to Aoife. She had thought to leave her but was afraid of what would happen to her if the soldiers took possession of the ship. Peering at the dock, she watched Alaric and the others be marched towards the fort. Her breath caught, a strangled sound came from her as they were led around the buildings and out of sight. Looking over at *The Croga*, Benjamin and his men, even the women and children, were led onto the same path. Not wasting another moment, she stepped over the edge of the ship and onto the plank that led to the docks. Drawing a deep breath in, she pulled the hood from her light cloak, over her hair. She had tied it back with a strip of fabric, but she felt it would still draw too much attention and did not know if the guards had been told to keep an eye out for her. She cautiously made her way towards *The Croga* where Amara was likewise making her way onto the docks.

"We must hurry. Alaric said there be a shop just up there. We're to tell the sailor and his wife we are friends of Captain Stein and Captain Harding. They will hire a carriage to take us to the plantation." Even saying the word made her stomach turn. She could tell it did similarly to Amara, her face paling even more.

Passing a group of sailors, Molly lifted her head a little higher. She did not wish to give them any reason to believe they were not familiar with the area or newly arrived. One of the men stepped forward, blocking their path.

His eyes travelled over her, "May I be of any assistance, m'lady?" He asked, a smile upon his face. Molly could not tell if he were being sincere or if he could see through their very thoughts.

"I do not believe so, Sir. We are merely strolling the stalls and shops." She looked up at him, surprising herself with how prim her voice had sounded.

"Very good then," His smile broadened. "Be sure to let me know if you change your mind and be cautious. There is word a notorious pirate and his son are in the area and conspiring with another heinous pillager. You'd do well to stay further inland." He cautioned.

"My thanks, Officer. We will head your advice at once." She said, returning the smile and giving a nod in way of courtesy. Making haste, they kept a lookout for the small building Alaric had described. It's slanted roof and blue painted walls were easy enough to spot. Though the paint was chipped in many spots and instead of a door, a canvas hung in its place.

"I believe we've found it." Molly whispered, pulling the canvas aside and stepping in. A man that looked as weather as the building peered up at them.

"What's it then I can do for two women such as yourselves?" He questioned.

"Are you an Albert Mason?" Molly asked, stepping further into the shop.

"That be me." He answered, looking at her suspiciously.

"Captain Alaric Stein told us to seek you and your wife out. He said we are to ask you to aid us is getting a carriage to take us to Captain Harding's estate." Her explanation seemed to surprise him even more than their sudden appearance into his shop had.

"Did he now?" Raising a bushy eyebrow, he chuckled, his voice crackly. "I can see to that, to be sure. Though, judging by the fact he's gone and sent you to me, I suspect those lads 'ave landed 'emselves in trouble once more." He stepped around them and through the canvas. Waving an arm over his head, he motioned for a rickety carriage to be brought up. Limping back into his shop, he returned his attention to Molly. "You let Ol' Mason know if those lads be needin' a hand." He held both his arms up, twisting one of them about. Molly realized then, he had a wooden hand. Opening and closing his other, he let out a boisterous chuckled, "I've still got one ta spare."

Molly could not help but laugh at the old man. "Thank you for your help," she said, dropping a few coins into his good hand and following Amara out the shop and into the carriage.

Molly rang her hands together, then pulling the sack onto her lap, she untied it a little and peered inside. Giving Aoife a quick scratch behind the ears, she sinched the sack closed again. "It won't be easy," She looked over at Amara who had remained stiff and silent since climbing into the

261

carriage. "Setting foot on a plantation again, no matter the reason." Molly watched the trees alongside the path, pass by. "Captain Harding and Catherine are very close with Benjamin. We have nothing to fear from them." Molly knew that was not the only reason for Amara's silence and fear. It would be seeing the slaves on the plantation. The men, women and children, working. Even knowing they were under the care of Miss Catherine. It would not be enough to make it any easier on Amara to see.

The carriage ride, though rather quick, seemed otherwise. Her nerves were causing her to tremble and her thoughts kept going to Alaric and what they might be doing to him or planning. The two women made their way up the sone steps. Looking up at the estate house. It was just as grand as the house she had been forced into before. The smell from the roses that lined the sides of the estate drifted on the breeze.

"Can I help?" A man stood at the base of the steps. His shirt billowed open slightly.

Amara and Molly exchanged a look. "Captain Harding?" Amara asked, her voice low and unsure.

"Aye?" Lucas began to smile. He took a couple slow steps up towards them. "How can I be of assistance?"

"Captain Alaric Stein has been arrested." Molly replied.

Lucas's face grew serious. He strode up the steps the rest of the way and opened the door. "Come in. Tell me everything." Waving a hand at a servant, he added. "Fetch Lady Harding, please."

The inside of the estate was even grander than the outside. A long rug stretched the length of the great hall. Candles were lit at every post, lighting the room in a warm glow. A vase of roses sat on a small table near the entrance. A sweet aroma wafting from them.

"Please, if you'll join me in here." He led them into a room. The fire burned low, not for heat, but to aid in lighting the room. "Tell me all. When? How?" Lucas asked, placing his hands on the desk in front of him.

Molly retrieved the letter from inside her gown and handed it to him. "He told me to give this to you. Alaric said you would know what to do."

Lucas glanced up at her from the letter, briefly. His gaze returning to the parchment in his hands. Reading over it, he folded it back up and placed it on the desk, tapping his finger on it in thought.

The door opened, Catherine entered, looking at Amara and Molly curiously. "Good afternoon, I do not believe we've had the pleasure of being introduced?" She stated, in more of a question, rather than a fact. Looking at Lucas for an introduction to their guests, he simply slid the letter across the desk to her.

"Read it, you'll understand all in a minute." Lucas replied. "We will need to move quick. They will not hold a trial. They'll want to hang them first thing to prevent them being spared. They will know they will be pardoned if they are made able to speak." Lucas reasoned. "You see to our guests. I'll take care of this." He held up the letter, his voice hard.

"I don't wish to be rude, Captain Harding, but we will be coming with you, if it's all the same." Molly said, lifting her chin slightly, at the shocked look upon his face.

Looking over to Catherine for explanation and aid, only to see her raising her brow at him. "Oh for pity's sake, woman." He breathed out. Exiting the room, he led the way to the stables. Digging a key from his pocket, he unlocked a chest. Inside, swords, flintlocks, and rifles lay. Opening a smaller chest beside it, he pulled out powder, cloth and ball.

Catherine reached in, grabbing a sword and flintlock. Motioning for Molly and Amara to do the same. "I trust Benjamin and Alaric taught you both how to use them?" She asked, doing little to hide her smile.

Lucas frowned, "I'm pleased you are enjoying yourself, love."

A boy, perhaps a few years young than Benjamin, came up to them, three horses in tow. "I saw you coming, and thought to meself, you may be wanting your mounts."

"Aye, thank you, Allen." He grabbed the reins, pulling himself easily onto the horse. "Keep a lookout. If something is amiss or a letter comes, find us at once." He looked at the women, a skeptical look upon his face. Molly tried desperately to hide her insecurity. It had been years since she had been upon a horse, and it was quite obvious that Amara had never ridden. Clearing her throat, she did her best to hide her discomfort, only wanting to show the thrill she felt about being on one of the beasts once again. "We will be at the gallows." He informed Allen. The surprise and curiosity evident in his eyes.

Molly felt the furry creature wriggle against her side. She had almost forgot she still carried Aoife. Untying the sack, she stretched her arm out to the young man that had bought them their horses. "I hope you do not mind but," She looked over at Catherine before returning her attention to Allen. "Could I entrust her to you for the time?" Allen gingerly took the sack from Molly and peered in. "Her name is Aoife."

Allen beamed, lifting the cat from her hiding place. "I'll take good care of her, Miss. You can believe me, I will." His eyes shifted to Lucas, "You really goin' ta the gallows?"

"We will be sure to tell you all the details upon our return." Catherine grinned at lad, kicking her mount and following Lucas out of the yard.

34

Alaric twisted his wrists, the coarse fibers of the ropes binding them, bit into the flesh. The breeze felt cool and refreshing upon his face. He closed his eyes, swallowing hard, praying Molly and Amara had made it to Lucas. As he had suspected, it had not mattered they had taken the French fleet down. They had hardly been given a moment to speak. The Admiral, along with the captain and lieutenant had been at the jail, ready to greet them and take them directly to the gallows. The only reason they had even stalled as long as they had, was because the Admiral had insisted the governor be there. If he had not been informed, it could have reflected poorly on the Admiral and could have even cost him his own position. It had bought them some time. The commotion causing a stir throughout the fort and the surrounding area. A crowd had already begun to gather. A steady buzz of whispers could be heard over the sounds of sea birds and the bustle of the nearby port.

Alaric stood on the stand, the rope looped neatly, swaying beside his head. On either side of him stood Benjamin and

Ethan. At the far end was Thomas. The rest of the crews from both ships stood lined up, their hands bound, their feet in chains.

A distant drumming drew his attention to the opening of the courtyard. As the sound grew louder, closer. The people that stood in the crowd, turned, curious to see what might happen next, already aching to see the so called, pirates hang.

"Let's get on with it," The governor waved a hand in the air, impatiently. He leaned over, whispering something to the Admiral who was beginning to look considerably uneasy.

Alaric swallowed hard as the rope was put around his neck. "Admiral, keep the lad out of this." He growled as a fist was brought down across his face.

"Shut up, pirate." The guard spat. Alaric swung his head forward, feeling the impact of colliding with the guard's face. Blood spurted from the man's nose. Alaric coughed, the breath leaving him as the guard's fist smashed into his middle.

"Admiral," Ethan began. "You know this does not involve the lad." Ethan's voice hard, his eyes challenging.

"On the contrary. He has been reportedly involved in a mutiny and has been founded allied with known pirates." The Lieutenant explained. "Allow us to continue, Governor. You cannot trust a word these traitors say."

The governor stood, his hand in the air, ready to give the signal. Alaric felt his chest tighten. It was not his own life he mourned or feared for. Molly's eyes shown in his mind. The feel of her lips on his. Fear gripped him at the thought of her and the pain she would feel. The guilt at not being able to save him. He looked over at Benjamin, the ache he felt when he had thought he lost the lad once before, coming back with even more intensity. Benjamin stared straight ahead. The deafening sound of jaunts and cheers were rising in the crowd

"That's enough!" A shot rang out. At the edge of the courtyard Lucas sat upon a horse, pushing his way through the crowd, ignoring the jeers and looks he received. Behind him rode Catherine, Molly and Amara. Alaric did not bother to hold back the smile, nor did Benjamin. The pride reflecting in his eyes at seeing them. "That's enough!" Lucas called out again, silencing the towns people. "Look at yourselves." His voice filled with disgust. "You are cheering for those men to hang!" He rode the horse into the crowd further, followed by the others. "Do you not know what these men have done?"

A voice from the crowd shouted, "They be pirates! Let them swing!" The statement causing a series of cheers to ripple through the crowd.

"You have been deceived, my friends." He began. "These men are no pirates." He looked about the crowd, the silence and anticipation almost too much to bear. "You've all heard about the French fleet threating these waters. This very island you all call home." A series of nods and acknowledgements were heard. "Our Royal Navy has tried and in vain they have not been able to capture the fleet or even find it."

"Get on with it!" A man called out. No one answered, their eyes locked curiously on Lucas.

268

"These men though, that only moments ago you were wanting and waiting eagerly to see hang. These men and their crews are the very men that just took on and defeated that French fleet, you all so feared. Will you stand here and let them meet their maker for saving these waters and this entire island?"

Murmurs swept through the crowd. "Cut 'em down!" A woman shouted, giving the rest of the crowd the encouragement. The sounds of the shouts and protests intensified, before the Governor, along with the other Lords on the bench stood.

"A brave speech you have made, Captain Harding." The Governor paused, "Perhaps this hanging has been done in haste and a proper hearing shall be made." He said, his hardened gaze on the Admiral. "Cut those men down!" He finally called out. A roar of approval and cheers went through the crowd.

Alaric's chest rumbled, "A brave speech indeed, Captain." He echoed, winking at Molly. "I think that was the closest one yet," he grinned, meeting Benjamin's gaze, his voice lowering.

Benjamin shook his head slightly, "Bloody close enough." He let out a shaky laugh. His eyes damp, his gaze on Amara.

"Git down, then, 'afore they do change their minds." The guard said in a gruff and put off tone.

Alaric looked over his shoulder at Molly, before being shoved down the steps and into the fort's jail.

"How long do you suppose we will be down here before our hearing?" Benjamin asked. The cell door being closed behind them.

"A few days, perhaps a week or two. Depends on how long the Admiral and the other kind and forgiving men wish us to rot and wait." Thomas scoffed.

"You could be grateful, laddie." Ol' Shorty spoke up from the cell next to theirs. "Captain could've condemned you. He didn't 'ave to speak up and not say a damned word about you and all you've done." He pointed a finger at Thomas, "And don't think those Lords out there don't know what ye've done. They know the truth 'bout it and that be why they let us to trial." Thomas scowled down at Shorty but did not say another word.

"The hearing will be held soon. They will want to get it over with. The scene in the courtyard did not bode well for the Governor or the Admiral." Ethan voiced, gripping the cell bars. Alaric knew Ethan felt guilty. He knew Ethan blamed himself for their current predicament, though judging by the look upon the Governor's face when Lucas rode up and his all too quick and almost sarcastic dismissal of the hanging, told Alaric there was more to the situation than the feud the Lieutenant had with Ethan.

Alaric leaned his head back against the cool, damp stone wall of the cell. Their wrists were no longer bound, and the chains had been removed from their ankles, giving some relief. Closing his eyes, he imagined the sway of *The Trinity*. The motion of the waves and how it carried the ship along the waters. The sun beat down, warming his body and the planks beneath his feet. He could almost feel Molly standing beside him. Letting out a slow breath, he kept the images in his mind and allowed his body to relax. As afraid and timid as she would be at the plantation, he knew it would not take long for her and Catherine to find their way into deep discussion. Probably along the lines of exchanging thoughts on boils, burns, cuts and all manner of ailments and treatments.

35

"Alaric says you are quite the healer," Molly began, studying Catherine. The ride back to the plantation was done at a far leisurely pace than the one had been getting to the gallows. She felt her body falling into the rhythm of the horse beneath her.

"I do enjoy it. A great deal, in fact." She smiled over at her. "Doc taught me a much."

"It's just, I'm worried about Alaric. He was wounded during the battle, and I stitched him up, but he was back out in the fray, immediately after. I'm afeared the damp of the cell will cause a fever. I did not have time to clean the cut well." She admitted.

"Oh, I had not realized." Catherine's eyes lit up. "You are a healer also?"

"Of sorts, I suppose." Molly felt herself flaming the color of her hair. "I prefer tending the animals." She caught a glimpse of Lucas's grin, though he kept his head looking straight ahead. The blush on her cheeks deepening.

"I admit," Lucas began, barely containing his laughter, "I did wonder what you could possibly see in him, but it is now beginning to make sense." He turned, resting a hand on the back of the horse, twisting his body to better see the women. "He does resemble the beasts in a most unfortunate way." Catherine frowned but could not hold the stern look for long.

"Did you see to the animals aboard *The Trinity*, then?" Catherine asked, her question sincere and the curiosity evident in her manner.

"I did, yes. I had begun to learn about the animals at…" she paused, "At the last place I was at, and I always enjoyed it, but truly formed a bond and enthusiasm for the animals and caring for them while on the ship. Doc too, instructed me."

"I should greatly love to hear all you learned. In many instances, the patients, whether we are speaking of people or animals, are much alike."

"Aye, that is what Doc says." Molly acknowledged. The rest of the ride was a short one. They returned back to the stables before Molly had even realized they had reached the plantation gates. The ride and talk had soothed her nerves. The events at the fort had shown her more than she had realized she would feel or witness. Seeing the noose around Alaric's neck had all but stopped the very heart in her chest from beating. She had felt as if she had suddenly ceased to exist, as if the world around her had stopped and she were left alone in shadow and darkness. Then, there was the look the Governor and Admiral had exchanged when Lucas had called out. They had looked exceedingly uncomfortable.

"You two must stay with us. I am sure you are worn out and could use a warm meal and rest." Catherine suggested, handing the reins off to Allen and leading the way back to the big house. "Come with me. I'll see to it that you are made comfortable."

The staircase wound its way up onto a balcony that over-looked the great hall. A large window gave a spacious view of the plantation. Molly's stomach turned slightly.

"We will eat at eight." Catherine came to a door and opened it. "This will be your room while you are here. I hope you find it comfortable and to your liking. If you should need anything, just pull the cord." Catherine told Amara, pointing to a long, yellow rope that hung near the fireplace. Looking at Molly, then, she said, "And your room will be just here." She smiled, glancing between the two of them. "You mustn't worry yourselves. Lucas will see things right and they will be released swiftly."

"Alaric was right. You are very kind." Molly admitted, entering the room and looking around. A seat with golden flowers on a beige backdrop, sat beneath the window. A green comforter rested atop the large bed, a chest at the foot of it. Opening it, she found hers and Alaric's attire from the ship in it.

Molly ran her hands down her gown, examining her reflection in the long mirror that stood in the corner of the chamber. Taking a deep breath, she strode over to the bed where Aoife had made herself a cat of leisure. "You rest here, wee one." She ran a hand along her soft, grey fur, before walking to the door. It was time for their meal, and she was not entirely sure she was ready. For so long, it had only been her and Alaric or her and Doc, eating together. Occasionally Ethan would join them. They would discuss the men on board, strategies, where they were headed next or talk of moments from their pasts. For many months though, it had just been her and Alaric, alone in his cabin. Sometimes sitting in peaceful silence. Sometimes talking and laughing into the late night. Before she had boarded *The Trinity*, she would occasionally eat with the other servants, but typically took her tray to the barn or into her room where she did not have to worry about being chided.

Coming out of the room, she met Amara on the landing. Her discomfort and insecurity apparent, on her face and in the way she stood. "Could you give my excuses? I'm tired, Lady Harding was right." She stammered, turning to duck back into her room.

Molly remembered when Alaric had insisted, she dine with the Captains and the Lieutenant. She wanted nothing more than to crawl under the hay with the animals and hide. "Benjamin would not want you feeling like you should stay in your chamber all evening." She coaxed, placing a hand on the young woman's arm. "He would wish you to enjoy yourself and the company of his family." Molly wrapped her arm around Amara's and drew her near the staircase. "Tis a grand house to be sure." She understood Amara's reservations and how she felt. Molly recalled the plantation estate they had dined at in the colonies and how uncomfortable and out of place she had felt then. This time it was different. She enjoyed Catherine's company and did not feel so different from her when they spoke, like she had with the Lady's at the other dinner.

"Grander even than the plantation we'd been at." Amara said, allowing Molly to lead her to the hall. A small giggle escaped her, "What would your old master or the Mistress think if they saw us now."

The night before had been a splendid one, despite the hearing looming overhead and knowing Alaric and the others were in the damp jail. The three women had found ample topics to discuss. Each of them eager to hear of the other's knowledge and experiences. It had been as if they had known each other for many years. They spoke with ease and contentment.

Molly adjusted her seat upon the chestnut horse. Reaching out, she pat the animal's neck, feeling his velvety fur beneath her hand. The trees swayed over the path, making the shadows dance upon the dirt. The sweet scent of flowers and green vines that grew along the stone wall filled the air. Their plantation was not the only one along the path, several lined the road. Occasional shouts or chanting could be heard, some of the songs sounding mournful and sending a chill down her spine. Some more upbeat, almost like the ones sung aboard the ship, encouraging the hard work being done in the fields. Glancing quickly at Amara, she saw her sitting straight and steady atop her mount. Her eyes were closed, her head tilted back, letting the warm sun beat down on her. The horse beneath her, soothing her mind and thoughts. Lucas had offered to have the carriage brought around but rather than being made to sit no more than a mere inch or two apart, they had chosen to ride to the fort on the horses instead.

Lucas had assured them they would be able to visit Alaric and the others at the prison. That preventing them from visiting would only cause more of a stir. Catherine had strapped a small, leather bag to her saddle, informing them that it was her case she carried everywhere as it contained some of her medical supplies. She intended to treat as many of the sailors as she could.

The courtyard was vast, the gallows sitting in the very center. The eerie stillness of the area, causing the hair on the nape of her neck to stand up. Approaching the guards that stood outside the wooden door, they did not even need to make introductions, knowing exactly why the party had come. Scowling at them, the larger of the two, his uniform fitting a bit too snug, fumbled with the keys. Grabbing hold of the heavy, iron ring, he pushed the door open with a loud creak.

"We will be requiring you, unlock the cells. These men need tending to." Catherine told one of the guards that had been standing outside the cells. He looked hardly old enough to be a soldier, perhaps no more than sixteen.

His eyes widening at the request, he looked about for a comrade, but the others had already began making their way towards the other end of the long corridor. "I apologize, M'lady, but I cannot do as you bit."

"And why not? You have a key, no? You are perfectly capable of unlocking a cell door, I am sure." She questioned, feigning ignorance. "These men have been gravely injured and require medicine and mending. I hope you are not suggesting that you will allow these men to perish while under your charge. The very men that protected this island from being invaded by an entire fleet of French ships." She looked at him is stunned astonishment.

Stammering, the young man quickly shook his head. His eyes moved to Lucas, who simply cocked his head, raising his brows in question. "Of course not, M'lady." Quickly reaching for the keys that swung from a single ring that remained clipped to his uniform.

"Very good," Catherine beamed at him, causing his face to flush crimson. Leading the way into the cell, she greeted the familiar faces of the men that she had grown to care for while aboard *The Trinity*. Doc came up, pulling her into a friendly embrace. "You'll be happy to see what I've brought, I'm sure." She said, holding up and patting her bag.

"I'm sure I will and so will the lads. Many of them are in need of fresh bandages and oils to aid in relieving pain. Any longer and I would not be surprised if they began coming down with fever." He answered, beginning to line the men up to be examined.

Benjamin, walked up to Catherine, his arm around Amara. "Miss Catherine, tis good to see you again." He grinned, as she spun around.

"Benjamin," She briefly wrapped her arms around his neck before giving him a light shove, "You did have us thinking the worst, all this time." Her eyes blurring momentarily. "The way you suffered." Her voice low with emotion.

He laughed in response, looking down at Amara, "It wasn't all bad."

"No, I can see that." She smiled in return, gently touching Amara's arm. "Now," She beamed, looking over at Doc. "Shall we begin?"

Molly stood in the dank cell, watching the scenes unfold before her. Alaric stood beside her, his arm protectively about her waist, eagerly talking to Lucas. Both of them having much to tell of their time apart. Alaric had told her many stories of all of them and having stayed the night with them, Molly felt she knew Lucas and Catherine very well already. She had long since begun to feel she belonged on *The Trinity* with Alaric and now she was beginning to feel she belonged to more. Was part of a friendship. A family.

"Molly, would you mind handing me the juniper salve?" Catherine asked, gently cleaning around a cut that looked even more red and painful than it had been before. Doc had been right, any longer and many of the men were sure to have come down with fever.

"Lucas, what of the women and children? Surely, they do

not need to be in here. They cannot be made to speak at the hearing." Benjamin spoke up, stepping closer to Lucas and Alaric.

"I spoke to the Governor of the prison after you were all brought down here. They are to be released into our charge. The man that olds their papers in the colonies is not to be informed. The Admiral and Governor were not pleased to be made to remain silent, but with the Governor's dealings with the French in the past," He looked over at Catherine briefly, "It is all too curious that the French fleet remained undiscovered by his Admiral's men. Then the very men that take the fleet down are nearly hanged." He nodded his assurances. "They will remain silent if they value their positions and reputations.

"We will take them to the plantation with us. Catherine will look them over when we get back to their estate and be sure they are well. Lucas and Catherine were kind enough to say they may stay as long as they like at the plantation or may leave to be where they choose. No one needs know of their past." Molly added, replacing the bandage on one of the sailor's arms.

"Thank you, for everything." Benjamin said, embracing Lucas once again. His gratitude evident in his voice.

"It is the least I can do." He put his hand on the young man's face. "I am only sorry we were not there for you sooner." He stepped back, allowing Catherine to come forward to examine Ben's head.

"Are you having headaches still?" Catherine asked.

He shrugged, "A bit, but I am fine."

"Here," Catherine handed him the oil of peppermint. "You won't need much. It's a bit strong."

Benjamin coughed in reply, "You don't say?"

"I've been sent to inform you that it is time you make your leave." The young soldier said, holding and arm out, pointing to the door.

"I'll do what I can to speed the hearing along." Lucas told them, putting a hand on Ol' Shorty's shoulder. "It was good seeing you all again." He stopped, looking around momentarily before his gaze landed on Alaric, a look of knowing in his eyes. "Eddie." He said, in neither a question nor a statement.

"He didn't make it. We lost him while fighting the French." Alaric shook his head, "And several others." He added, his jaw tightening.

"I'm sorry," Lucas ran a hand over his face. "He was with us a long time." He put a steadying hand on Catherine's back. "We can talk more about what transpired when you've been released and had time to think." He led Catherine from the cell, beckoning the women and children to follow them. Amara held tightly to Imani, guiding her steps through the dark corridor.

Molly blinked, the bright sun hitting her face. Her eyes had adjusted to the torch lit jail, now having to adjust back to the light of the day. Molly reached for the young girl she had met those months ago, aboard *The Croga*. It seemed a lifetime ago, yet somehow, strangely felt as if it had only happened a fortnight ago. Lifting the girl onto the horse, she kept a hand on her until she was ready, her eyes alight with excitement and nerves. "Hold here to steady yourself." She placed a handful of the horse's mane in the girl's palm. Then lifting another girl, a few years older, onto the horse behind her, she reached for the reins. "I'll lead the horse. You mustn't fear." She told them, seeing the uneasiness in their eyes when the horse backed away from the post it had been tethered to.

"What will it be like? This new plantation?" The youngest girl asked. She was filled with curiosity and a glow that despite all she had faced at such a young age, never lessened or dimmed. "The Master and Mistress seem kind." She whispered, watching Lucas and Catherine cautiously.

"They are. Very kind. You have no reason to be afeared. Not of this plantation. Mistress Catherine will see to it you are not unhappy or unwell." Molly assured her, then looking up at the girls again, "Mistress Catherine has a maid and she told me that the Mistress ensures all on the plantation, especially the children, are given delicious fruits, sweeter than you've ever tasted afore." She smiled at them, enjoying the looks of hope and anticipation.

36

"What is it, Allen?" Catherine asked, slightly startled by the young man's sudden appearance. Molly, Amara and Catherine were at a small hut that Catherine had constructed so she could properly and privately see to the slaves that had been injured or unwell. The room held four beds. Curtains divided each one, giving them a sense of calm and seclusion. A wooden table sat in the middle of the room. Opposite it was a water pitcher and basin with fresh cloth next to it. A cabinet rested in the corner, containing an assortment of herbs, salves, ointments and oils. Most of them Molly had never heard of. A chest sat next to it with various instruments used for healing and mending. Each rolled carefully in canvas or leather to keep them separate and clean.

"Tis Sunny, M'Lady. He still not be acting himself. The Ferrier, he's been sent for but I fear what he'll do." Allen said, twisting his hat in his hands.

"Right, I'll will be right there." She said, removing her apron and hanging it on a hook near the cabinet. "Molly, perhaps you'll accompany me. You may be able to help more than that retched man that sees himself as Ferrier."

Molly nodded eagerly, "We won't be long," she told Amara, who had her hands full, telling a group of children of the adventures aboard *The Croga*.

"What has Sunny been doing that is odd, exactly?" Molly asked, quickening her pace to be able to keep up with the anxious lad.

"He not been at his feed for some time. He be lookin' scrawny. The Ferrier, he had a look at him but says he just not thriving no more. Says his minds gone. He half been actin' like he's gone mad." Allen informed her, leading the way into the stables. Each stall was filled with fresh straw. Ornately carved walls separated each horse into their own area.

"Lady Harding," A man strode up, a leather bag in hand. "I understand I've been summoned to see to this horse again." He cleared his throat, giving Molly a curious look. Approaching Sunny, he held a hand out, allowing the animal to get a whiff of him. Sunny stomped his foot anxiously, letting out a loud whinny that seemed to echo through the stables. Flinching slightly at the sudden reaction, the Ferrier stayed his steps briefly. "Tighten that lead, boy." He demanded, flicking a hand at the ropes that tied Sunny to the stall. Moving quickly, Allen did as he was bid. The man took a step forward, all but lunging at the strap at the horse's mouth. A swift kick from Sunny sent the man howling in pain.

Staggering to his feet, he retreated to his bag. An obvious limp to his gate. He picked up a long rod that had been bound in leather. A few strands of the brown hide falling off the end of it. "What is that to be used for?" Molly stepped forward, pulling her brows together.

"Tis to teach the beast a lesson. His mistress has been too soft on him, and he needs to be reminded of his place." He went to strike at the horse who attempted to rear out of the way.

"You'll do no such thing!" Molly grabbed the rod from the man, tearing it from his hands, tossing it into the pile of manure that had just been scraped from the stalls.

"You'll hold your tongue!" His hand raised, poised to strike her.

"Mr. Grant, you'll conduct yourself in a gentlemanly manner." Catherine ordered, her face flushed with surprise and anger. "Allen, fetch Captain Harding." Her eyes not leaving those of the Ferrier. He pulled at his coat in an attempt to regain his composure.

Molly cautiously approached the young horse. Her voice low and calm, she began to hum a tune she had sung to the animals on the ship. A slow, rhythmic one that seemed to quiet them with ease. Gently sliding her hand along the animal's neck, she examined him. Trying to remember all she had read. The imagines of the sketches she had been working on and studying. The conversation with Alaric flashed through her mind. The book spoke of horses being killed for turning, 'mad'. She ran a hand along his legs, not feeling any heat or oddities. Molly suspected his upset had little to do with his mind or his legs, but rather his mouth.

"Catherine," Molly asked, careful not to startle Sunny. She felt the woman move into the stall beside her. "When a person is in pain, they can act out of sorts, even become quick to anger."

Catherine raised a brow, thinking this over, "Yes, of course, but I am not sure I follow." She placed a hand on Sunny, looking back at the Ferrier who stood, scowling at the two of them. "He looked him over. Said he could not find anything amiss, therefore it must be of the mind." She looked from the horse to Molly.

"Aye, but I believe tis due to a tooth. It explains him being off feed and his change in behavior." Molly explained.

"That's the most absurd thing I've heard." Mr. Grant stepped forward, throwing a hand in the air and scoffing. "The animal is too young to have tooth problems and even if he did, t'would nothing that could be done a'fore it." He shook his head, "He must be killed."

"That will be quite enough Mr. Grant." Lucas said, coming in, his face hard. "Molly, please continue." He came up to stand beside the Ferrier, assuring he would not interfere again.

"Allen, Catherine, you two keep him calm and still. I'll have a feel in his mouth." She instructed, placing one hand under his mouth, the other stroking the side. Slowly sliding her hand into the side of the horse's mouth, she felt around. Sunny tossed his head slightly, not liking the invasion. She tried to count the teeth, visualizing the sketch she had studied. Reaching further back, she slid her finger along the inside of his mouth. His teeth felt straight and relatively short.

"Shhh, Sunny. Please," Catherine soothed, the horse flared his nostrils, pawing at the ground.

"I feel it." Molly whispered, relief flooding her. "His teeth are as they should be, save one. Tis sharper. Pointed. Tis rubbing against his mouth." She explained, pulling her hand from his mouth. Giving him an affectionate rub and brief reprieve.

"Use this." Mr. Grant pursed his lips, handing Catherine a file of sorts while avoiding Lucas's hard gaze. "It's not used for teeth, but I've heard tell of folks in Edinburgh speaking of such like instruments."

Molly looked from the file to Sunny. She felt the rough edges of the file. It was heavy and the thought of putting it in the horse's mouth and driving it across his sore tooth was not a thought she relished. Her eyes met Catherine's. The trust and hope she felt showed in her eyes without a single sign of doubt or hesitation. Dipping the file in a bucket of water, somehow feeling that if it were wet, it would not be as bad, she reached her fingers into Sunny's mouth. Guiding the file in, careful not to harm him further, she worked the iron across the pointed tooth.

"It's alright. It will be alright." Catherine soothed, keep the animal from trying to rear again.

Molly removed the file. Reaching in with her fingers to feel the tooth. She smiled, "Tis working. The point is nearly gone." Slowly replacing the file, she whispered to the calming beast, "Just once more now, laddie."

The rough scraping of the iron against tooth all but sent a chill through her. It was not a pleasant sound or feeling. As the tooth ground down into a proper and smooth size, it eased and so did the horse. The relief and comfort clear in his golden eyes. She removed the file and ran her hand between his ears. Sunny let out a soft snort, pressing his nose gently against her chest in gratitude.

"Thank you, Mr. Grant. For the file." Handing him the instrument, she beamed, much to his displeasure and wounded pride.

Lucas stood, his arms crossed over his chest, his legs spread wide apart, as if he were still aboard a ship. "That was quite something. Alaric was not exaggerating your talents." He voiced, coming up beside the horse and his wife.

"Thank you, so very much." Catherine said, her voice low and filled with emotion. "You've saved his life." Wrapping her arms around Molly, she squeezed her tight, trying to get ahold of her emotions.

"I'm just pleased I could," She smiled sheepishly, "I had never done anything quite like that and it was not spoke of in the book Doc gave me. The book gave the same diagnosis as Mr. Grant did." She admitted. "It were my own thoughts that made me think it were right and your trust in me." She returned the hug. "We best see how Amara is getting on."

37

It had been more than a fortnight. Their assumptions in believing they would want to get the hearing over and done with had been a great misconception. Instead, the Admiral and the Governor had decided to drag it out in wanting to prove a point. Lucas had done what he could. Even Lord Benedict had dined with the Governor to try and sway him, but it became evident that it would be of no use.

Benjamin scratched the back of his head, his hands chained together. The irons pinched uncomfortably. He sat in the front row, along with Ethan, Alaric and Thomas. Their crews behind them. The room was large. The judges sat at a long, solid table against the back of the room. All chairs and benches faced them. A balcony stretched around the top, allowing more folks to listen to the hearing.

Amara sat between Catherine and Molly, her body rigid, trying to hold her composure. Even if the others were released and enough witnesses testified and vouched for their characters, it was Benjamin who had more being held over her head. He had not simply been accused of crimes he did not done, but in fact had committed them. He had escaped and freed several other slaves as well. Not to mention causing a mutiny and taking a ship. It was he and Thomas that may not be spared, for their crimes had not been fabricated. The Governor and Admiral were angry. Their pride and reputation compromised when Lucas had challenged them at the gallows, and this was not the first time Lucas had faced the Governor. He was now wanting his revenge.

One of the Lords hit the gavel down, ceasing the murmuring and whispers in the room. "Captain Alaric Stein, Captain Ethan Clarke, Captain Thomas Banning and Captain Benjamin Stein, you have been accused of piracy in His Majesty the King's waters. Captain Benjamin Stein, along with piracy, you have been charged with fleeing your master's plantation, releasing fellow slaves and creating a mutiny." The judge spoke, the words reverberating off the stone walls. Benjamin's jaw tightened, sitting a bit straighter. He did not want to give Amara anymore reason to fret. He had not missed Catherine pulling Amara's hand into her own or the slight shiver that had brushed through her body. "The witnesses testifying against these men will now be called forward." He hit the gavel against the block and sat back, staring straight ahead as a man was motioned forward.

"Christ," Alaric muttered, glancing at Ethan.

Benjamin looked the man over. He did not recognize him but had little doubt of his profession. It was clear he was a sailor and a seasoned one at that. He wore a loose, white shirt that hung open. He sneered at Alaric, catching Lucas's eye next. His dark beard was long, reaching down passed his chest. Rings filled his fingers and a leather band wrapped about his left arm.

"What have you to say, Captain Howard?" One of the Lords asks, his voice dull and unamused by the proceedings.

"That man," He spat, jutting a finger at Alaric, "And his brother," tipping his head in Lucas's direction, "Wrongfully took me ship from me a few years back. I'd been injured in a battle a few days before." He looked about the room, "Protecting these waters for you lot." He looked pointedly at his audience. "When they came along. Not even giving me men a chance and me too wounded to do anythin' 'bout it. They were ruthless. They plundered me ship and claimed it as their prize. When it be taken to the Govern'r, I wasna able to dispute it as I was still near to death." He looked about the room, meeting the gaze of anyone that dared. "I've been trying to seek justice and revenge since that day." Captain Howard stood down from platform, returning to his spot in the crowd, a scowl upon his face.

"Thank you, Captain Howard for your accounts of your dealings with Captain Alaric and his crew." The judge spoke up, summoning the next witness to the stand. "Mister Wyatt, what have you to say?"

"Captain Banning be a right sinful man." To this, Thomas let out a loud laugh. Catching the startled eye of Mister Wyatt, he gave a fake bow from his seat.

"Please, continue Mister Wyatt. Captain Banning, one more outburst will see you thrown from the room and into your cell." The judge spoke firmly.

"As I were saying," He began again, shooting Thomas an uncomfortable look, "We was aboard a merchant vessel, heading towards the islands from England when he came upon us. The mist was thick, and we could no see more than a few feet from the bow. His canons tore through the ship. We be all but unarmed compared to his ship. We did no even have a chance to fire a shot. He boarded the ship, his men slaughtering the crew and passengers alike. I was knocked out from a blow to me head and awoke only to find no one be left but me." The man's lip quivered slightly. Refusing to meet Banning's gaze, he waited to be excused. Benjamin watched Thomas's expression at the retelling. His jaw had tightened, and he had looked down, his gaze unmoving from the railing in front of them.

"Was it *The Trinity* that fired upon you? Did you see Captain Stein and his men?" One of the Lord's asked.

"It be *The Amity* that fired upon us. I seen the name when it drew close, the cannon fire lighting it in the mist."

"You paint a vivid picture, Mister Wyatt. You may stand down." The judge said, waving an arm in the air as a dismissal.

Man after man came forward, speaking words against Banning. The occasional witness would go up, looking uneasy, their gaze flicking from the Admiral, lieutenant or Governor to Alaric and Ethan. Most of these accounts were clouded, unsure. A few speaking of the wrecked ships they had come upon, much to Thomas's surprise. He cocked a brow and choked on a laugh during one particular retelling. It had been of the vessel they had found young MacKay on.

The man at the stand spit on the floor, moving his tongue along his teeth.

"I was caught up in the rigging. They must've been thinking me to be dead. They drove our ship onto the shallow sandbar where we be nothing more than a sittin' gull. They came aboard and killed the remainder of the crew, leavin' no survivors. Them did steal valuables from the captain's cabin. Jewels, I suspect and the like." He sneered at Ethan.

"And whom do you say did this?" The Lord from before asked, his gaze curious. He had been watching them closely with each account told. His wig was powdered but not as white at the others. His brow pinched together a doubting look upon his face.

"Twas that there Captain Stein and Captain Clarke. They be on *The Trinity*."

"Tell us, what reason do you suspect a proven privateer and a loyal Captain of His Majesty's Royal Navy have for destroying, ransacking and murdering a merchant vessel?" The Lord asked.

"Dunno, gone rogue I suspect. Figured they'd make more wealth in pirating." He shrugged.

"And what is your profession, exactly, Mister Gutter?" He questioned.

The sailor rocked on his heels, running a hand along his jaw. "Uh," he chuckled, "A simple whaler, M'lord, not more." He replied.

"Right," He looked at the others seated next to him, tilting his head and leaning back in his seat. "Next." He called out.

Lieutenant Mason stood up then. His gaze a near to triumphant one. "My Lords, Ladies," He began, he voice smooth. "I had the privilege of serving under Captain Clarke for some time now. He has been a great mentor. He is…" he paused briefly, "Was a truly respected and loyal Captain of his Majesty the King's Royal Navy." He let out a slow breath, his eyes fell upon Ethan. His face appearing sincere. "But, after his sister's unfortunate accident." Ethan stiffened at this. "I am afraid he became unsettled. He asked for leave to track down and find the man that committed the heinous crime upon his sister." His voice rose with emotion. "In his search he found himself upon Captain Banning's ship," He gestured to Thomas. "Where he was corrupted by the man's vile ways."

Thomas raised a brow and laughed low, "Clearly he does not know you as well he says, mate."

"Aye, he does not," Ethan responded dryly.

"During a battle, he was recruited onto *The Trinity* with Captain Stein. He too was once a valued and respected privateer of these waters. He and his brother, Lucas Harding," He motioned to him. "Were the Governor's top men. However, during a time of grief and revenge, Captain Stein and Captain Clarke found a common bond. They then both sought Captain Banning who was believed to be the murderer of Captain Clarke's Sister and of Captain Stein's adopted son, Benjamin, who now sits amongst them, alive and well." His voice rose with each statement. Murmurs spread throughout the room.

"Captain Hanes and I were patrolling the waters in search of the French fleet. We knew of what direction *The Trinity* was headed and found ourselves in the same area. We had seen smoke swirling in the horizon and sought to see if it had been them and if they were in need of any aid. What we saw instead was far worse." He let his words hang in the air. Let the men and women in the crowd come to their own guesses and conclusions of what the men were about to be accused of. "We came upon the very vessel Mister Gutter had been aboard. We witnessed what he spoke of. We were too far off still to prevent it. By the time we reached the ship, *The Trinity* had sailed off. That is when we came upon Mister Gutter and brought him to the nearest port, where we sent him off on another Naval Vessel to return back to the islands."

"And what happened next?" One of the Lords rustled through the papers that sat in front of him. "I have it here that it says you dined aboard *The Trinity*."

"Yes, we did. It was not long after the dreadful attack that we were able to flag them down. We were in mind to dine with them and see what they had to say for themselves. To which they of course denied the acts. It was then we discovered Miss Maclean, who sits just there."

Alaric suddenly stood. His knuckles white as he gripped the railing. "As you are well aware, Lieutenant, Miss Maclean is not the one on trial. She is innocent in all of this. We have sat silent during your ludicrous accusations, but I will not allow you to bring her into this." His gaze was steady, his eyes hard.

"Though I cannot condone Captain Stein's outburst, I

would have to agree with him. Miss Maclean is not on trial. Furthermore, we are aware of what transpired between her and Lord Willington. We also are aware that he in fact followed Miss Maclean and kidnapped her. Captain Stein and his crew, as we understand it, were the ones that rescued her. During the fight, Lord Willington was killed. Our counterparts in the colonies have already sent us a letter informing us of the dealings they had."

Lieutenant Mason cleared his throat. "Very good, Lord Harlem. I apologize, Miss Maclean." At this, Alaric slowly sat, nodding his thanks at the Lord.

"I believe we've heard what we need to from you. Thank you, Lieutenant." Lord Harlem said. The judge remained silent but the Lord on the opposite side of him, watched the Governor closely, his lips twisted into an unpleasant look.

"Who is the man at the end?" Benjamin asked Alaric, curious at why the man appeared so angry at the Lieutenant's dismissal from the stand. It had been clear he had more to say.

"That is Lord Anderson. He is new to the bench. He was the man Catherine had been engaged to before she came aboard *The Trinity*. I wager he is just as desperate to see us condemned to get his revenge on Lucas as the governor is." The judge shot them a silencing glare.

"Is there anymore witnesses against these men? If so, please come to the stand." The judge spoke.

"Aye, I have something to say." Captain Stoll stood up from his seat near the back. Benjamin had not seen him in the crowd, his breath catching. Beside him stood Mister Luggnar. Benjamin watched the two men step forward. Captain Stoll took his place beside the bench, first. Benjamin's gazed shifted to Amara, she had grown pale, her eyes fixed on Benjamin.

"Aye, I have a few things to say about Benjamin. I cannot bring myself to call him a captain as he is a mere boy and did not earn the right to be named such." His eyes narrowed. "My crew and I came upon him, floating in the sea, near to death, shot in the shoulder. We pulled him aboard. Gave the boy, food, drink and my surgeon fixed him up proper like." Doc scoffed audibly to this remark. The brutal scar on his shoulder told a different story to the mending of the wound. "He was not aboard more than a few days before he began making trouble. I am a trader of slaves. I bring only the best and healthiest to the colonies. My goods are highly sought after and cannot be compromised on the journey by disease or dishonorable behavior by a whoremongering lad. Not a fortnight after retrieving the boy from the sea, he sought to stop us from throwing a sick, diseased and already dying slave from the ship." A few gasps spread through the room. Captain Stoll raised a hand, "I can assure you, the boy was punished accordingly. From then on though, he continued to make trouble from me. He insisted on being with the slaves, particularly one rather lovely one that was sure to fetch a fine price, and so she did." He looked pointedly at Amara. "The boy even tried to tell me he had medical training and knew how to properly care for my slaves." He smirked and a rippled of laughs flowed through the room. "In the end, I had no choice, seeing as how he caused so much trouble for me and tried in vain to compromise my entire cargo, I sold him at the market with the others." He paused, looking around the room. "I will now hand the stand over to Mister Luggnar, who will inform you of his dealing with the troublesome lad."

Mister Luggnar stepped up, his gaze shifting from Benjamin to Amara. He eyes traveling over the slaves in the stand that had become part of Benjamin's crew. "I cannot attest to Captain Stoll's accounts of the boy. However, according to the body of his first mate that was found the very morning after his and the other's escape, I am in no doubt there was much trouble aboard the vessel. Furthermore, my foreman and his wife gave me many accounts of his rebellious nature. At the hands of my foreman, the boy was punished accordingly. This did not seem to tame or dampen the boy's traitorous behavior. He led a band of more than twenty slaves from my plantation, God only knows how they did it, as no other slave has ever escaped my grasp. It was from there they boarded Captain Stoll's ship, some days later and mutinied." He concluded. Pointing a finger at Benjamin, his gaze hardened, "You'll swing boy, mark my words. You and the rest of them will swing."

"That's enough Mister Luggnar. You are not the one who decides that." The judge said, before turning to Captain Stoll. "Captain, pray tell, did the mutiny take place at sea or in a port?"

"In a port, my Lord." He answered, his brow furrowing in question.

"I see. In the colonies, correct?" The judge continued.

"Uh, yes, that is correct." He stammered.

"Right, then I say the mutiny, however inexcusable they

maybe, cannot necessarily be held against the boy at this particular trial." The judge reasoned.

"That is absurd!" Captain Stoll stepped forward. "I demand my ship back and that boy hanged for his crimes." He ordered.

"You may command your crew as you wish," Lord Harlem bit back a grin, "Correction, I apologize for being insensitive. Seeing as how you no longer have a ship, you seem to have no command at all, especially not in this room."

"And what of my slaves? Am I to sit back and allow this creatine to be excused for all he's done? The bounty upon his head is well over a thousand pounds for that alone." Mister Luggnar looked at the judge, appalled.

"I can assure you. Your accounts have all been heard with the most sympathetic of ears. We will discuss what is to be done with these pirates, betwixt ourselves." Lord Anderson assured the audience.

Lord Harlem leaned over, whispering something to the judge. Slamming down the gavel, he brought the murmuring to a quick halt. "We will now hear what the prisoners have to say for themselves and if there are any witnesses that can attest to the good nature of these men, they may step forward now."

The room remained still, silent. No man or woman moved. The Admiral began shifting in his chair, catching the eye of Lord Anderson. "Perhaps, my Lords, there are in fact no witness that can testify to their good nature."

"Then we move forward to the men themselves." The judge said, slamming his gavel down once more.

"If I might, M'Lord?" Doc stood up. "I am the surgeon aboard *The Trinity* and have been for many years." He paused, waiting for permission to continue.

"You may take your place at the stand." The judge informed him.

"Thank you. I would begin by informing all of you that Lieutenant Mason and many of these so-called witnesses are gravely mistaken in their retellings, however, who would believe a surgeon that has been branded a pirate, over a man from His Majesty the King's Royal Navy?" A chorus of agreements whispered through the room. "So, I will not tell that story, I will tell you what I saw from trained eyes. I believe Captain Stoll informed us of how he so heroically saved young Benjamin." Again, whispers of agreed spread through the crowd. "He informed us that his surgeon mended and so graciously healed Benjamin's wound. I find this to be untrue, well, untrue in a way. It is true he stitched the boy's shoulder, as the lad himself told me so. However, it was done not in a way to save the young man or keep him in good health. The stitching was done in a careless manner, any surgeon who looked upon it would tell you so." Doc looked about the room curiously, "Pray tell, do we have any surgeons in this room today?"

"What are you about?" Lord Anderson asked.

"I am a surgeon, here, on this island and have tended many of the folks here in this room today." A man stood up, straightening his vest with pride.

"Please, may I continue?" Doc asked the judge. He gestured for him to do so. "Benjamin, please, will you remove your shirt?" He asked, a sympathetic look upon his face. Benjamin hesitated, his eyes on Amara. Pulling his shirt from his person, he bundled it in his hands. The room all but exploded in gasps and murmurs of shock. "If you please," Doc gestured for the surgeon to move come forward. "What say you of the wound upon his shoulder?"

The surgeon took out a pair of glasses from his vest and peered at the wound curiously. Letting out a conclusive sigh, he motioned for Benjamin to turn, examining his other scars. "I would have to agree with *The Trinity's* surgeon. He is correct in saying the wound upon his shoulder was not properly mended, even an unskilled surgeon or apprentice could do a better job." He announced, replacing his glasses to their spot in his vest. "As for the other marks upon this poor boy's body, I would not say they are of just punishment." He nodded to Doc before taking his seat once more.

The two men prior, adjusting their seating, uneasily. "Thank you for your opinion," Doc said. Stepping from the stand and back to his seat.

"I'd like a say," Thomas stood. "I've been accused of some vile acts, and in truth, aye, I've committed each and every one of them." He let out a laugh, "Lieutenant Mason however, I believe has been at the rum more than I." Laughter erupted from the crowd.

"Can we stop this?" The Admiral stood, "This pirate has

confessed to the accusations."

"Aye," Thomas raised his voice before the judge could speak. "I have confessed, and more than that. The acts the good Lieutenant accused Captain Stein and his men of were not performed by them, but in fact were committed by myself. They happened upon the ship stuck upon the shoals because they were after me and following my path." He leaned forward, "See, they believed I had murdered young Benjamin here," He gestured to him. "But also, Captain Clarke's sister. As much as I had intended to kill the lad during battle, I am pleased to say, that particular soul does not rest over my head. As for the sister, I did not commit that crime either. Captain Stein and Captain Clarke have proof of that and discovered the true culprit after they took my ship." Thomas shook his head, not bothering to hide his smile. "It has also been said that the good and noble Captain Clarke was in fact corrupted by my despicable nature, however, I am ashamed to say, he did not fall prey to my vicious ways. In fact, he ended up upon *The Trinity* because I imprisoned him in my brig, along with Captain Harding." Thomas's brow furrowed in mock questioning. "As his Admiral, I would think Captain Clarke included this information in his report to you before asking to take leave once more." Thomas shrugged, "At any rate, I be the gruesome pirate they claim me to be. These sailors don't have what it take." He returned to his seat, the room near to silence once more. "Haven't I told ye lads afore?" He stretched his arms wide, "I aim to please." He laughed, "And I do hate to be predictable."

"Well, thank you, Captain Banning for your confessions." The judge said, "Have we any other accounts?"

Alaric stood, "I would like to address the folks here today, my Lord. If I may." The judge nodded.

"Parts, bits and pieces of the testimonials you have heard today are true. Some entirely true, as Captain Banning has so openly told you. My men and I are being branded as traitors, pirates. Tell me though, would a traitor turn in a Spanish ship? Would a pirate so easily turn in other pirate vessels? Lieutenant Mason has informed you they were in the same areas as us. I wonder why he has not thought to tell you all of the ships we took on, leaving as many onboard alive, locked in their brigs so the Navy ship that was following us," He pointed to Lieutenant Mason and Captain Hanes who had curiously chosen not to say a word during the entire trial. "Could take them in and dispose of the crew and the ship as they saw fit. I ask you, Lieutenant, what did you do with those men?" He raised his brows, "I should hate to think of those men still sitting in their rat invested and fowl smelling brigs. Did you not come across them while you trailed behind us?"

Captain Hanes fidgeted nervously. Lieutenant Mason stood, "I am not the one on trial here and as you so harshly pointed out earlier, we may not call upon those that are not on trial."

"Tis a bit different I should think. Particularly since you already stood and testified against us." Benjamin spoke up.

"Lieutenant Mason, I will remind you that you chose to be a part of this trial when you gave your accounts and may be called upon at any time." The judge added.

"Very well, yes, we came upon those men. I assure you.

We took them into our charge and did as we saw fit." Mason pursed his lips.

"Good, I am glad to hear of this." Alaric grinned, "By taking them into your charge, I wonder if you could enlighten the folks here today as I am sure many of them are not aware of the customs of the sea."

Lieutenant Mason cleared his throat, "We saw that they were seen to by our surgeon and then we sent them back on the ship with a few of our men to bring the prize ship in."

"I see. Seems you did the right thing." Alaric looked down, still smiling. Meeting Mason's gaze once more he asked, "And are any of those men here today? I am sure they would tell you we were not savages and in fact took mercy upon them and killed as few of them as possible during the battle. Their captain could even inform you that we were merely stopping them and questioning them as to the whereabouts of Captain Banning's ship." He waited, "Or did those men already testify today? I wonder, Lieutenant Mason, how much did you bribe those men today with to tell such out-landish stories before a judge?" Gasps and more whispers ran through the room.

The Judge hit the gavel hard, several times before the room came to silence once more. Ethan stood, "May I?"

"If you must," Lord Anderson snarled.

"Captain Hanes, you have not said a word. Surely, as the captain of the very vessel Lieutenant Mason was on, you would have notes in your logbook of all accounts." He looked at him, his brows drawn together. "You and I have never truly had any qualms against one another. As captain, I should think you were in more of a position to speak than your Lieutenant." Ethan shifted his gaze to the Lords at the bench, before sitting.

Benjamin had thought as much himself. He thought of how he had rescued Alaric and the others from the Naval ship. *Why had that moment not been brought up?*

"Captain Hanes?" The judge called out to the man who was growing paler by the moment. "Do you have anything to add?"

No one moved once again, waiting in anticipation of what this next man would have to say. The room had grown humid, the air almost as stale as that of inside the ship.

Captain Hanes stood, making his way up to the stand. "Captain Clarke is correct in saying he and I have never had any true qualms. I was tasked, along with Lieutenant Mason to gather witnesses against these captains, as we were the ones following the progress of Captain Clarke in his search for his sister's murder. The Admiral," He swallowed hard at the narrowing eyes of the man. "Was not pleased that his most highly trained captain was asking for leave once more to search for his sister's killer when the French fleet was in the area. Lieutenant Mason suggested that he and I trail behind *The Trinity* and under the Admiral's orders, bring Captain Clarke in if we believed it necessary."

"And did, believe it necessary?" Lord Anderson asked, leaning forward.

Captain Hanes clenched his jaw. "We tried. We flagged them down on their return to the islands. We imprisoned Captain Stein, Captain Clarke and Miss Maclean in our brig and set officers to command the other vessel. We were unaware of the younger Captain Stein's presence at the time. He led the rest of *The Trinity's* crew aboard our ship and freed the prisoners.

"Typical of the disrespectful urchin." Captain Stoll hissed.

"Silence!" The judge ordered.

"We chose not to pursue, knowing they would return to the islands. We decided to return and await their arrival. While collecting evidence against them." Captain Hanes let out a shaky breath. "It was during this time, I discovered something I had not known before." He looked at Ethan, "Lieutenant Mason has always been jealous of Captain Clarke, sought to bring him down so he could rise. That is why he suggested we follow him. He had planned to have a fleet of pirates attack their ship, but I convinced him to spread the rumors instead. I did this and allowed the Lieutenant to continue his pursuit of the captain for my own selfish gains."

"Would you kindly share with us what you discovered?" The judge was clearly infuriated at the deception and lies. Benjamin shifted his eyes to the Admiral and Lieutenant who looked near to exploding.

"During my search to find the sailors from the ships and convince them to testify against these men, I discovered the truth behind Lieutenant Mason's actions. His dislike for Captain Clarke runs far deeper than even Captain Clarke is aware." Ethan stood. His face hard. "Lieutenant Mason sought the attentions of Helena Clarke. She refused him numerous times, saying she could not possibly be with a man her brother did not approve of, not after all her brother had done for her." He gave Ethan a sympathetic look. "It was lieutenant Mason that ordered Jonathan to attack her that night. It was meant as a warning, he was not to kill the girl. Lieutenant Mason believed in courting Helena, he would be able to convince Captain Clarke to approach the Admiral for captaincy. His plans quite obviously did not go as he had planned. He then focused on bringing Captain Clarke down in other ways." Captain Hanes concluded.

Alaric remained still, staring in disbelief at Captain Hanes. His eyes moved to the spot where Lieutenant Mason had sat, the seat now barren. The Admiral sat is silent shock of the turn of evets.

The judge hit the gavel, "Well, seeing as how half the accounts today were lies and the other half to do with a plantation in the colonies and a ship captain that does not even make port here. I say this trial is over. He stood, sweeping his robes around the chair, readying to make his exit.

"Surely not!" Captain Stoll stormed forward. "You cannot possibly excuse the boy or the slaves of their crimes."

"I can and I will. In fact," he looked back at them before returning his gaze to Captain Stoll. "I declare them to be free so long as they do not return to the colonies. There, I cannot help you." He said to them. "What they did for the islands. Aiding in defeating the French fleet excuses them of their crimes of escaping, in my books as does it the rest of the men." He motioned to the others. "Now, if you will excuse me, I have other engagements I must tend to. I suggest you find a new ship and return to your previous dealings. Perhaps, with a bit more grace." He looked Captain Stoll and Mister Luggnar over.

38

"What's this then?" Ethan came to an abrupt halt as he rounded the corner of path. He looked the men before him over. Each of them having a sword or ax strapped to them, as well as a flintlock or two.

"You stood with us through many of our battles. It is our turn to return the debt." Alaric said, rocking back on his heels.

"There is no debt to repay. You aided me in finding Banning and with him, Jonathan. If you come with me now, you may find yourselves back in those cells for treason and murder." Ethan advised.

"We will take our chances." Lucas stepped forward. "Now, where is he said to be?"

Ethan sighed, running a hand over his face. "The old sailor that sits outside *The Rusty Anchor*, he saw Mason stow away on the merchant vessel, *The Brachner* early this morning." He nodded his thanks to them.

"Are you the captain of this vessel?" Ethan asked, hopping from the plank and onto the ship.

The small man's eyes widened. "I am and I don't want no trouble. What are you playing at?" He stammered.

"I've been informed a man boarded your ship this day. Where can I find him?" Ethan's voice was firm.

"I…I have no idea what you be speaking of. We not even recruited new crew this time." The man's eyes grew wider as Ethan stepped closer.

"If you are not hiding him, then you have no problem in us searching your ship." Ethan raised a brow, waiting for the man to dispute it. Alaric looked about the rigging, being sure Mason did not hide amongst the men readying the sails. He noted Benjamin doing the same.

"I, I swears," The man began, only to stop himself. Gesturing with his head, he nodded towards the captain's cabin.

Ethan frowned, he and Alaric exchanging the same look. Of course Mason had sought to hide in the captain's very quarters, no doubt he planned to take over the timid man's ship in time. Smashing his boot into the hatch, it flew open. "Ah, there you are." Ethan stepped inside the cabin. "I would say you are under arrest, but I feel settling this like a pirate is more suitable to the situation. Do you not agree?" Ethan gestured with his blade, towards the opening in the hatch.

"First blood then?" Mason swallowed, his gaze roving over the other three men that stood, guarding the plank and preventing him from running.

"To the death." Ethan replied, his face calm.

Mason cleared his throat. "Very well," stripping the vest from the shirt beneath it, he drew his sword. Not bothering to bow to one another, they circled. Waiting for the other to make the first move. Ethan feigned a lunge, causing Mason to react. He would have blocked the blade had Ethan continued the jab. Instead, it opened him up and left him fighting harder to block the blows that came. Ethan lunged forward. The rage clear in his eyes. Mason swung up catching Ethan's shirt, grazing his middle just enough to draw a trickle of blood.

He smirked, "All this time with them and your skills still haven't improved?" Mason goaded.

"It appears not," Ethan grinned, jumping back from another swing. Pulling the shirt from his body, he stood ready once more. There blades clanked together, the commotion drawing a crowd of onlookers at the docks. Men exchanged coin and whatever possessions they had, wagering on which of the men they believed would win.

Mason leapt forward, jabbing his sword at Ethan. His precision was off. He misjudged the blow. His blade sliding deep into Ethan's leg. Ethan snarled against the pain, plunging his blade into Mason's middle, just below his chest. The man's eyes wide with shock as his body fell limply against Ethan's sword. Withdrawing the blade he stood there a moment, staring down at the Lieutenant's lifeless body. Turning to the merchant captain, he dropped a few coins into his hand. "For your trouble," he flicked his head at the body, the blood beginning to pool around him. "And for the mess. I'd be grateful if you could inform the officers that there was a misunderstanding between this man and a pirate." The man simply nodded, quickly doing as he had been commanded.

Ethan stepped from the ship, the others following close behind. His limp worsening as he walked. The blood soaking through his clothes. Lucas rose an arm into the air, waving at a carriage driver to come forward. Helping Ethan in, they rode for the plantation. Alaric could see Ethan swaying in the seat. Benjamin removed the strap that held Ethan's sword. Pulling it tight around his leg, he tried to stem the bleeding, but it did little. Ripping a strip of fabric from his shirt he pressed it firmly against the wound. The carriage ride rattled them, causing Ethan to fall forward. Alaric pulled him back, "Stay awake, mate. We are almost there." The carriage turned off the dirt path and onto the gravel. Before it even came to a complete halt, Lucas jumped up, bounding up the steps, calling for Doc and Catherine.

Alaric grabbed Ethan from behind, his hands wrapping under his shoulders. Benjamin held tight to Ethan's legs as they hauled him up the steps. Catherine and Doc waited in the great hall. "Bring him up, the servants are preparing a chamber." Catherine called over her shoulder as she led them up the staircase. "In here," She stood aside so they could go into the chamber. Laying him down on the bed, Alaric and Lucas exchanged glances. He could not help but feel they were back aboard *The Trinity* together. A white sheet had been laid out over the bed and one on the floor next to it. A bowl and pitcher sat on the table beside the bed. "Lucas, get him some whiskey in case he wakes while we are stitching him up. Ben, Alaric, stay here in case he tries to fight back.

Lucas returned with the whiskey. Pouring a generous amount on the wound, Ethan groaned, moving his head against the pillow. Grabbing the needle Catherine had set out on a clean, white cloth, she began to stitch the wound. It was clear Ethan had awoke, but he remained still, he eyes closed.

"You are a lucky lad. A wound as bad as this one in the correct spot on the leg could have bled you dry." Doc explained, handing Ethan the bottle of whiskey.

"Feels as if I lost plenty already." Ethan grumbled.

"I will have a tray brought up to you." Catherine said, gathering the bowl of water that was now tinged pink from the blood on the cloth, and her kit.

"We will leave you to your bottle," Alaric said. He knew Ethan had not had much of a chance to clearly think of all that had happened and all that he had found out over the past couple of days since and during the trial. Ethan nodded in replied, taking another long drink.

39

"Lucas," Alaric announced his presence. Lucas was in a section of the field that had just recently been planted. Bent down and looking at the fresh shoots that broke through the rich soil. "How are they looking?" He asked, nodding to the greenery, when Lucas looked up at him, squinting in the bright sun.

"Well, I should think." His gaze scanning the rest of the field. Placing his hands at his hips, he beamed. "It is going better than I had hoped, to tell the truth."

"I'm glad to hear it." He ran a hand through his hair, the other holding a small box.

"What do you have in there?" Lucas asked, turning his attention to the item in Alaric's hand.

"Red's things." He said, then lifting the sack he had placed on the ground beside where he stood, "Along with the other sailor's things. I am going to return them to the families and give my condolences. I wondered if you'd want to accompany me, seeing as how they had served under you as well." Alaric dropped his gaze. He could not help but feel none of them would have lost their lives had it not been for him. If Lucas had been captaining the ship during that year and especially the battle, maybe they would still be there.

"Whether it be you or me, lives would have been lost all the same. You know that." Lucas spoke up, leading the way out of the fields and all but reading Alaric's thoughts. "How many days and nights after battles have you had to assure me?" He scoffed. "Those men knew what they signed on for and would not have wanted to part this world any other way." He said, speaking the truth. "Any rate, I'd be honored to go with you." He clapped him on the shoulder, "If only to ensure they know I am the superior captain." He grinned, giving Alaric a teasing shove.

"Aye, we'll see about that," Alaric returned, shaking his head at the jest.

"Red's house is closest. We can stop their first. Eddie does not have a next of kin, did he write where he wanted his things delivered to?" Lucas asked.

"Aye," Alaric looked straight ahead, "He wants his earnings to go the orphanage. He wrote that since he did not have a child of his own and the orphanage took such care of Ben, that he thought it only right."

Lucas cleared his throat, "Aye, very generous and fitting, I should say." The gravel beneath their feet changed to the dirt of the path. The trees making a canopy above them, giving a brief reprieve from the sun. "What of Key and the others?"

"Their notes spoke of a couple people," Alaric shrugged, "A mother, sister, an uncle. I have the places of residence marked down," he handed Lucas a parchment, "I cannot say where they'd be if they no longer reside in those places, though."

"Not much we can do at that point." Lucas admitted. The houses they neared were far less grand than the plantation ones but still far nicer than most houses privateers resided in. A vine of sorts grew up the side of the farthest house on the path. The door was painted once a bright blue but not faded and chipped from years in the sun.

Alaric took a step up, knocking on the door. He knew the families of the fallen sailors, if they were still on the islands, would know already of their loved one's passing. Not how or when but not seeing them at the trial or having them return to them after the ship made port, would have told them. Alaric ran his fingers across his forehead. He could hear footsteps nearing the door.

"Captain Stein, Captain Harding," Red's wife stood in the opening, "Please come in," she bid them, stepping aside to allow them entrance. A fine, green rug, beige swirls and leaves decorating it, lay in the entrance upon the wooden floors. A young woman stood at the base of the stairs, her face searching theirs, flicking to the plump woman who had opened the door for them. Alaric guessed the girl to be one of Red's daughters. He knew him to have three girls, how old, Alaric could not remember. "Please, have a seat in here, I'll have tea brought in." She walked from the room, leaving them standing before a small fireplace. The room a light from the sunshine that streamed in. The room was small, hardly bigger than his cabin aboard the ship, but more finely decorated.

"Mistress Fiener," Alaric began.

She held a hand up. "I am aware of what you are to tell me. Please, spare myself and my daughter's, the details, I do not think we can bear it. I do appreciate you coming to inform us yourselves and bring his things." She explained, gingerly taking the box Alaric held out. She ran her fingers gently over it, taking a steading breath in. "He loved what he did and we both knew one day it was likely to end this way. I know it could not have been easy to whiteness. He thought fondly of you both and the boy." She said, a tremor in her hand as she patted the box. "I thank you, for coming and giving your condolences." Her voice growing quieter. She gestured for them to accept the tea that had been brought in.

Awkwardly, they both reached for a cup from the tray. "He was brave and one of the very best and most loyal of sailors. We were honored to have him aboard our ship." Alaric voiced, Lucas echoing the sentiments. Finishing the cup in a single swallow, they each set the cups back down, giving their apologies and sympathies one last time, knowing there was no more to say.

The orphanage rested in the center of the town. Alaric looked up at the building, shaking his head and expelling a light laugh. It had not been that long ago Ben was there, a book in his arms about the oceans and sailing or a wooden ship or sword in hand. He could hear the laughter and shouts

317

from kids inside. His knock nearly going unheard.

"Yes?" A young boy opened the door, his face filled with excitement at who the two visitor could possibly be.

"We'd very much like to speak with the Mistress in charge." Alaric told him, biting back a smile at the other children that peaked around the doorway, their curiosity getting the best of their manners.

It was not long before he and Lucas returned to the plantation. They had been able to track down Key's mother, but the family of the other sailors had not been at the given addresses. Notes had been left in case the family went searching for answers, but it was not likely it would happen. Chances were they would hear of the trial or find out *The Trinity* was in port and know what the absence of their loved one meant.

40

"I can't possibly accept this," Amara said, holding up the gown. The oranges and golds complimenting her skin and eyes remarkably. "Tis too much. Tis too grand."

"Nonsense," Catherine took the gown from her and gestured for her to turn so Emma could help her out of the gown she had worn since their voyage to the islands. "Molly and I each got a new gown for tonight's dinner. We thought you should have one as well." Catherine beamed at her.

"I shouldn't even be present at the dinner. I should have a tray in the chamber." Amara stammered. Molly sympathized with her. She knew exactly how she felt. Her own emotions not being far from those of Amara's, but she found she had also been greatly looking forward to the dinner.

"You certainly will be at the dinner, and you will enjoy it more than you think. Trust me," Molly assured her.

Amara gave a timid smile, "You'll show me to dance?"

The laughter echoed joyfully in the chamber, "Most definitely," Catherine giggled.

"There. How does that feel, now?" Emma asked, adjusting the waist on the gown, slightly.

"Truly wonderful." Amara replied, running her hands along the fabric.

"Come, let's go down. They'll be serving drinks soon and the most delicious petit fours." Catherine told them excitedly.

Following her down, Amara next to Molly, she took a deep breath to steady her nerves. Molly looked down at herself. Alaric had insisted she purchase a new gown with Catherine. It was a lighter green than the other she had and was a bit grander but not by much. She had not wanted one too extravagant. A delicate lace sash went about the waist. The fabric swayed gently against her legs as she walked down the stairs. Her hands covered with white, tight-fitting gloves that went to just past the bend in her arms. She placed a shaky hand upon her chest, trying in vain to steady it. She had scarcely seen Alaric since the trial, almost a fortnight ago, now. He had been busy helping Lucas with the plantation and overseeing much needed repairs on *The Trinity*. While she had been assisting Allen with the animals in the stables at the plantation. She had even seen to it that the ones aboard the ship had been taken off and were brought to the plantation for the time being. Catherine had kept busy with her work in the medical room at the other end of the plantation with Doc, while Amara had taken to teaching the children. The days had gone by quickly, all of them coming and going from the estate and only seeing one another for meals in the evenings.

"You look exquisite," Alaric whispered against her ear. Placing a hand on her back, he guided her near the fireplace, where a man and a woman stood, talking with Lucas. Amara was smiling up at Benjamin who seemed to be enjoying himself greatly, already. Talking with another lad who could not have been much older than himself. "Molly, may I present to you, Mister and Mistress Neemus?" He looked to the couple, "This is Miss Maclean."

"Oh, it is lovely to meet you, my husband told me he had heard of your adventure at sea." She looped her arm in Molly's, "Come, we must sit, and you must tell me everything. It sounds most thrilling." She whispered excitedly. "My husband owns his own ship but refuses to take me aboard, says it's no place for a woman." She rolled her eyes and snorted. "Perhaps hearing your tales, as well as Lady Benedict's, he may allow me a chance." She took a delicate sip of the champagne in her hands. "Captain Stein told my husband that he would not have fared nearly as well upon the voyage if it were not for you. He says you are a vital part of the ship, as much so and Captain Harding claims Lady Harding to be." She went on.

"Tis most good to hear such things. One always wishes to be needed as well as wanted. Don't you agree?"

"Oh, indeed." She nodded in agreement. "Tell me, what is the most trying part of being aboard a ship. I should think it does not smell too agreeable and pirates are most terrifying and unsavory." Her eyes widened, her face turning scarlet, "Oh, Miss Maclean, please forgive me. I did not mean. That is." She stammered, taking another sip of her Champagne, this time less delicately.

Molly giggled, quickly covering her mouth, "Tis alright, I took no offense and I think you will find neither would Captain Stein or the others. Twas a simple rumor, no more than that." She assured her. "As for the most trying part of it, I am not quite sure. You are correct, the smell is rather unpleasant and the air in the cabins is hot and sticky. There is little privacy, and the men certainly can be loud," She laughed, "but you get used to it all in time."

Mistress Neemus nodded eagerly, "I've heard tell of storms at sea. Is it true, the waves are grand enough to sink a ship in a single moment?" She scooted closer on the bench seat that sat in front of a large curtain. Behind it was a window that looked out onto the garden path.

"Oh aye, we saw many storms, some nearly rolling the ship right over. They are terrifying right enough, but with a crew and Captain so well trained, there tisn't as much to fear."

"That is encouraging. Please, go on." She beamed, smiling politely at Catherine and Amara who had come to join the conversation.

"The various small islands and thrilling ports all over, make up for any inconveniences or fears. They offer some-what of a refuge and break from the trials of the ship, but after a few days in port, it is easy to begin to long for the simplicity of the ship once more." Catherine added.

"Do you miss it?" Amara asked, curiously.

"At times, yes. I do enjoy my life here and my work on the plantation, but there will always be a part of me that longs for another adventure. Longs to be aboard the ship and never knowing what the day will bring." Catherine smiled, her eyes seemingly far off. Molly caught Lucas and Alaric listening in. Alaric winked at her.

"Ah, Ejiah, will that be supper ready then?" Lord Benedict asked, alerting everyone it was time to go into the dining room.

"It is, M'Lord." He responded, standing straight and holding the door for the Baron to lead the way. The room had become far more crowded and quite a bit louder. Molly had been enjoying the conversation so much that she had not realized.

Taking their seats, Molly looked about the table, Alaric sat directly across from her, a kind, older woman on his right and a young, rather homely and timid young woman to his left. He smiled politely to her and addressed as if they had met in the past. The girl kept glancing at Benjamin who sat further down the table. Molly wondered on the connection, it soon becoming clear when the girl mentioned the orphanage and the Mistress that owned it. The woman on Alaric's right, looked to the girl and smiled warmly, adding a bit of information to the topic they had been speaking on. Amara was all but glowing. She was enjoying herself and talking fervently to Lucas who sat beside her.

"Tell me, Miss Maclean, what is it you did to occupy yourself aboard the ship, during such a long and trying voyage." The gentleman beside her asked. She wracked her brain, trying to remember what Catherine had said his name was. He was tall, lanky, with his hair hidden under a wig with an enormous amount of powder. Nearly every time he turned his head, a cloud of white would plume over his head. On the other side of her sat Lord Harlem, a pleasant smile upon his face.

"I mended sails, assisted Doc and Cook when needed and tended the animals aboard." She cleared her throat at the shocked expression upon his face. "I also enjoy reading and sketching." It was the first time she had told anyone about the sketches, aside from Doc and Alaric.

"Ah," Lord Millner seemed to recover from his lapse in manners. "And what do you read and sketch, Miss Maclean?"

Molly bit back her smile, knowing her response would once again cause the man's eyes to bulge. "Animals and their anatomy and I read texts on treatments and illnesses of animals."

"How," He adjusted his seating, "Peculiar." He finally said. "Pray tell, before your life at sea, where was it you lived? By the manner of your speech, I take it you hail from Ireland? Is that originally where you met the captains?" He asked, obviously trying to figure out how she came to be aboard *The Trinity* and what she did before that. No doubt by the look upon his face, he thought it must have been a life of ill repute and Alaric must have taken her in to keep him company on the voyage.

"Yes, I lived in Ireland when I was young. I was sold by my uncle to a tyrant of a man. I struck him upon the head one day and escaped. I stowed away aboard Captain Stein's ship and by the time he discovered me, it was too late to turn the ship around." Molly explained boldly, knowing very well it was not proper but not being able to stop herself at the man's impertinent and rude manner.

"I, uh, I see. And could not, the captain drop you off at the next port?"

"Oh aye, and leave me stranded and at the docks alone?" Molly replied, looking at him in disbelief.

His face turned crimson, "Quite right, Captain Stein clearly made the honorable decision."

"He is most honorable in all things," She paused, taking a small bite of the meat that was soaked in a cream sauce. "I must admit though, I gave him little choice in the matter."

"Oh? What's it you did to secure passage?" He asked, lifting a brow in curiosity, looking her over.

She shrugged, not bothering to look up from her plate, "I held my wee dagger to his throat." Lord Millnar blanched. Beside her, she heard Lord Harlem stifling a laugh by covering his face with the cloth and feigning a cough. Alaric sat back in his seat a wide grin upon his face, clearly enjoying the display exceedingly.

"Shall we go through?" Catherine's voice spread across the table. "I do not think we will split. What do you say to some music and dancing?" She stood, leading the way into the hall.

Amara stood off to the side, watching the partners lining

up, waiting for the music to begin. "I would be honored if you would share this dance with me?" Benjamin stepped in front of her, offering his hand. Seeing the surprised look on her face, he was quick to reassure her, "Lucas has been giving me lesson," he grinned, "Just follow along, you will pick it up quickly."

"And what about us? Should we join them?" Alaric whispered beside Molly.

She slipped her hand into his and gazed up at him. "I won't be an embarrassment to dance with? I fear I already shocked enough tonight." Her eyes shifted to Lord Millnar, briefly.

"You could never be such. You are the most lovely woman in the room." He led her onto the floor, "And as for earlier, I could not have been more proud or more entertained." He grinned, stepping apart from her and lining up beside the rest of the men.

The dancing had continued for well over a couple of hours. The spinning and champagne making Molly feel lightheaded and giddy with excitement. She could scarce stop herself from smiling for even a moment. Her and Amara had danced nearly every dance and had finally slowed to find a seat.

"Once you catch your breath, I wonder if you might sing for us." Catherine suggested, sitting next to them.

"Oh, I would enjoy that." She surprised herself by saying so and actually wanting to sing in front of so many faces. She let her mind wonder, going back to how she had felt when she first came aboard *The Trinity*. Her fear and nervousness had all but consumed her then. She still felt it on occasion but mostly she felt happiness, contented, joy, and even love.

Setting her glass down, she walked up to the piano, Catherine sat on the bench in front of it. Whispering to one another, they decided on a song.

"My Lady," Elijah stood beside Catherine, now. "One of the slaves is downstairs. She asks if you can come immediately." He frowned, at even having to suggest she leave the party and guests. "She says the laboring mother is struggling." He straightened. "I would be happy to send a servant for another doctor, so you do not need to leave the party under such circumstances."

Catherine stood, "Of course not. That will not be necessary. I have told you before. I know them. They trust me and I will be there for them when they need me. No matter the circumstance." She reminded him, looking pointedly at the guests. "Thank you for coming and getting me. If you will have a lantern ready for me, I will be there shortly." He bowed and took his leave.

"I will come with you, in case you need anything. Shall I tell Doc?" Molly asked.

"Yes, please." Catherine replied, turning to Lucas to let him know what was happening.

"I will come as well," Amara added, following them out the door as Catherine made her excuses.

327

"She will be in the surgery. They know when a mother is beginning labor, to take her there. Usually, the other women they are close with will handle the labor and deliver the baby, but if there is a complication, then I am summoned. This particular mother labored while I was aboard the ship. The baby was born still and not breathing. The mother was very weak, and the labor had lasted several days." Catherine explained as the woman who had come to fetch her held the lantern and led the way.

"It appears whatever was the trouble last time is happening again this delivery. That is not uncommon." Doc informed.

Stepping into the hut, Catherine immediately began speaking to the women in the surgery. Asking questions about the mother and labor as she pulled an apron over her head and tied it quickly. Molly stood off to the side, each pulling an apron on as well, in case they were needed. The water basin was already prepared. Warm water and a fresh cloth were ready. Waiting to receive the new baby. The mother's screams of pain and stress were almost unbearable. It was not just the pain of the labor but that fear she would once again lose her baby. Molly looked over at Amara, a tear ran down her cheek. Catherine had not been told about the baby she had lost and could not know the memories that were being brought forward. Memories buried and not spoken of until now.

"Amara, would you like to return to Benjamin?" Molly asked, placing a hand on her back, giving her a slight hug.

Amara breathed in, wiping the tear from her face. "No, I'd like to stay." She looked at her. "I've lost a baby once too, maybe I can help her in some way." Amara stepped forward.

Speaking softly, Amara gestured if she could sit beside the mother. She looked surprised, overwhelmed with emotion, yet nodded for Amara to sit beside her. Amara's voice was her own, different from the one she spoke in, to the others. Now, to the mother, she spoke her native tongue. Though Molly could not understand her, she could tell the words spoke of understanding and confidence.

"Keep talking," Catherine whispered, "Give her your strength." She turned to Doc who had been keeping back in case Catherine asked him to do otherwise, giving her space with her patient. "The baby is presenting the wrong way." She told him.

Molly looked between them and back to the mother. Sweat beaded from her head, mixing with the tears she shed. Her face pinched in pain. "What can I do to help?" She asked.

"You get ready to receive the baby while Doc and I see to Sona." She said, her eyes still on the mother. "Sona, I need you to come to the end of the bed. Don't be afraid, we will help you." Catherine instructed. Doc went over to help the woman move forward. She was tired and running out of strength. Molly turned around, she needed to busy herself but she was unsure how. Spotting a kettle that hung from a hook above the fire, she grabbed it off with a cloth that lay on a nearby table. She smiled to herself, remembering once when she was very young. She had been running down the trail that led to the rocky beach. She had been in search of shells to string up and kelp to dry. The shells they used as decorations for inside their small cottage and the kelp they used for many things, from eating it in soups or with other meals, to scraping the salt from it when it dried. They even sold some on occasion to an elderly healer in the area that swore by it's medicinal uses and could no longer make it down the rocky path. Molly had just made it down to where the water reached when her foot slipped, sending her leg into a sharp rock. By the time she had made it back up to show her mother, the thin fabric of her dress skirts was saturated with blood. Her mother had comforted her and made her a cup of tea while she cleaned the drying blood from her leg and wrapped the wound. More than anything, Molly remembered the tea making her feel better. She hoped it would have the same effect on Sona and perhaps even give her a little bit of energy.

Sona sat on the edge of the bed her hands gripping the sheets tightly. Catherine knelt on the ground in front of her, another white sheet on the wooden floor. Examining Sona once more, she stood, turning to Doc, gesturing for him to step aside with her.

"Might I give her some tea?" Molly asked awkwardly, realizing the helplessness she felt now must have been similar to how Catherine felt while she tended her horse.

"That would be most welcome, I'm sure. Thank you." Catherine smiled, returning her attention to Doc.

Molly stepped over to Sona, looking over at Amara. Molly made out her name in the speech and noticed Amara point to the tea. Nodding and smiling weakly, she accepted the tea, "I, thank you," she whispered, allowing Molly to tip the cup to her lips and let her drink. Listening closely to Catherine as she did so.

"Doc, I'm afraid I've only delivered one baby born the wrong way. He did not live." Catherine's voice was filled with emotion and worry.

"I will be with you every step of the way, but I must confess, being aboard the ship the majority of my time, I have not delivered many babies, myself. Only occasional ones in various ports." Doc admitted. "I'll follow your lead."

"Very well," She lifted her head, returning to her patient. "Did the tea help?"

"Mmmm, very much, I thank you." Sona said, groaning as another labor pain hit.

"Alright, Sona, with the next pain, you push. Just enough, mind you. We want baby coming slow." Catherine instructed, a cloth in her hands. Sona squeezed her eyes such again, her head rocking back. "That's it. Little push." Catherine encouraged, hooking her fingers around a leg, she brought it forward. "There we are. Now again, when you are ready, Sona. Gentle pushes." She guided. The other leg came free, the body slipping out and into the cloth Catherine held. "Now just a moment. No pushing. Not yet. You are doing splendidly, Sona."

Doc and Catherine exchanged a look. Doc finally nodding to her. "Alright Sona, just now, with your next pain, you'll push. Little ones now, Sona, little ones." The baby came. Sona rolled her head back, a sob escaping her at the sound of her baby's piercing cries. Tying and then cutting the cord cleanly and quickly, she stood with the baby in her arms. "Molly, wrap the babe in a fresh cloth, please." She said, handing the babe over to her. "Well done, Sona, well done. Tis almost over." Catherine said, placing a bowl beneath the mother, in order to catch the placenta.

As Catherine tended the mother and Amara helped to clean her up, Doc saw to the baby. Looking him over and ensuring his was in fine health. "I clean him. I wish to clean my baby." Sona said, holding her arms out.

"Alright," Doc smiled, walking over with the babe. Molly grabbed for the basin and a fresh cloth. Amara and Catherine helped Sona sit up against the head of the bed as Doc lay the now calm baby in her lap. Dipping the cloth in the warm water, Sona gently wiped the infant down.

"When you are ready and have your strength back, you and baby may return to your hut, but only when you feel ready." Catherine said, taking a step back and gathering the cloth that had been on the floor beneath her, covering the bowl that held the placenta. "Will you wish to bury the after-birth in the naming ceremony?" Catherine asked.

"Yes, I wish to." Sona smiled, still staring upon the small babe that lay in her lap, sleeping contentedly. "Thank you for all you do." She said, looking up at Catherine, her eyes, roaming over all of them in thanks.

Molly put an arm around Amara, giving her a hug. "We will leave you be now. You've the most beautiful wee lad." Molly told Sona. Taking the dirty linens for Catherine so she could place the placenta in a cupboard to be safe until the naming ceremony.

"There is a bucket just outside. If you put them in there, they will be washed." Catherine instructed them. Looking her patients over one last time before taking her leave and following them out of the door with Doc. The other women would be back to check on her in case Sona needed anything.

"Tis my turn to be impressed." Molly beamed at Catherine. "You did remarkably." She said, holding up the lantern for them to see their way along the path, though the early morning sun was already beginning to peak through the trees.

41

Benjamin hung from a rope that was tied about his waist. He on a long piece of wood that dangled from the bow of *The Croga*. Painting the lettering a gold that nearly matched the letters of *The Trinity*. Both ships having fresh, green paint on them that wrapped around the entire vessel. Brand new masts and sails had been properly fitted, along with a new helm on each. Twisting knots for luck, bravery, speed and love had been intricately carved into the wheel. He had the interior of the ship refitted as well. It now matched that of a proper privateer ship, rather than the slave ship it had been.

A day or two after the dinner party, the Governor had summoned he, Alaric and Lucas to his estate. Apologizing for the misunderstanding, as he put it and inconvenience that had met them upon arrival to Barbados. He granted them brand new letters of Marquee, ensuring them the mistake would never happen again.

"Ben," Alaric called out. "Come down here, there is a letter for you." He waved the parchment in the air.

Signaling to sailors on deck to lower him to the dock, he swung his leg over the plank he sat upon and walked up to Alaric, the others stood close behind him. "What's this then?" He asked, taking the letter from Alaric and looking from him to Lucas.

"Appears you have your first orders, Captain." Alaric grinned, crossing his arms over his chest.

Benjamin broke the seal, tearing open the letter. Reading the words in a low voice, hardly believing it. He let out a low laugh, "I did not expect to be tasked with a voyage so soon."

"Aye, well, we will be accompanying you, aboard *The Trinity* of course." Alaric said.

"As will we," Lucas stepped forward, his arm around Catherine.

"On what vessel?" Benjamin asked, confusion and excitement in his voice.

"That one," Catherine pointed to a Brig that bobbed in the port a ways down from *The Croga* and *The Trinity*. The coloring matching theirs. "Lucas and I purchased her just after the dinner party. She grinned at Amara and Molly, a knowing look on their faces.

"We've named her *The Eachtra*."

"We will leave port on your command, Captain."